Steampunk Stray

Kaybee Pearson

The Rural Publishing Company

Dedication

To my daughter, my inspiration
and a talented Steampunk ceramic artist.
With all my love.

Acknowledgements

The author acknowledges the Traditional Custodians of country throughout Australia and their connections to land, sea, the sky, and community. She pays her respect to all Aboriginal and Torres Strait Islander peoples today along with her gratitude living in rural Tasmania on Tyerrernotepanner, Panninher and Leterramairrener country.

A huge thanks to Lisa Bolton, proofreader and editor of my many books. Also, to The Rural Publishing Company for their excellent work taking on this big job with such professionalism.

Chapter One

Paisley Wildmoor shrugged off ISLE FM's weather report droning on the car radio. She didn't need to be told road conditions were bad and that there were warnings across the whole of Eden Isle north. It was obvious from the rain slick roads littered with debris and the bursts of lightning crisscrossing the windscreen and temporarily blinding her like a camera flash from some demonic paparazzi.

Turning down a laneway past the Town Common of Lower Teasel, Paisley winced as the car hood lit up once again, this time from an especially dramatic booming flare just to prove the weatherman's point and reminding her of a lecture from a particularly hateful and patronising high school teacher several years ago. At times like this, Miss Butters' booming voice needled in her brain stuck on repeat, going on about her inadequacies as a student, not paying attention to instructions and stubbornly doing everything her way, meaning 'the hard way'.

Another sheet of lightning reflected across the hood and then quickly dissipated into sparkles of black and silver fairy lights that danced before her eyes.

Magical but leaving her with a pounding stress headache nonetheless from too much concentration.

Street gutters were becoming choked with leaves and twigs, and black puddles formed into slippery hazards across the bitumen. At the back of her mind, Miss Butters' disembodied voice harangued *slow down* but Paisley, being a self-confessed good driver and in a rush, ignored the reprimand as usual. Defiantly, she pressed her foot on the gas pedal anxious to arrive at the Club before Marianne.

The motor of Paisley's old car refused to be hard-pressed; it sputtered and threatened to stall before heroically catching and taking off like a plane on a runway. Unfortunately, not as a passenger jet or a racy spitfire lifting up to the sky, she sighed. More like a cumbersome and tired WWII bomber heaving and groaning as if debating the whole notion of lift-off was a bad idea. A signal that retirement to a salvage metal graveyard was long overdue. 'I'd never do that to you,' Paisley voiced out loud offering reassurance to her trusted set of wheels.

For encouragement, she patted the dashboard of 'Rolla', her turmeric and rust coloured Datsun 1200 with Granny visor, hotted-up with an applied adhesive black racing stripe, and named after the cassette jammed in its retro tape deck. An old cowboy song, 'Rawhide' was on a continuous play loop with the lyrics stuck on *roll-um, roll-um … raw-hide.* She hated that song and had tried everything she could think of to eject the cassette, including trying to pry it out with a dinner knife. No such luck. It remained firmly wedged and determined to drive her mad. This left the only alternative – the radio tuned to ISLE FM for music, not much improvement with its Elvis Presley and Frank Sinatra playlists from the sixties.

She thought of her car as one thinks of a pair of old boots, that comfort one gets from a supportive ally where you are both in it together. *Like two peas in a pod*, one of her foster dads used to say – never sure what peeing had to do with anything. It sounded gross but for some reason the phrase had stuck around a lot longer than she had in that home.

She and Rolla were two of a kind. Although never likely to be a hot, racing model herself, Paisley reasoned they were the same age and had been together for the past seven years, Rolla being her first car and first home of her own in fact.

Rolla was one constant in a lifetime of so many changes it was hard to keep track. Therefore, Paisley felt a warm attachment to the old bomb the same as she would feel towards an aging family pet, if she'd ever had a family or a pet for that matter.

It wasn't Rolla's fault Paisley was late for the Steampunk Club meeting, ruining a chance for a majestic entrance to impress Adam – before Marianne dug her paws into him. As if Adam would even notice the new outfit.

'*Or care*', Bernie would say, constantly remonstrating that she was wasting her efforts on a buffoon with a capital B.

Dependable Bernie would have arrived early, all prepared with agenda papers and speaking notes for the meeting, patiently waiting for her. He took life safe – and much too seriously when it came to the Steampunk Club. But he understood how to make it a success. She trusted his judgment.

Except about Adam who wasn't good enough for her apparently.

Bernie, best friend since high school and the most honest person to reside in Eden Isle, constantly teased Paisley of being a perfectionist and consequently always running late. As usual about most things, he was right particularly tonight. She'd totally lost track of time when designing the best ever outfit. In hindsight, she kicked herself for wasting precious minutes sewing on that last leather strap and buckle to the handmade tartan skirt, the finishing touch that turned it into Steampunk chic. Adding a gypsy blouse with flounced sleeves and a laced-up leather corset, and killer boots of course, her outfit was awesome. But its perfection also made her late.

Bernie had become attached to Paisley in high school, sharing the honour of being the bullied kids – the dork and the weirdo respectively. Apart from that dark time, Bernie had experienced a secure and stable childhood unlike Paisley. This stability countered her wayfarer spirit. She was lucky to have him as a friend.

Despite his gold wire rimmed glasses and mussed up, stringy blonde hair framing chubby cheeks, he was not as staid and boring as he might appear, nor such an unlikely friend for the deliberately outrageous Paisley. It turned out Bernie had an entrepreneurial streak that aligned with her creative endeavours. Together, they'd come up with the idea for the Steampunk Club and it was proving to be a growing success with the locals.

Distracted, Paisley took the corner wide and too fast on outer tyres, before righting the car. Speeding towards the corner of the Village Green and Convict Crust Bakery, she pumped the gas again. "Come on baby, you can do it," she whispered. Rolla hiccoughed and jerked before plunging onwards, skidding and correcting, then drag racing down the narrow laneway. Strong gusts of wind rocked the car body and showered a wet greased road with Spring green leaves and fruit tree petals.

She told herself, the thrumming beat of her heart came from being dressed to impress and feeling fabulous. Nothing to do with excitement at seeing Adam again. After all, it had only been a few weeks since he did that man cave thing where he went dark and didn't go out to the pub or text until he got over it. Whatever 'it' was. He never gave fair warning when this was going to happen, so it still hurt a bit even if she tried not to take the abandonment personally and tried to be understanding. His separation and divorce, sole parenting his kids, being rejected by his wife and her going off with another woman, being Catholic and everything, must have been a bitter blow to his self-esteem. It had only been a couple years.

Zipping past the Convict Crust, she noted it was lit up like a Christmas tree. Unusual. Each fortnight at this precise time she drove by on the way to a Club meeting. Always in a hurry; always late. She wondered what was going on at the bakery, especially on such a stormy night. Maybe an event?

Not that she'd know. She never went there to buy their expensive loaves of sourdough olive bread or fancy French pastries. Not on part time wages working as a bar assistant at the Draught Horse Pub where scrounging happy hour beer nuts often counted as dinner on some nights. Maybe when her Steampunk jewellery business took off, she'd feast on boutique eats. Lower Teasel's town folks may see her as that loser, foster kid from Stubblefield with no place to call home but all that would change when her big plans came together.

Distracted by these musings, she faintly glimpsed an apparition waiting on the grass verge. Under the dim, orange glow of a street lamp, privet hedges outlined the sidewalk and cast long shadows, obscuring a ghost grey creature blending into the nightscape. Luckily this time, Ms Butter's incessant chatter foreboding disaster overrode Paisley's cavalier defiance. As if on auto pilot, she slammed the brakes before consciously registering the spectre streaking in front of Rolla at the precise moment a flash of lightning burned across the windscreen in a blinding boom.

With squealing tyres, she turned the steering wheel abruptly to avoid disaster. The car hit a pothole causing it to fishtail down the road out of control.

Paisley's heart flipped in a rush of adrenaline. Over-correcting sent the front end of Rolla in the direction of a high curb that edged the Village Green. A premonition of the car flipping as it hit the curb made her jerk the wheel the other way causing the car to spin several times in three hundred sixty degree circles. Screaming for dear life and evoking every prayer she could remember taught in Catholic primary school, she gripped the wheel and pushed harder on the brakes making the fishtailing worse.

Big mistake. This was not working. *Dumb, dumb. Focus.*

Taking a deep breath, she willed focus. Resisting knee jerk reactions against all natural instincts, and with superhuman single-mindedness, she managed to make a few small steady corrections and brake more gently. Miraculously, Rolla responded. The Datsun straightened enough for her to gain control, slow down and pull over to the side of the road, stopping abruptly. It was all over in a matter of seconds.

Turning off the ignition, Paisley slumped a pale forehead on the cold steering wheel, hyperventilating, heart hammering in her throat.

She succumbed to big fat baby tears and therefore missed seeing a scrawny dog standing safely under a camellia bush on the Village Green, its narrow head cocked to the side as if in sympathy.

Headlights illuminated the interior of the car. Paisley continued to sniffle, feeling like an inept eight year old, hearing taunts of *useless, pathetic, unlovable* play on a continuous tape at the back of her mind.

A few minutes later, a soft tapping on the driver's window startled her *feeling sorry for herself* gloom. Glancing out the side window, at first all she saw were knuckles decorated with black tattoos, then long hair obscuring a man's face as he peered in. With a shriek, she quickly locked the door.

"Are you alright?" he shouted through the glass, trying to be heard over the pattering of rain and bouts of wind showering the road with twigs and leaves. He stepped back a few steps in deference to her scream.

Paisley frowned, peering out the window into an eerie orange mist. Through watery red eyes, it was difficult to make out details of the stranger except for his biker leathers against a backdrop of bleak shadowed blackness. Squinting, she noted tall, long limbs and strong, taut thigh muscles, wet strands of thick hair hanging past his shoulders – and awesome knee high boots with zips and buckles – *I wonder where he bought those?* she thought and then immediately shook her head at the non sequitur. She must be in shock admiring boots at a time like this.

He cut an imposing figure. Could she trust a guy with tattoos on a dark laneway in Lower Teasel? Even if it was a small town in the middle of nowhere?

Wiping away tears using the sleeve of her coat, smearing black mascara across the white pancake makeup on her cheeks, she scrutinised the good Samaritan for signs of danger. Sensing her fragile state, he stood back from the car posed with hands upright, as if to show he carried no weapon and therefore, was harmless. He seemed to have a kind and caring face. From long experience, Paisley had learned to be wary of people, even those with kind faces and well-meant intentions.

"Impressive hooning. What I'd give to be able to control a three sixty like that." He bent down, peered at her, smiling reassurance. Not handsome but he had presence. The confidence of someone who knew his place in the world and had no reason to prove it, or fight for it. Momentarily, a pang of envy coursed through Paisley, quickly suppressed.

He was young, younger than her by a few years. He didn't seem so scary. She'd risk it.

She rolled down the window.

"It wasn't my fault," she whined, immediately regretting sounding like a P-plater. "Some animal ran in front of the car."

"Yeah, I saw."

"I'm pretty sure I missed it. A possum or something."

"You did good missing it." He shook his head as if he couldn't believe it. "A stray dog it was. I thought for sure it was a goner."

Expecting criticism, conditioned to believe everything was due to some failing on her part, his compliment acted like a healing balm. A heavy weight of guilt at driving too fast for the road conditions lifted from Paisley's chest and she began to breathe more normally.

He pointed across the Datsun's hood to the parklands. "It's cowering in the bushes." He whistled and shouted, "Come girl."

A ghostly grey dog with its ribs showing watched suspiciously from the bushes, wet and shivering, and probably hungry, but not easily trusting. Paisley, relating to strays all her life, wanted to reach out and give it a big hug.

Compassion for the stray overrode Paisley's reticence to engage with this stranger. Opening the car door, she emerged on jelly legs. A light mist quickly flattened her fine cherry red hair and dampened the military-style overcoat with a soaking chill. Shivering, she wrapped her arms in a self-hug and stood wondering what to do.

"It's ok. It's ok," the young man crooned. "Come."

He slapped a hand on his thigh and whistled. The dog cocked its head, puzzled.

Taking a deep breath, Paisley joined in calling to the dog. It slunk closer and stopped.

"Hey, what about that? She likes you."

"Us *strays* recognise one another," she quipped, instantly regretting giving too much away.

The young man turned to Paisley with a quizzical look before asking, "You wouldn't happen to have any food in your car that we could use to coax it over? It looks like it hasn't eaten in days."

Not quite over the whole fishtailing experience, Paisley's brain was slow to engage. Befuddled, she vaguely recalled a box of stale cheese crunchies wedged under the front seat. Couldn't remember how they got there. Or why she'd never thrown them away – they were awful. "I think so, maybe," she said, fishing around under the seat. "Will these work?" she asked, pulling out the pack and giggling from suppressed hysteria. Hellfire. Did she really giggle like a teenager with a crush?

"Let's try and see," he grinned, pleased. And held her gaze. "Cool earrings," he said.

Was he flirting? She couldn't be sure. Shock caused her inner woman instincts to go into dormancy temporarily. It wasn't like he could see the awesome outfit underneath her long coat. This thought was surprisingly disappointing. As if she wanted to impress the young tattooed stranger.

"Thanks, they're my design, Steampunk," she answered. Get real. Looking like a drowned rat wasn't going to arouse any romantic inclinations in the guy. What was she thinking? Adam was the guy she was rushing to see. Adam. She smiled to be polite and pushed wet strands of hair behind her ears.

"Thought so," he gushed and suddenly looked sheepish. "The name's Lance by the way." He reached over to shake her hand. "I love dogs. Do you like dogs?"

Still recovering from shock, in a daze, Paisley sat in the car parked outside the Draught Horse Pub debating whether to even bother going to the club meeting. The whole point of rushing to get to the meeting was to impress Adam with her new outfit. She'd spent all week designing and sewing it. It was awesome, too. The best yet.

It was too late. Marianne would have her hooks into him by now, with a bar stool pulled up close between his knees, batting her lashes, waiting on his every word, giggling like a schoolgirl. And Adam would pretend to be oblivious as always. Forget a grand entrance. She'd be lucky to even catch his eye.

Bedamned. What a disaster. Her hair was plastered to her head in threads. Underneath her coat, she imagined an outfit wrinkled out of shape, matted – and bedraggled like a stray caught in the rain – that was the word for it, she felt like a stray, an all too familiar feeling.

Worse yet, Lance had convinced her to take the mutt home before she could formulate a refusal. Before placing it in the backseat, he'd checked to see if the stray had a name tag or owner contact details on its collar. When it didn't, he'd proposed they name it. Jokingly, he suggested 'Mist', for the obvious reason Paisley had *missed* hitting it with her car. She thought it poetic because the dog was a skin and bones grey streak that could appear and disappear as if into the mist.

Mostly being practical, they had to call the dog something.

She wasn't a complete idiot. Obviously, the gorgeous guy had taken advantage of her befuddled state of mind with his easy smile and his kind-hearted attitude to Mist – as well as to her. Who could say *no* to that? Even if she'd been able to, watching him shrug his shoulders in a most attractive and apologetic way while pointing to his Harley made it obvious it was impossible for him to cart a dog home. That sealed the deal. The responsibility fell to Paisley. She couldn't leave Mist out in the cold, shivering and homeless. She knew all too well how that felt.

She shook her head in disbelief. She had a dog. What was she going to do with a dog?

Daydreaming, her brain conjured memories of Lance. She wondered if their paths would ever cross again. Kicking herself, she'd not thought to ask for his number. It would have been cool to update him on Mist, an easy excuse to keep in touch. But he hadn't asked for her number either. So that was that.

Casting a glance over her shoulder, she watched Mist snuggle into cloth shopping bags bundled into a doggie nest making itself at home on her backseat. One paw rested on the box of cheese crunchies protectively. The beast snored, totally content with its new owner, not worried about a proper feed or a warm dry rug to sleep on. Its simple faith in her created an overwhelming fondness. Any residue of reluctance on becoming a new dog owner dissolved with the rain streaming down the windscreen.

With the motor shut off, the windows fogged up from a damp over coat and moist breath. The car smelled like musty, wet dog and stale cheese crunchies. She sniffed and grimaced. *She smelled like wet dog and cheese crunchies.*

Paisley pulled out her phone and stared at it. Bernie would start to worry if she didn't text him soon. A bleep broke into her stupor with notification of a text message.

It read:

Mtg started. Adam asking where r u? xB

Bernie had beat her to the post. Paisley took in a deep breath wondering what decision to make. She smelled of wet dog, wet hair and damp coat. And cheese crunchies. And lost heart. Any excitement at seeing Adam was gone, submerged beneath the night's upending events and turmoil.

Bernie could handle the agenda on his own.

She texted back:

Not coming now. Will explain tomorrow. Hugs P

Turning on the ignition, Paisley drove home slowly as if there was a baby on board.

Chapter Two

"Don't get too attached. You know you won't be able to keep her," Bernie was saying. Paisley frowned but kept quiet and continued in a semi-run across the mowed interior of The Common, trying to keep up with Mist who pulled on the leash despite its three meter lead. Uncannily mirroring her new owner's personality, Mist made up her own mind about how things were going to go. Despite her slight, undernourished build with ribs sticking out, the stray demonstrated dogged strength and one-eyed determination in towing Paisley along, avoiding the easy walkway with its levelled path and tidy gravel, choosing instead to gallop across the less travelled path being a paddock of potholes and prickly weeds.

Bernie had been invited along on their Sunday walk around The Common as a gesture of friendship. Not for a lecture about how her landlord would have *kittens* when he discovered Paisley was keeping a pet in her tiny unit. However well intentioned, her BFF was being a pain in the proverbial. At any rate, she had that one covered. If the landlord complained, she'd say Mist was only visiting; that the dog belonged to her ex-boyfriend's son. Often Heath stayed for weekends when his father was working shifts.

How would her landlord even find out about Mist? There'd never been an inspection in all the time she'd lived here. And he'd have to give her a week's notice. She knew the rules. If she was careful it would be fine.

She and Eddy lived together for two years before their breakup last June. Eddy had been twelve years her senior, probably a father figure. He'd come as a ready-made family package which was part of the attraction. Over the course of their relationship, Eddy's son, Heath, became the little brother Paisley never had. At the end their split was amicable – Paisley grew up and didn't require paternal advice any longer – and she remained a steadfast and loyal friend. In return, Eddy allowed her visiting rights to Heath on a regular basis. They got on like *two peas in a pod*.

Ten year old Heath would adore Mist. He was due for a visit next weekend. It would be so awesome playing fetch and teaching her tricks. The kid would be in seventh heaven.

She knew her little brother would happily collude in the misdirection with the landlord if problems arose. He'd see it as a game.

Bernie could be too uptight at times. Not that he gave her the chance to explain the plan about handling the landlord, going on like he was. If he had, true to form, he'd probably give her a side lecture about honesty and not bending the truth to suit the circumstances. That was the last thing she needed right now.

"And then there's registration, vaccinations, worming tablets as well as dog food. You can hardly afford food for yourself let alone a dog." Bernie kept up a monologue in an unmistakably *dogmatic* manner.

"Thanks for your vote of confidence," Paisley murmured. The truth hurt, she thought, somewhat alarmed, realising she'd spent her last ten dollars at Shiploads buying the retractable dog lead that didn't seem to retract. Pay day at the Draught Horse Pub was three days away. She regretted giving Mist those cheese crunchies from under the car seat. Stale cheese crunchies filled an empty tummy even if it was a stretch calling it food.

In the distance she spotted another dog, a Westie toddling along with its owners, at the same moment as Mist. Reading her dog's mind, she gave the lead a jerk and began to reel it in before Mist did a runner resulting in her arm being pulled out of its socket. The leash felt as if she'd hooked a log when out fishing and was pulling its weight against the current. "Come Mist," she shouted, all hope and optimism waving a doggie choc treat in the air.

Alongside, Bernie puffed from exertion, his sweaty hair matted to his head. Not used to vigorous exercising, he spent most days of the week at *Light Up*, his Tobacco Gift Shop at Stubblefield, a business inherited from his grandfather last year. With that kind of head start in life, what would he know about lack of money? Paisley envied the fact he had a big, generous family; any one of them would bail him out if ever he was short on cash. She had no one but herself.

Except now, she had Mist. A family responsibility.

The lead went slack and then coiled around the wheel with a whirring sound. Mist panted at Paisley's feet with a pointy toothed look of adoration. "Good girl," she said, handing out several choc treats and patting Mist's head. She figured the dog could use some fattening up.

"She's a whippet, you know. A purebred. Pedigrees cost a lot of money. Someone will be missing her," Bernie scolded. Paisley grunted.

The walk would do Bernie good if he'd chill out about the dog. She set her jaw and refused to engage in conversation. Bernie was being practical in his own way, but he was still pissing her off. He was saying stuff she already knew, just didn't want to hear.

Finally, she said rather defensively to shut him up, "I posted a note on the pub's noticeboard. It's been two weeks and no one has claimed her."

"That scrap of paper with the tiny writing that said, 'Stray dog found – all enquiries to Paisley at bar'?"

"Yeah, so?"

"Well for a start, the owner obviously doesn't frequent the pub. Not everyone does in Lower Teasel."

"Well I figure, if they really missed their dog, they'd be making enquiries all over the place and someone would have told them about my notice. There must be a reason Mist ran away. She was probably abused. Look how skinny she is, with her ribs sticking out. They probably didn't feed her." Paisley stared defiantly at Bernie but he was used to *the double whammy look* and refused to back down.

"Whippets all look like that. It's the breed. They like to run. In the UK, I heard they race them like greyhounds."

"Exactly. We know how mistreated animals are in the racing industry." Paisley gave him a triumphant smile.

"Not all animals …" Bernie stopped mid-reprimand. "You've grown attached to her. That's what this is about. You don't want the owners to be found," he accused.

Ashamed, tears formed in the corners of her eyes. "What's wrong with that? Growing up the way I did, I never had a pet of my own. Except for a goldfish I won at a primary school fair and it died after a couple days, probably because the jar was too small. Or maybe I over fed it. But anyway, Mist and I have bonded. I love her." Paisley wiped the tears and marched away, roughly pulling Mist along.

Bernie didn't give up. "I know how it is, but maybe her owners love her too. You have to try a bit harder to reunite them. It's your civic duty."

Civic duty? Paisley glared at him with a look that said *you've got to be joking.*

"Let me post something on Facebook. There's a local site called Quamby Bluff Shire Lost and Found. I can handle enquiries and vet the bogus ones," he offered, being a good friend after all.

"I'm sure lots of people would claim a pedigree whippet if they got it for free." Paisley thought about Bernie's offer, then reluctantly nodded. "Maybe post it for a couple weeks. But if you don't get any legitimate bites, please can I claim Mist as my very own?"

Bernie's face lit up with a broad smile, having won the argument. Not an easy achievement when it came to his stubborn friend. He stopped to give her a high five. At the back of her mind, Paisley thought that the way Mist liked to run, she probably travelled many kilometres before ending up in Lower Teasel. All the way from Plover Point or Whaler's Cove, with any luck. No one from that part of Eden Isle would think to look at Bernie's local Facebook site. Fingers crossed.

Chapter Three

Paisley threw a bright orange tennis ball overhand with all her might across the Common and watched both Heath and Mist run after it. Heath's playful screams mimicked the Masked Lapwings in the paddock. The birds dive bombed anyone getting too close to their nests hidden in the tall grass. Mist leaped in the air with a toothy grin trying to catch a bird when it dived down with wings flapping menace and shrill warnings. Heath kept running, waving his arms in the air to scare them off, not the least worried.

She placed bets on Mist getting to the ball first; although there was a smidgeon of concern about whether the dog would return with it. There was as much chance she would change tact and chase after a bunny rabbit – or keep running for no other reason than sheer joy.

She turned to Eddy with a smile. "Heath loves Mist as much as me, like she's his dog, too." Her ex wasn't much of a talker but after hearing his grunt, which she believed indicated a positive response, she decided to risk it. "In my lease agreement, I'm not meant to have pets. But I was hoping maybe if an inspection was coming up, you guys wouldn't mind babysitting Mist to keep her a secret; you know, like pretend she was Heath's. It would only be for a couple hours tops – so my landlord didn't complain."

Eddy frowned, not unexpected whenever she asked a favour. "Is that the right message to give Heath?"

Paisley looked puzzled. "Message?"

"You know, blurring the lines between pretend and reality. Mist isn't even *your* dog."

Paisley cringed. Eddy was a stickler for following the rules and always made her feel immature and judged by her unconventional suggestions that challenged the system, even if they were petty issues where it didn't make any difference one way or the other. It was frustrating.

He didn't stop there. "I don't want Heath getting close to Mist if you have to give the dog back. Unlike you, he's not used to parting from those he loves. He'd take it hard."

Eddy was oblivious to delivering a remark akin to a punch to the gut. Referring to her history of being in and out of numerous foster homes throughout her childhood was a low blow. As if comparing losing an adopted, stray dog to losing one adopted family after another was in the same ball court. Okay, Heath would be upset if Mist had to go, but he lived in a secure and stable home. That would help him cope with a fact of life – people, loved ones, left, disappeared, even died. He'd come through loss better than she ever did given her wacked out parents. Give the kid some credit.

Would she ever be allowed to escape her past, or would it be used as an excuse to challenge her judgment forever more? Why couldn't people accept her the way she was, for who she was, damaged but loving and creative just the same. She wanted to be seen as normal like everyone else. That's why she hid her feelings. It didn't mean she was stoic and immune to hurt. It didn't make feelings less painful. All it did was protect her vulnerability. Why was it hard for Eddy to understand this?

Raising her eyes to the grey sky and taking in a deep breath calmed her disappointment. She was being uncharitable. Eddy was meeting her halfway by agreeing to consider the request. He had to keep Heath's best interests in mind. That's what a good dad did. It was true – she'd never experienced a caring father. She was happy Heath had one as protection from a self absorbed *pretend* sister. It was good to be reminded now and then about what normal relationships looked like. Dysfunctional ones had been her normal for too long.

In her heart, she knew Eddy meant no harm. Generally, he was kind, not cruel. In fact, of all the people she knew, he was one of the good guys which is why they'd remained friends after breaking up. Although, it would be a stretch to place him in the same class of friendship as Bernie, her very best friend. Eddy was more like a relative than a bosom buddy. But he and Heath were all the family she had left.

The remark was his way of winning an argument – a *man-thing* – and shouldn't be taken personally. By rubbing in her up-bringing and criticising her character, he didn't have to feel bad about saying 'no'. That was all it was. She got that.

It was too exhausting fighting. She didn't have the fortitude to argue. Giving in to Eddy's opinion was easier.

"You're right. I don't want Heath to get hurt. I'll think of some other way," she said sullenly. Eddy picked up on her tone.

"Look. I'll think about it. Okay?"

No actual decision. Typical Eddy. Keep her in suspense and in guilt waiting for his paternalistic gavel to fall. Some things never changed.

The mood was broken by heavy panting from a slobbery dog and an out of breath ten year old, both manifesting like apparitions at her side. Heath held up a soggy tennis ball as if it was a prize. Bending over double, he gasped, "She didn't want to give it up, but I got it off her. Can I give her a treat? I need a drink."

Paisley dug into her satchel and extracted a handful of choc treats for Mist who waited dutifully. "Sit," she commanded before they were gobbled up in seconds. Wiping a hand on her jeans, she grabbed a drink bottle from a side pocket and passed it over to her little brother. "Here you go, bro."

"Thanks," Heath gushed, gulping noisily. Handing back the bottle, he heaved the ball in the air and ran after it. Mist followed, starting the game all over again.

Eddy gave her a look, as if to say, *see what you've done – it's already too late*. The gavel had fallen. She was judged and found wanting.

Chapter Four

Paisley stood staring at the Olde English lettering on the weather worn oak panelled door of Bernie's shop, '**Light Up** – *Tobacco Merchant and Reliquary*' – and couldn't make herself pull the tarnished brass *Jules Verne-style* octopus handle to enter. Locals walking past screwed up their faces at her leather cap with goggles, worn bomber jacket decorated with Steampunk clockwork cogs, WWII aviation jodhpurs, and chunky Doc Martin boots. This came as no surprise; she knew old timers on Eden Isle frowned upon differences and individuality. Their attitude only dared her to try harder to be outrageous. At any rate, Steampunk may be different but it was a culture – not just a fashion style; she liked it. It made her feel like a strong Warrior woman. What was the big deal about fitting in and belonging anyway?

The text message Bernie sent earlier in the day said 'Good news re Mist. Call me'. This could mean only one thing.

Normally, she couldn't wait to visit Bernie at his shop at Stubblefield, with its old polished floorboards, reclaimed brick walls, and barn weathered shelves hanging from wrought iron brackets filled with Steampunk paraphernalia. There was nothing to compare to that first hit of old leather mingled with cured tobacco as she walked through the door. Steampunk heaven.

Not today.

Despite Bernie's eagerness, for Paisley no news was good news. Two weeks and three days of *no news* to be exact. It was not going to be a good day. Heath would be heartbroken, the poor kid. Eddy was right, of course. Guilt ridden she wasn't sure how to break it to him.

She waited for Bernie to finish serving a guy purchasing a pouch of bourbon infused tobacco leaf imported from Kentucky. He was going to be a while. They were having a deep discussion about the best spots for fly fishing, and comparing notes on previous catches, not that Bernie ever went fishing. Bernie's dad was an avid fisherman but hadn't managed to pass on his love of the sport to his youngest son. Nonetheless, Bernie, the businessman, could talk the talk when required.

In the meantime, Paisley browsed through the aisles looking for new stock on the shelves. Since taking over from his grandfather, Bernie had made several improvements. Now he carried a large selection of vape mods, fruit flavour shots and e-cigars, as well as herbal cigarettes. On display were black cigarettes from the Philippines, very Goth, branded 'Black Bat' that were liquorice flavoured. Paisley didn't smoke, however, peering into the glass cabinet she was tempted just a little to indulge for the dramatic impact; however, they were not for sale anyway. Next to the Black Bat cigarettes were vintage lighters shaped like old fashioned kerosene lamps, sundial ash trays, cigarette holders shaped like pistons, and Sherlock Holmes style e-pipes decorated with skulls – all in keeping with the Steampunk theme.

With an excellent head for business, Bernie had expanded his stock, branching out to gift items unrelated to smoking paraphernalia. Strolling to another section of the shop, Paisley picked up a pot bellied tea pot shaped like a Jules Verne airship and studied it for several minutes fascinated with its intricate design. She set it down again next to an antique hourglass. Alongside on the shelf were hand worked leather journals with Celtic knot locks, copper flasks encrusted with barnacles, anchors and starfish looking as if they'd been dug up from a shipwreck, Raven shaving brushes, statues of tiny stag beetles made from blue titanium, metal screws and clockwork parts, and black umbrellas with skull handles.

Bernie's pure indulgence – much to the shock horror of his parents – was in another section of the shop. Here his inner child went wild with Steampunk fashion accessories based on retro-futuristic inventions and pre-industrial Victorian mythology: cyberpunk pirate guns, warrior leather breastplates and forearm guards, sundial and compass wrist watches, wide leather belts with straps and tarnished buckles, corsets and lacy blouses, re-fashioned army coats dangling clockwork cogs on chains, and Mad Hatter top hats decorated with aviation goggles. A veritable feast of Steampunk sub-cultures ranging from Goth, cyberpunk, and neo-Victorian. This was the section Paisley spent the most time, and the most money when she could afford to splurge. It was the inspiration behind setting up the Steampunk

Club as a marketing ploy. It was also about sharing their passion for Steampunk with other adventurous, like minded people.

It took some time for Club membership to grow and for Bernie's flair for entrepreneurship to show steady profits. And for his scandalised family to tone down their objections. Now they were his biggest supporters. It was advantageous to have doting parents, Bernie admitted.

If this were her shop, Paisley thought, she would never have to go anywhere else ever. Bernie promised that as soon as he could afford an assistant, she'd be hired. In the meantime, he supported her nascent Steampunk craft initiatives, stocking her Victorian-style necklaces, rings designed from clockwork gears and cogs, hair combs with cyberpunk futuristic decals, Alice in Wonderland hats and smoking vests. This was her passion and it made good pocket money. But not yet enough to differentiate it from making a living rather than a hobby.

"Greetings from the Laudator Temporis Acti," Bernie said walking up from behind, interrupting her daydreams.

She finished the ritual. "Salutations from the Guild of Artificers."

"If you're looking for your stuff, most of it has sold. I've been meaning to see if you can make a few hats and vests for the window display."

"Sure. Now that Mist is settled into a routine, I should have more time," Paisley said while inspecting a ceramic mug with a red heart and the phrase *Drink Me* splashed across it. "I could use the money, too. You're right about the cost of keeping a dog."

"Yeah, about that." Bernie hesitated. Paisley knew what was coming. "I got a hit on the Facebook post. A girl from the bakery in Lower Teasel says it's her parents' dog." Before Paisley could argue and put up barriers, he added, "I think she's legitimate."

"All this time, she was caught only meters from her home and wasn't lost at all," Paisley whispered into the room. "I feel terrible."

"Don't. Anita, the girl who contacted me, said the dog was in their backyard but got spooked from the thunder that night and managed to jump the fence. They didn't bother looking for her straight away because they figured she'd be long gone. They left all the lights on hoping she'd find her way home once the storm cleared."

"I expect they'll want Mist back as soon as possible," Paisley said, heartbroken and pale.

"Anita said to bring her around tomorrow. The bakery's closed on Sundays. If you're up for it, I can go with you," Bernie said, patting her shoulder.

"Best to get it over with," Paisley said with a sigh. "I'd better go and pack up Mist's gear and say my farewells." She hugged Bernie and left the shop, determined not to cry. This was life. You learned not to get attached. *You let go and moved on.*

Chapter Five

The next day, leaving it to the last minute, late morning, Paisley drove Rolla slowly as a hearse to the Convict Crust, accompanied by Bernie holding Mist in the front passenger seat. To match her mood, she dressed in Goth black: black t-shirt, a wide belt with several buckles over a short pleated black skirt, black and white check leggings, and black ankle boots. Her eyes were outlined in ebony kohl and her foundation was as pale as the moon. To make a point, she'd chosen a necklace made of heavy chain that dangled a weighty anchor and red enamelled earrings heart shaped stuck with arrows. Their significance wasn't lost on Bernie.

Unexpectedly, a silent but deadly dog fart permeated the car interior. Mist's innocent expression caused a smile which Paisley quickly suppressed. *That I won't miss*, she thought then changed her mind. *I'll miss everything about her.* Bernie rolled down the window letting fresh air in. No one uttered a word.

He kept quiet knowing better than to give her a pep talk about the virtues of being a good citizen. Paisley refused to look at him. With watery red eyes and sniffles, she was doing all she could to hold back tears. One word and she'd be a sobbing mess. Mist stuck her nose out the window with glee as if on a fun adventure. *Traitor*, Paisley grumbled in her thoughts.

Nearing the bakery, Paisley pulled up the car opposite a row of Harley motorcycles parked along the footpath. A gang of leather clad bikers with bushy beards and elaborate tattoos lounged on outdoor chairs around the side of the old brick building drinking mugs of coffee. "I thought Anita said the bakery was closed on Sundays." She turned to Bernie with a frown looking for an excuse to accuse him of something.

Mist began to whine and fidget from excitement. Bernie secured the lead and opened the car door, allowing Mist to jump free. "Let's go find Anita," he said, all business and no nonsense. Paisley wasn't sure if he addressed the dog or her. Taking a deep breath, she followed them across the street towards the bakery.

A young woman dressed in jeans and a white apron over a camisole, with short black hair and a neon green fringe, pushed open the screen door of the bakery with a hip. She carried a tray laden with an assortment of pastries to an outdoor barbeque area sheltered under massive, old oak trees. She didn't see them at first and proceeded to hand out plates to the bikers with deliberate care. With a tail wagging like a fan blade, Mist whined and pulled on the lead. Bernie struggled to hold her back and she gave a sharp bark of frustration. The young waitress looked up with a wide smile and waved. "Hi there," she shouted. Depositing the tray on a spare table, she caught up with them outside the bakery's front door.

"Missy!" she said and crouched down to scratch Mist between the ears. "Where've you been, silly girl." Within a few minutes, the front door opened and a gangly young girl ran out and encircled the dog in a bear hug. "My sister, Noelle," Anita explained.

The way Mist's tail was wagging, Paisley didn't have to be an animal psychic to see that the whippet belonged here with her family.

Bernie was introducing her to Anita, weirdly blushing deep red while doing so. Then Anita was coaxing them round to the barbeque area, saying "You must meet my parents, Tobin and Monique Swan. They'll be thrilled at Missy's return. Don't mind the biker horde. I forgot; the club stops here once a month on their tour of the north. Tobin opens specially; he loves motorbikes, especially Harleys."

Chaos erupted as Mist, now reclaimed *Missy*, broke free and leaped into the arms of Tobin, licking his face and generally being totally out of control with happiness. Howls of laughter followed from the crowd of onlookers. Noelle trotted after Missy. Anita motioned Bernie and Paisley away from the commotion to meet her mother. "She's the one dressed like a flight attendant from the nineties," she quipped.

Monique was sitting on the edge of a picnic table with legs crossed, leaning rather flirtatiously over a young member of the biker gang in intimate conversation and not demonstrating any particular interest in Missy's return. With hair cut in a smooth blonde bob, wearing a red, white and blue scarf knotted around her neck, a white blouse tucked into a knee length, straight skirt, and swaying a foot tucked into a low-heeled navy pump, Anita was correct. Definitely a classic corporate airline look. Paisley felt young and immature in comparison.

Her second impression of Monique formed after receiving a plastic *customer service* smile. *Umm* far from genuine. Maybe the lady wasn't exactly pleased with being interrupted mid-chat with the young biker. There was definitely a lack of excitement at being reunited with the wayward whippet. Paisley had a bad feeling about it.

Bernie was introduced to Monique, all the time grinning like a fool at Anita and making small talk. "We didn't know her name so we named her Mist, which is cool because it's so close to Missy, her actual name," he bragged – using the royal 'we' as if he was responsible for picking the name. Before Paisley could protest, Monique started gushing thanks.

"You're our heroes," she exclaimed with dramatic flair. "That dog's my heart and soul, and I've missed her so much."

Anita rolled her eyes. "Sure MM, you loved Missy so much, you just accidentally left the back gate open during a storm—"

"—I was just explaining to my dear new friend how heartbreaking it was believing she was gone forever. My beautiful feral beast," she crooned, gazing coyly at the young biker.

Cynically, Paisley thought the *beautiful beast* comment was too coquettish to be meant for Missy. And then the guy turned around, stretching his long legs out from under the bench, and casually leaned elbows on the picnic table. And Paisley totally related to the woman's blatant female attentiveness, even if Monique was old enough to be his mother.

The young man looked Paisley up and down with appreciation. "The Steampunk chick, we meet again," he said cheerfully.

"You know each other?" Monique asked, dismissively.

"One dark and stormy night," Lance waxed poetic.

Paisley put a finger to her chin and looked to the sky. "That's right, it's Lance, isn't it? I remember the boots."

He laughed. "It was night and pissing down; suppose I looked like a drowned rat at the time. Not very noteworthy."

He had a deep, charismatic laugh. Paisley thought there was nothing drowned about him now, except for the dripping sex appeal, steaming up the surroundings and making it hard to breathe.

Bernie pointed to Lance. "Here's your other hero," he said to Anita. "This guy helped Paisley catch Mist – I mean Missy."

"I knew there was something special about you," Monique cooed, trying to draw Lance's attention. "Why didn't you say something before?"

His focus was on Paisley who he smiled at like an old friend.

"You left before I could leave my contact details," Paisley said too sharply, trying to hide the discomfort of a budding attraction in front of a jealous Monique. "I thought you'd like to know what happened to Mist, err *Missy*."

"It's intense we ran into each other. Nice coincidence," he said, holding her gaze with lightning intensity a few seconds longer than necessary. Paisley felt a flurry of fairy sparkles in the pit of her tummy.

Monique interrupted their moment. "Well, we've got the reunions out of the way. I believe Paisley and I should get to know each other better. It seems we share a common love of feral beasts," she said smoothly but rather too brazenly for Paisley's liking.

To cover a blush creeping up from her neckline, Paisley quickly asked, "So, is this your awesome bakery? Everyone in town goes crazy over Convict Crust's famous pasties."

"My husband and I purchased it last year after moving from Queensland. I came into an unexpected windfall. My parents died in a car accident and being an only child …" She left the implications hanging. In the background, Anita inhaled loudly as if about to argue but then remained silent when Monique frowned.

"I'm so sorry," Paisley murmured, embarrassed at the personal nature of the conversation.

"Don't be. They were losers, never did anything for me while they were alive," she said bitterly. "It worked out for the best. My motto is *cut your losses and move on*. It was a chance for a new start someplace special. I've always loved baking and this is my dream life."

"I can imagine," Paisley mumbled, gazing at the Federation building with its brick chimneys and painted walls gleaming bright white in the sun. Although taken aback at Monique's pragmatism, Paisley related to what she was saying about letting go of loser parents and moving on.

"Really? You can imagine?" Monique was asking, gazing intently at Paisley who as a rule never volunteered private information to strangers and felt uncomfortable when conversations become too personal early on.

Bernie covered for his best friend's reticence by explaining, "She grew up in foster care and moved around a lot." Paisley shot him a double whammy look which he shrugged off.

"Oh my, then we have so much in common," Monique gushed enthusiastically. "Like we're both orphans!"

Thrown by Monique's effusiveness, Paisley didn't have the heart to correct the misapprehension that her parents were dead. They were very much alive and living in a govie rental at Crows Marsh, not that she ever visited or that they kept in touch.

An awkward lull in the conversation was filled by Bernie asking Anita, "Does the bakery have a convict history?"

She looked puzzled before laughing. "Oh, you mean why did they name it 'Convict Crust'? That's Tobin's sense of humour—"

"—It used to be a coach house in the old days. A half way stop on the high road between Plover Point and Whaler's Cove," Monique cut in.

"Highway robberies were a thing back then," Anita said. Everyone nodded.

"The kitchen has its original wood fired brick oven and stone hearth where I bake the artisan bread and French pastries," Monique said with pride. "The accommodation around the back needs some renovating—"

"Yeah, she's been pulling up floor boards and tapping the walls, as if looking for something lost!" Anita whispered to Bernie.

"—but I'm decorating with period furniture," Monique finished saying, ignoring the interruption.

After a moment's pause, Lance turned to Paisley and asked, "Do you have a place to call home nowadays?"

Inside Paisley winced. Lance had zeroed in on her most sensitive issue. True to form, she deflected an answer with a teasing comment. "Whoa, trying to get my home address – that's a fast move. Let's take this a step at a time, cowboy. If you ask nicely, I might see about a phone number first."

Monique's fake smile returned. "I'll bet my new friend, Paisley, would love a tour of the bakery. Come on," she said, grabbing her arm and pulling towards the back door of the building.

Lance gave Paisley a mock look of woe at their parting before moving from the picnic bench to sit next to Tobin and a couple older bikers who were comparing tattoos and telling the stories behind each one.

Monique announced in a voice that carried in Tobin's direction, "Some help clearing tables would be appreciated."

Tobin growled, "In a minute, *Moaning Mona*. I'm in the middle of a conversation you might have noticed." This got him a round of applause from around the group.

Monique rasped to Paisley, "Typical guy. Sits on his ass sipping coffee, entertaining customers, expecting me to do all the work from the crack of dawn baking, serving, cleaning up."

"Hellfire. His nickname for you isn't exactly flattering," Paisley whispered back in female solidarity. "You must hate it."

Monique shrugged, seemingly not bothered. "Well, that's not the worst of it. We've been together for many years. I'm used to it. It's rubbed off on my daughters – they've started calling me *MM* for *Moaning Mona* as well."

Bernie leapt at the chance to impress Anita by offering to stack dishes and carry the tray to the kitchen. Paisley couldn't help but notice the attraction there. She was happy for him and hoped it worked out between them. Maybe a new love interest would mean he'd stop vying for Marianne's attention at future Steampunk

Club meetings. Whatever it was about Marianne, the guys in Paisley's life certainly were attracted to her. She couldn't decide if she disliked Marianne because of Adam, or for ignoring her BFF's qualities as a boyfriend. Maybe it was both. In Paisley's view, this new chick Anita seemed a better match for Bernie.

The tour felt like it took hours instead of twenty minutes. Monique hammered her with so many questions by the end of it, her whole life story had been extracted despite Paisley's reluctance to share. With each answer, Monique enthused that they were so much alike. By the end of it, she was gushing that *they could be sisters*.

When they finally emerged, most of the bikers had left but Lance remained, sitting next to Tobin bouncing Noelle on his knee, with Anita and Bernie nearby. Missy sprawled at Tobin's feet sleeping. "We should be going," Paisley announced to the group.

Tobin waved a twenty dollar note in the air at Bernie insisting it be taken *for their troubles*. Bernie shook his head adamantly refusing charity. Although Paisley was the one with empty pockets due to buying a lead and dog food, and therefore not as inclined towards humbleness under the circumstances.

He must have heard her stomach growling from hunger because Lance spoke up on her behalf. "It's okay to let Paisley accept a well deserved reward for finding and caring for Missy these last couple weeks." Bernie blushed, chastened.

Monique nodded. "Absolutely. She's our hero. Tobin, twenty dollars is not enough. She deserves more. Noelle, come with me." Disappearing into the bakery, Monique returned with Noelle carrying a large paper bag wafting the delicious smells of chocolate croissants, unceremoniously grabbing the bag and shoving it at Paisley.

After getting a stern look from his partner, Tobin dug deep into a jean pocket, pulled out a fifty dollar note and folded it into Paisley's palm, earning a satisfied look from Monique and a relieved look from Paisley. She'd be able to buy groceries before pay day.

"Thank you," she mimed, kneeling to give Missy a tummy rub. "Farewell. I'm going to miss you so much," she crooned with tears threatening to spill down her cheeks.

"Maybe Tobin would let you visit her now and then?" Lance asked sympathetically.

"I know!" shouted Bernie. "Let's get a photo of Missy with all of us." Whipping out his phone, he posed for a selfie, snapping a photo of himself and the grinning faces of Anita and Noelle along with Paisley hugging Missy. Inadvertently, he also captured Tobin's surprised concern and Monique's frown in the background. "I'll post it on the *Lost and Found* as a happy ending story."

Tobin mumbled something about not liking his photo taken but Monique cut off his complaint, talking over him.

"I have an idea," she said. "I walk Missy around The Town Common every morning after the baking. Why don't you join us?" Tobin screwed up his face as if this was a revelation, earning a glare. Monique continued with more fervour. "Please say 'yes'. I feel we have this connection already, like Missy escaped for a reason because we were destined to be friends." As Paisley hesitated, thinking over the offer, Monique pressed some more. "Or do you work? This wouldn't be a problem. We could walk after work?"

Paisley had to smile. This was a new experience for her, meeting someone who wanted to become a friend straight away. She understood how Mist must feel during a tummy scratch – all mushy and happy inside, not wanting it to end.

Considering how her first impressions of Monique were not that favourable, her attitude flipped one hundred eighty degrees. This morning, she was being forced to give up Mist and therefore her mood was particularly cynical and distrustful. But now, she knew the bakery was clearly Mist's home.

The dog wagged its tail and gave a stamp of approval.

Tobin and Monique were Mist's owners and they seemed to be lovely people. Lance was here, too; another sign that this was meant to be – fate, as Monique suggested. It was all good.

Paisley decided to let down some of her defences. "Okay, I'd like that."

This simple agreement had a momentous edge to it. By saying *yes*, Paisley entered a new chapter in life, one she imagined would signify worthiness; by becoming friends with one of the owners of a successful business in town, she would transform into *a someone to be noticed* rather than a homeless wayfarer. In her heart, she knew Monique's offer of friendship foreshadowed a stability and connection to Lower Teasel's community that she would never earn in her own right. For the first time, a long-held dream of belonging was on the cusp of manifesting as a day to day reality. *Yes.*

✿ ✿ ✿

Sidelined to a backrow seat by Monique's dominance and her effusive chatter about wanting to become Paisley's friend, Lance failed to register the moment the show was over and the scarlet haired Steampunk girl was walking away. Tongue tied, he watched Paisley and Bernie get into an ugly mustard coloured Datsun parked across the street and drive off, kicking himself for missing the opportunity yet again to get her phone number. Anita's gaze followed the car until it turned the corner, also looking momentarily bereft.

"What's the story between Paisley and that guy, Bernie?" he asked Anita, trying not to sound too obvious.

Monique answered instead. "Paisley told me they've been sweethearts since high school. So romantic." Looking shrewd, she rubbed it in. "Inseparable, I believe she said."

Lance watched Anita open and then close her mouth, biting back a dissenting retort after deciding it wasn't worth arguing with her mother over something that might never eventuate. He understood the feeling.

Then Tobin with unexpected empathy turned to Anita and said, "Didn't I hear something about him working at a tobacco shop in Stubblefield?" Ignoring the fury burning behind Monique's glare, he prompted, "Wouldn't hurt to do some tactical reconnaissance sometime. Never know when things could change."

Lance nodded, thinking it wouldn't hurt to take a detour to Stubblefield next road trip and check out this guy who was so special to Paisley. Sure, he was a likeable dude, if a bit serious. Safe.

But *safe* didn't seem to be her style. He wondered what she saw in him.

43

Chapter Six

By the time Paisley arrived at the Steampunk meeting, small groups stood huddled around the crowded room humming with dozens of random conversations. Late as usual, she'd given up on the notion of making a striking entrance for Adam's benefit. Scanning the crowd, she found him, or at least the back of him, wearing a khaki army coat, his distinct zig zag buzz cut and trendy rats tail ensconced in a far corner. As if by magic sensing her arrival, he turned and smiled a greeting, causing Paisley's heart to flip just a bit. He was so gorgeous. Then he resumed his deep and meaningful with Marianne who wore her blond hair tied in two pigtails with oversize bows, dressed like a cutesy Alice in Wonderland. Paisley felt like a tomboy by comparison in her go-to jodhpurs and army bomber jacket. Knowing his attention was monopolised, she sought out Bernie, her trusty BFF.

Ever faithful, Bernie looked relieved to see her. He waved and motioned to the head table, set up for Committee members. "Greetings from the Alchemist's Sanctum!" he shouted.

"Salutations from the Guild of Artificers," she replied. Pushing agenda papers aside, she plonked onto a chair next to him with a sigh, elbows on the table, chin in cupped hands. "What's up? You look nervous," she asked. Tonight, they were putting forward an idea that would test the group's commitment to the cause. But she couldn't see anything going wrong. Their idea was brilliant. Then she saw a neon green fringe sticking out of a bowler hat worn by a slim young woman in a top coat with tails.

Now it made sense. Bernie dressed to impress in his long leather coat with cyberpunk arm guards and the Third Reich monocle; the explorer binoculars dangling from his neck. The cunning devil needed this meeting to be a success for more than one reason.

She leaned a shoulder into his in a gesture of camaraderie. "Mmm, I just saw the reason for your butterflies," she teased, nodding in Anita's direction.

Bernie grinned sheepishly. "Bedamned. She turned up at my shop out of the blue," he whispered in awe. "We got to talking and it seemed so easy. I invited her along tonight but I wasn't sure she'd come."

Paisley smiled across at Anita. "We'd better get this party started before we bore her to death," she said. Bernie gave a signal to another committee member, Conan, who called the meeting to order by clanging an elaborate Celtic sword encrusted with rhinestones onto a shield.

When the buzz in the room dimmed, Bernie sat up straight and affected a look of authority. "Welcome adventurers within the Grand Mechanism, all ye' daredevils, gypsies, pirates, saboteurs and warriors of the sanctum of magic, fantasy, and theatre. I know the business side of our meetings can be a tedious necessity." He paused for a few snorts and jeers, smiling in empathy.

Part of the double act, Paisley declared, "But tonight, it will be short and sweet." More chuckles, this time of friendly incredulity.

Bernie held up his hands in a gesture of *trust me*. "I have good news. This time our agenda has only one item listed – raising money for our charity."

"Or as I like to call it *fun* raising for the Street Kids of Lower Teasel," Paisley said in a voice similar to a spruiker on a TV shopper channel, winding up the crowd's enthusiasm.

Bernie signalled Conan to beat out a drum roll of sorts with his sword. "We've teamed up with the Shire's Steam Fest organising committee. And – we are going for a Guinness Book of Records this year at the Steam Festival! For the largest gathering of Steampunk costumes in one spot!" Bernie waited for the applause to follow this announcement. Paisley whooped and wolf whistled along with cheers and clapping from group members. "All you have to do is turn up—"

"—along with all your friends, family and work mates," Paisley added.

"Watch this space for further details. Let's do this people of the Sanctum," Bernie ended his speech with a flourish. Getting the message Conan banged his sword on his shield to symbolise the end of business and the start of feasting. "Godspeed. See you at our next meeting."

Club members surged through amber glass double doors that separated the meeting room from the front bar. Their thoughts focused on the real purpose of the night's get together – to line up to order drinks and meals. For once, Bernie abandoned his committee papers scattered across the table leaving it for Paisley to clean up and instead jumped up to intercept Anita before the masses wrapped her into their fold as they herded out. For most, the real business of the evening was to get merrily sloshed and to provide the night's entertainment for the gawking local patrons on slow Tuesdays.

"Hi," he said blushing a brilliant red before stammering, "I'm glad you could make it. I like your hat."

"Thanks. I hope it's *Steampunk* enough," she said, trying to make conversation. An awkward silence ensued.

Bernie shuffled his feet, then had a light bulb moment. "Come and say hello to Paisley," he said, dragging her over to the committee table where Paisley was slapping notebooks and folders in a pile in haphazard order, not being an admin-type of person.

Anita said to them, "That Guinness Book of Records idea is really awesome. If you need any help with it, let me know. I may be useful."

"Hellfire. We can always use help," Paisley groaned theatrically. "We've started getting in proposals for catering but haven't made any decisions, so if you're thinking of a waitressing role, we'll need to wait until they start hiring staff for the Festival," she explained.

"Oh, I wasn't thinking of that. I mean, I only help out at the Bakery in exchange for room and board. And only when I'm not at uni and my study schedule allows it," Anita said.

Bernie added with pride in his voice, "She's studying PR and marketing. I was thinking we could use her to do up posters, work on social media, you know, drum up enthusiasm for the Festival around the area."

Paisley studied her BFF's face with a secret smile. Clearly, he had fallen hard for this neon green fringed girl. "That sounds awesome," she said as much for Bernie's benefit as for Anita's. "Now, I suggest we get ourselves some well deserved drinks before our people drink the place dry."

In the back corner of the dining area, The Pocket Watch Fiddlers, a local band that Mel always booked for Steampunk nights, finished playing a reasonable rendition of Rihanna's 'Diamonds'. They gave it a dark brooding quality, more like Steam Powered Giraffes' cover version. Their Irish fiddler and electronic keyboard player dressed as Steampunk pirates and the rock cellist and banjo player wore Lord Nelson military jackets and naval hats. Their lead singer began a new song, 'Wicked Games', in a deep forlorn voice accompanied by a fusion of robotic synthesised rock, a didgeridoo, and the sounds of industrial gears and cogs cranking. An odd mix but it seemed to work. Dinner patrons tapped their feet enjoying the show.

Paisley pushed her way to the bar. A heavenly fragrance of cedar mixed with wood smoke and Irish Whiskey wafted across the back of her neck up to her nose. It was Adam's unique masculine scent. She could suck in that liquor all night long. He stood behind, not touching but effectively pinning her to the counter. "I missed you at the last meeting," he drawled in her ear in that sexy, 'just got out of bed' voice that never failed to instantly cause warmth between her legs. "Bernie said something about a lost dog?"

Paisley stiffened and didn't answer straight away, waiting for the bartender to plonk a schooner of frothy beer down in exchange for a handful of coins. When she turned, a hair's breath separated her body from his firm physique. She caught her breath, knowing there was no hiding the effect the man's flirting had on her sensibilities.

"I bought something for you at the markets," Adam said, holding up a rusty pocket watch for inspection. "It doesn't work but I was thinking you could use the parts for making your Steampunk jewellery."

Finally, he stepped back to allow her to push through the throng to a clear space with fresh air. Paisley was too caught up processing the heady fact he'd missed her and had bought a gift to study the pocket watch with any professional objectivity. She held it in her hand and stared blankly for several minutes, unable to utter a simple *thank you*. Over the noise of the crowd, a sugary voice called *'over here'* and the magic of the moment was broken.

Adam turned towards the voice and then quickly smiled at Paisley before joining Marianne at a sofa in the corner, drinks and two meals waiting on a coffee table. Leaving Paisley alone, standing in the middle of the dance floor with a silly grin on her face, exposed like an idiot. The Pocket Watch Fiddlers sang a parody about never falling in love again, in synchronous sympathy.

Chapter Seven

Monique puffed frosty breaths into the cold Spring morning, shuffling to get warm and impatient to continue their walk around the Town Common.

After snuffling through tufts of grass along the path, Missy had finally chosen the right spot to relieve herself and was taking her sweet time about it. Paisley stood by holding the lead and making all sorts of encouraging noises as if talking to a toddler. When the job was done, Paisley pulled a plastic shopping bag from her coat pocket and collected the smelly offerings.

Disgusted, Monique cringed. Paisley would have to carry it with them around the circuit, odiferous dog poop mingling with Monique's Opium perfume. *Remind me again why I thought this was a good idea?*

Paisley smiled at Monique as Missy jerked the lead and was off like a shot. Finally, the girl got the dog under control enough to stroll along and have a conversation at the same time.

"I imagine working at the pub is much the same as working at the bakery," Monique began. "I learn all the dirty, small town secrets of Lower Teasel's good neighbours: who's having affairs with whom, who's paying off an official to get a development approval through Council, how much to give out as a bribe," she prompted.

Paisley refused to oblige. "Not really," she said. "The pub on Friday nights gets packed and I'm too busy pulling pints to socialise."

"You must get blokes chatting you up all the time." Monique persisted in her mission to extract salacious gossip. Her philosophy was that there was less chance of being the subject of gossip in a small town if you were the main source of it. No one wanted to cross you when you knew everyone's secrets.

Paisley shook her head. "That's a common misperception of the job. My boss, Mel, ensures patrons are PC at all times. It's an OH&S thing. If anyone tries it on, there's a bouncer in the wings."

"How boring!" Monique gave a brittle laugh. "I guess the benefit of being my own boss is making my own rules. My customers can flirt with me any time. One bloke, married for twenty years with four kids, comes around every Monday supposedly for a coffee and meat pie, and a wink and a nudge. He never fails to hint we could have a fuck amongst the bags of flour in the store room. It must be a kitchen maid fantasy of his, I suppose." She waited for Paisley's reaction.

"Hellfire. His poor wife!"

Satisfied, Monique continued. "He's not the only one. There's a guy high up in Quamby Bluff Shire Council waiting for me to say *yes*. He trapped me against the kitchen bench once, hands all over me like an octopus, got so far as pulling down my knickers." She chuckled. "I stopped him by grabbing a bowl of hot melted chocolate meant for the profiteroles and dumping it on his hard on. I keep waking up in the middle of the night dreaming of licking it off. The man had a donger the size of a horse." She sighed theatrically. "He's not married but he's been rooting his assistant for a year now. I told him *I don't share; come back when you're free.* He will one day; you can bet on it."

Paisley stopped suddenly, anger shooting out of her eyes. "Tell Tobin. He'll put a stop to these guys harassing you!"

The girl's protectiveness – no, actually her unconditional adoration – was touching. "Don't worry. Tobin knows. When we met, he was Special Ops, very sexy – but that was a few years ago, before PTSD changed him, forced him out on a pension. He's our social director entertaining the regulars nowadays. His favourite saying is that most men would root a dead cat in the gutter given half a chance."

"Euww, that's not very complimentary to you!" Paisley exclaimed.

Monique was touched by the display of female solidarity but wanted to reassure Paisley. "He reckons there's nothing wrong with keeping our customers happy, even if it means entertaining their fantasies." She preened at the thought of the male gaze on her firm boobs and taut butt cheeks but seeing the displeasure on Paisley's face, quickly added, "Despite his PTSD, I'm devoted to Tobin and completely loyal." She winked. "It adds spice to our relationship knowing other men want to fuck me if only in their dreams."

Paisley didn't look convinced, but she was young and not as wise to the world. Monique would change that soon enough.

"Talking about being fancied, how about that biker the other day. Lance, I think his name was." Monique watched the blush creep up Paisley's neck, impressed at the girl's deadpan expression refusing to give any feelings away. "I may be old enough to be his mother, but holy hell, he was a mother's wet dream for bonking the lad next door," she said, trying to get a rise out of Paisley. "Leathers, tattoos, a Harley. What's not to lust after?"

The girl flinched but didn't say a word, just resumed walking, a stoic expression on her face. Monique was enjoying the moment. "I'm thinking of getting a tattoo for Tobin as an anniversary gift. Something war-like and heroic. Did you know Lance is a tattoo artist? A total bad boy. I can't wait to spend time in artistic liaison with him, experimenting with imaginative configurations, roughing out designs for Tobin's tattoo. I'm sure it will be something special."

"A tattoo sounds romantic; what a whimsical idea." Paisley deflected the conversation to a safer tone to Monique's amusement. "How many years have you and Tobin been married?" Paisley prompted.

Monique ignored the question. "After you and Bernie left, we got to talking to Lance. He asked a lot of questions about you." She paused for effect. There it was – a slight crinkle of happiness in the corners of Paisley's eyes. "The bike club rides through Lower Teasel more or less monthly, always stopping for a break at the bakery, so we see a lot of him. Of course, his girlfriend usually comes with, riding on the back. They both live in Whaler's Cove, I believe. It's harder keeping a relationship on fire if you live kilometres apart."

Paisley seemed to mull over this. Finally, she spoke, once again trying to change the subject. "Sometimes it's just as hard when you are close by. I mean, I can't even seem to light this one guy's fire let alone stoke it to an inferno."

It was a plaintive entreaty for help. Monique was instantly intrigued. "I can't wait. Tell me everything. Who is this bloke you've set your heart on?"

Paisley slowed to a snail's pace and began to confide. "There's this guy in our club. I think he likes me and we text a lot; he'll do something nice like buy me a pocket watch from the markets but then he pulls away, leaves me hanging in mid-air and goes to sit with Marianne. I can't figure him out. I've tried to talk to Bernie but he just says Adam is a buffoon and refuses to discuss it further."

Monique concealed a sense of victory. "Well, Bernie's not much of a friend then. You can talk to me about anything. That's what girlfriends are for." She put an arm around Paisley's shoulder in a hug of camaraderie. "Tell me more about this Adam. He must be gorgeous if you like him?" They continued walking a second lap around the Town Common, a skinny whippet tugging along two new best friends, lost in girlie conversation.

Chapter Eight

At the next Steampunk Club meeting night, Paisley paused for a moment outside the Draught Horse Pub to breathe in confidence and exhale the *wow factor*, as instructed by her new mentor, apparently guaranteed to transform Adam into a soulmate.

Although after pouring out her heart to Monique about Adam, Paisley felt slightly weird. She wasn't sure if this queasiness was guilty pleasure at finally knowing how to play the game to win him over if she got the courage to follow Monique's advice. Or, if it was just qualms about divulging a lot of private stuff about Adam to a third party and betraying confidences without permission. She didn't like to think about herself as a gossip. This went against her better nature. Throughout childhood when she was part of the system nothing about her personal life was kept confidential; there were too many third parties involved.

As an adult, privacy had become a non-negotiable value. Or so she believed.

It was just that she had all these pent-up emotions around the guy – confusion, lust, anger, loss, hope – and for once, there was a girlfriend ready to hear it all, piece it all together and tell her what to do. Like the big sister she never had.

And Monique was such a good listener. She had a way of asking questions, not in a nosey way but in an understanding way like she really wanted to know. It was so cool having a girlfriend to confide in. So different from talking about stuff with Bernie. Guys just didn't see things in the same way.

According to Monique, despite a tough Steampunk girl image, Paisley was not worldly, even after living with a guy for two whole years.

During their walks around the Town Common, her new and very enthusiastic girlfriend had taken it upon herself to provide coaching on how men think about women.

According to Monique, Eddy had been her first and only relationship and therefore unconsciously set the standard for future romance. A worry if true. Eddy's charm was his slow and somnolent nature – what Paisley needed when they first met with her own restless spirit running from everything. Sex had been uninspiring – his idea of passion was waking her up for a quickie at two in the morning after spending a night gaming and downing a few glasses of cask wine. They'd been a comfortable, safe couple which was what she needed at the time. She'd harboured no illusions of a grand passion with him. In his defence, he was quite a bit older and split his energy between being a father to Heath and a partner to Paisley. And he was kind. This was more important. They'd remained friends for the sake of Heath.

Yesterday, somewhere along the gravel circuit with Missy pulling her along and Monique lecturing on passion, it had dawned on Paisley that Monique was around the same age as Eddy. A mother with two kids no less, and yet she exuded sex appeal and apparently men passionately desired her body. So maybe it was an Eddy-thing rather than an age-thing that dampened the flames of passion in their relationship.

Clearly, Monique knew what she's talking about when it came to men. Paisley would be foolish to ignore mature advice from an experienced authority.

According to her new life coach, Monique, it all was a game. Paisley had to start seeing love like a competition. To win Adam, Marianne had to lose. Simple as that. Forget Bernie's advice that Adam was a loser, too fucked up by his ex-wife being a dyke to love again, obviously so depressed he quit his job as a cop and now had to support three kids on a single parent's pension.

Bernie never said it like that; he was much too PC. Monique was paraphrasing, rather harshly in Paisley's opinion. Nonetheless, her point was made.

Even if at the end it turned out Bernie was right and Adam was a loser, according to the coach, Paisley could always dump him. It was the winning that counted.

Monique insisted she assert her rights to Adam's attention, pushing Marianne from centre stage. Take some risks, show she was available and willing. Why wait for Adam to do all the work?

So, this is where all of Monique's lecturing got her. In front of the pub, taking in deep breaths of confidence and *wow*-ness. Paisley began to feel light headed. Hyperventilating had not been part of the plan. She could do this. Dressed in the self-proclaimed *awesome* Steampunk outfit, with the right attitude, miracles would happen.

This time the weather colluded with the universe and her affirmations – it was cool and dry, no storms or stray dogs to dampen and wrinkle the effect of her sex appeal. No tattooed biker with a crooked smile and the best buckled boots … *Where did that thought bubble come from?* She couldn't be thinking of Lance at this moment.

Plastering on a wide smile, she entered the pub with a flourish, head held high.

Adam was not in a corner of the meeting room talking to Marianne, as anticipated in the 'war plan'. He was sitting on a bar stool, shoulders slumped, nursing a Southern Comfort and cola. Alone. Marianne was nowhere to be seen. He looked so lost; so vulnerable. Like he needed a hug. Paisley recognised the signs of the man about to hole up in his man cave again.

Thoughts of winning some stupid game, besting Marianne, being some kind of sexy poster girl for Adam to notice, all dissipated into the pub's grungy hops and nicotine fug. In an instant, Paisley comprehended what Monique would never realise about Adam. Not all newly single dads know how to transition from husband to dating, or for that matter, want to go on a sex rampage to alleviate grief over a lost love. It was possible for all of Adam's sexy dreamy gorgeousness, he hadn't had a lot of passion in his marriage. His skill set could be lacking or he was out of practice. Paisley wasn't the only one needing confidence. Recognising a kindred soul softened Paisley's recent resolve, at Monique's insistence, to push him into something before he was ready to move on.

Taking the bar stool beside him, Paisley signalled the bartender for a beer. "Are you joining the meeting, or do you need some alone time?" she asked quietly.

Adam's smile, the sort one gave to an old friend, indicated he was happy to see her. "I'm fine, just a lot on my mind. I needed to clear my head."

Paisley waited, no pressure. If he wanted to talk, he would.

After a few minutes of silence, where they both sipped drinks and stared at the counter, he said, "My ex is getting married. They'd like the kids to move in with them after the wedding. She wants me to ask the kids about it." He turned his face to Paisley showing one of those smiles men do when life sucks but they won't admit it and they refuse to expose their true feelings.

"Hellfire, that's major. Would the kids want that? I mean, how do you feel about the idea?" Paisley asked, realising too late to tone down her initial gush of concern so as to not sound too alarmist. She wondered how conflicted he would be feeling about his wife remarrying, being Catholic and having a strong faith in all its religious values.

"The kids miss their mum. I imagine they'll be thrilled." The look of bleak resignation on his face said it all.

"Bedamned, Adam, I'm so sorry." Paisley resisted the urge to hug him, not wanting to take advantage of a vulnerable moment. Monique would call her a wimp. But she didn't want to spoil this surreal moment of sharing and caring with Adam. The man needed a friend right now. *Girlfriend* would have to wait, probably a long spell from the sounds of it.

He slugged the last of the Southern Comfort and cola, thumped the empty glass on the counter and stood up. "Best be getting to the meeting," he announced, abruptly marching off across the bar room and pushing through amber glass doors leading to the meeting room.

Not waiting to see if Paisley followed. Which was disappointing. Maybe he was suddenly shy after their deep and meaningful.

A burst of laughter-filled conversation from Steampunk members filtered into the bar area before the amber doors swung shut and the back of Adam's broad shoulders dressed in his Steampunk military long coat disappeared down the shadowed corridor. With a sigh she thought *I wonder how long he'll man cave this stretch?*

Chapter Nine

A grey blanket of clouds hid the early morning sun, keeping the air as chilled as an esky filled with ice. A low mist hung in patches around the Town Common giving the car park a lonely vibe. Cold and wanting to get moving, Paisley waited for Monique and Missy wondering if she should hop back into Rolla and turn on the heater. It had been at least fifteen minutes already. Looking up the road in the direction they usually strolled in from, she was met with an empty street devoid of life apart from a black cat stalking along the gutter. Was it possible they'd arrived early and had continued to walk around the Common without her? No chance. Her friend had never arrived on time, let alone early, the entire while she'd known her. This had to mean they were late. Later than usual. Something may have happened. Checking the phone, there wasn't a message.

Deciding to tough it out, she wrapped a chunky knitted scarf around her neck twice and then shoved her hands into the pockets of a bomber jacket that was doing very little to repel the cold. In some ways, Paisley was relieved for the few minutes of respite to get her thoughts together. Monique would want to know how well the 'war plan' had worked with Adam and Paisley dreaded being a disappointment. She wasn't sure how to exactly explain all her good intentions unraveling as soon as she got through the Draught Horse Pub's front door and saw him sitting there. How to admit the likely truth that there wouldn't be another opportunity to win over Adam for several weeks because he'd be man caving again.

If Monique judged her a wimp or started criticising her soft heart, Paisley couldn't predict how volatile the reaction would be. Exhausted from being up all night obsessing about her interaction with Adam, analysing every piece of their conversation, his body language, how he up and left her to go to the meeting, the conflicting messages first confiding and then distancing himself, consumed what should have been sleep time, leaving her an emotional pendulum. If Monique disapproved – or judged Adam – Paisley knew in her heart she'd defend the guy even at the risk of ruining a budding girlfriend-ship. Or worse, maybe whine that she wasn't up to playing Monique's game and therefore would quit before making another fool of herself. Or maybe both defend and whine.

Now that was confusing. She needed a girlfriend's advice to help sort out these conflicting feelings. An older and wiser sister to listen and understand.

A Land Cruiser sped into the car park, pulling up next to Rolla spitting dust and gravel against the side panels. Before Paisley could swear at the gate crasher, a dishevelled Monique tumbled out, hair askew, looking as if she hadn't slept all night. Her first words at seeing Paisley were *'Tobin's left me!'* Then she doubled over and burst into wailing.

All Paisley could do was let Monique's pain run its course. Surreptitiously, she scanned the backseats of the Land Cruiser for Missy but found them empty. Disappointed, she understood today was all about Monique.

As she gained composure, Paisley patted her back and suggested taking deep breaths. "Talk to me. Why would he leave you?"

Monique went still, a calculating expression crossing her face so short-lived Paisley wondered if it was imagined. Her girlfriend inhaled tremulously. "It was all so sudden. A phone call at midnight from his father woke us up. Tobin's mother was dying from cancer and he had to make a mercy dash to the UK to say goodbye." Monique's voice choked up. "He packed his bags and caught the red-eye this morning to Sydney on standby for the next flight to England." Tears ran down her cheeks.

"That's terrible!" Paisley said.

"I know. How could he do this to me? What am I going to do?"

"I meant, terrible for Tobin losing his mother," Paisley amended, envious that some people had mothers they'd willingly drop everything to help.

"That too," Monique hiccoughed. "But what about the bakery? I can't do it on my own. I'll have to close it down and then how will I live?" She began to wail again.

Paisley's common sense kicked in. Indulging Monique's drama queen theatrics was not going to get them anywhere. "Hang on. How long is he going to be away for? There must be something you can do in the interim? What about Anita helping out?"

"Anita? You're joking, that piece of baggage? That girl's never pulled her weight a day in her life unless I get on my hands and knees … I'm not begging her!" Monique's voice screeched to hysterical levels.

Impressed by Anita's dedication to studying at university and taking breaks to help out at the bakery on weekends, Paisley wanted to suggest she ask Anita before reaching that unhelpful and unnecessarily negative conclusion. But in the same space, she realised this would pour oil on the pyre of Monique's self-imposed misery. Her friend was not about to be consoled or talked into solutions too soon.

Nonetheless, Paisley was finding difficulty making the connection between Tobin's absence and the bakery not operating. Didn't Monique say she was the baker and Tobin was the PR guy who helped with the washing up occasionally? Monique already did the bulk of the work.

"He could be gone weeks! Who knows how long his mother will be dying!" Monique twisted her neck to gaze at Paisley from the corner of her eyes with a beseeching look meant to tug heartstrings.

Paisley was more confused than moved. Her friend was resourceful, intelligent and hardworking. Why was she so upset about Tobin's temporary absence? In her experience, no man could be depended on for continuous love and support. Eventually, you were left on your own to fend for yourself. What was the big deal?

The one and only good thing her parents taught her was self sufficiency. There was this independent streak in Paisley's personality that made her hard hearted and unsympathetic towards others falling apart in crises. You didn't moan and wail when someone let you down – you let go and moved on. Simple.

And the guy was coming back. What was all the fuss about?

That was cold. She sometimes hated this pragmatic lack of sympathy in her character, seeing it as a flaw rather than a virtue. It was no wonder she had few friends. For 'normal' people there was no shame in missing someone, being lost without them, allowing emotions to erupt in tears and wailing. Like Monique was doing now. It was a sign of trust and friendship to be so honest and open.

Giving Monique superwoman status had been a mistake. An abundance of charisma didn't necessarily mean Monique was self confident or strong or self sufficient. Paisley had over inflated her qualities in the first flush of enthusiasm at having a girlfriend. The woman needed her to be the strong one, the caring one. To be there for her. Being needed was a new experience for Paisley.

Monique's tears started flowing again. "What am I going to do?" she kept repeating in whispers of despair.

Against her natural inclinations to not get involved in other people's problems, Paisley softened. Of course, Monique would be in shock at Tobin's sudden departure. The guy had chosen his parents' needs over his spouse's without a second thought. That had to hurt deep down. She'd be missing him and full of doubts about managing the business without his support. That's what a husband was meant to do.

And what friends were for, Paisley decided in a rush of loyalty. With Tobin gone, Monique needed a friend more than ever. True, she hadn't known Monique and Tobin for long. But if she wanted a girlfriend and confidante in her life, then she needed to be a good friend in return. This was a confluence signalling Paisley to step up to the mark.

Chapter Ten

After sorting out Monique's breakdown by agreeing to help out while Tobin was away, Paisley headed to *Light Up* to share the good news with Bernie. It was exciting having another paying job to supplement the bartender's job even if Monique warned she couldn't pay Award wages. This didn't matter. Working at the prestigious Convict Crust bakery alongside her girlfriend was going to be fun, not work. And she'd see more of Missy, too. It might mean putting her Steampunk craft work on hold but it would only be for a short interval.

Of course, Bernie did his best to pour cold water on her enthusiasm. Paisley stood next to the counter, trying to get a word in edgewise to explain her snap decision in between constant interruptions while Bernie served customers and passed on gossip from Auntie Sheryl about the new owners of the bakery.

Auntie Sheryl was Lower Teasel's Post Mistress and a notorious gossip. She was also Bernie's actual great aunt, unlike other residents who called her *Auntie Sheryl* but were only distantly related, if that. Therefore, Bernie put a lot of weight into what she told him. And his auntie was worried about any association with the bakery and therefore strongly encouraged him to leave

Anita well enough alone. *Sins of the fathers* and all that stuff and nonsense. It was already too late; he was smitten. *Children couldn't be blamed for their parent's flawed past,* he debated. Paisley couldn't argue with that, given her own parents' history.

Nonetheless his defence of Anita didn't curb a lecture to Paisley about heeding Auntie Sheryl's advice and steering clear of the bakery before getting in too deep. She smirked at his double standard and refused to be alarmed. "I don't believe that Tobin was an ex-con who learned to bake in prison. Just because they named the bakery 'Convict Crust' doesn't mean anything sinister. It's a reference to Lower Teasel's convict past." When Bernie didn't look impressed with the argument, she added more forcefully, "Monique told me she's the baker, not Tobin. So, it can't be true." It was staggering how rumors evolved from a simple shop sign. The creativity of small town gossips spinning madcap yarns flabbergasted her.

Bernie wasn't finished though. "You have to wonder where they got the money to buy the historic roadhouse and turn it into a bakery, plus all the other renovations going on. That would take some serious cash. Not something you'd have from being pensioned out of the army." He gave Paisley a sympathetic look to play down his pernicious horrible-ising. "Auntie Sheryl says it's drug money, that Tobin served time for a drug deal that went wrong."

"Don't be ridiculous, Bernie!" Paisley exploded in outrage realising her BFF, the most sensible person she knew, was indulging in Chinese whispers like a school kid. "You were there when Monique explained her parents were killed in a road accident and she got an inheritance."

"I'm just saying—"

He was interrupted by the shop door opening. Anita walked through with a big grin on her face. He blushed, returning a guilty smile.

"Hi, guys. I was getting cross eyed from my nose in books all morning so I decided to go for a drive. Look where I ended up," Anita said laughing.

An awkward silence ensued, with Bernie looking like he'd been caught out gossiping. *Which he had, served him right.* To save face for her BFF, Paisley quickly said, "I'm sorry to hear about your dying grandmother in the UK."

A puzzled expression crossed Anita's face before she blurted, "Oh, you mean Tobin's mother? Didn't even know he had a mum in the UK, let alone that she was dying." This confused Paisley. Why wouldn't Anita know about her grandmother? Oblivious, Anita chatted on. "Yeah, it all happened rather suddenly after their fight, him disappearing into the night, leaving poor Moaning Mona in a lurch."

"A fight?" Bernie asked.

She turned to Bernie. "I don't know what she and Tobin were arguing about specifically this instance but it sounded like the usual stuff. Tobin's shouting woke me at around midnight. *What have you done with the money*? he was yelling at the top of his lungs." She paused to reflect. "He sounded downright scared, which was different."

"Do you think the bakery is in financial trouble?" Bernie asked, ever the businessman.

"Maybe. Money goes through MM's fingers like water. Her credo is *the best of everything, bugger the cost.* Tobin likes to lay low and not flash the cash. She would often accuse him of being a petty penny pincher and he'd retaliate by calling her a petty thief." Anita laughed as if these revelations were normal family dynamics and nothing odd or concerning.

Bernie and Paisley were lost for words. Anita was happy to carry the conversation.

"MM says you're going to help out at the bakery until Tobin returns. Just so you know, we'd be OK without you. Tobin taught me all the recipes, even the fancy French pastries. MM is panicking for no reason. I'm all the help she needs." Anita's kind expression contradicted the rejection. "I've been told to train you to make coffees and clear tables. Seeing as you work at the pub already, that will be like teaching you to suck eggs. But just go along with it. She's freaking out enough about having to get up at the crack of dawn to bake the bread. This will be a first for her. It will do her good." Anita raised her brows with a look of mean delight.

"I thought Monique was the baker," Bernie said with a pointed stare at Paisley.

"God no. She loves to give that impression, you know, a martyr doing *all* the work. But Tobin does all the baking. He learned a few years ago in Queensland through a job training program. Not really a passion; I'd say more of a vocation for him." Anita kneeled down to study descriptions on various tobacco pouches displayed in the glass cabinet, bored with discussing her parents.

At the mention of a job training program, Bernie glanced at Paisley with a knowing look. She responded by sticking out her tongue.

"Blueberry infused roll your own tobacco. That sounds good," Anita gushed, in an attempt to regain Bernie's sole attention. Not looking up but out of the corner of her mouth she whispered to Paisley. "You'll hate working for her. MM's got a bad temper and she holds grudges. Take this as a warning – don't get her offside." Then snuggling up to Bernie, in a loud voice, she said, "One pouch, please, Bernie baby. I've decided to extend my habit to rolling and smoking tobacco for a change."

"Might not give the same kick," Paisley murmured. From the sidelines, she watched the two love birds absorbed in each other's company, feeling superfluous. Second thoughts about whether to help out at the bakery dampened the happy mood she'd arrived in. After a few minutes she decided to leave and give them space. Bernie hardly noticed.

Lost in thought, Paisley sat in the driver's seat staring out Rolla's windscreen, restless but not sure where she wanted to go or what she wanted to do. Despite having ruined her good cheer with his concerns about the nefarious goings on at the bakery, Bernie seemed extraordinarily happy to liaise with the baker's daughter. Good luck to him. She couldn't wish her BFF ill, not when she knew in his own way, Bernie was trying to look out for her. *Damn Auntie Sheryl, the busybody casting doubts.* Why couldn't something go right just once for a change? Working at the bakery was her chance for self-esteem, to fit in as one of the locals. As per usual, ignorant judgements from townsfolk trashed Paisley's dreams.

And stoked defiance. They needed to be proved wrong. She'd show them up.

Anita didn't sound that happy with the generous offer to help out which was a bummer. Paisley didn't want to step on anyone's toes, especially when those cute little digits belonged to Bernie's new girl. On the other hand, Anita was planning to train her in the art of waitressing, so maybe the resentment about her incursion into Convict Crust's family affairs only went skin deep. This was something to sort out later, if it became an obvious issue.

She decided to ignore Anita's comments about Monique being difficult to work for. She was only helping out a friend; not an actual employee. It would be a short stint. Therefore, hopefully, Monique's expectations were not set too high.

However, if the other stuff Anita said was true, Paisley needed to consider what this signified. If Monique wasn't the baker and the bakery was running into financial difficulties, and Tobin's frugal business sense would be missing for – however long – was Paisley getting in over her head, as Bernie suggested?

There was only so much she could do to help, but she didn't want to ruin a chance to form a true and lasting friendship by letting her friend down either.

She had to give it a go, no matter what.

Except, just after this thought, a cartoon impression of Tobin in orange overalls on a dusty prison quadrangle scrolled past her mind's eye like a TikTok video. Bernie had messed with her head.

Even considering Tobin as a criminal was silly of course. What was he thinking? Determined, she'd set him right, somehow.

Racking her brain and coming up blank, suddenly the answer became clear. Adam was an ex-policeman. She would ask his advice. He was the one person she knew who was emotionally distanced from the bakery. He'd be good at putting all the facts and innuendos into a semblance of order for her; maybe even clarify the best course of action. Opening her phone, she sent a text before regretting the decision.

> Can we meet for lunch today? I need your help.

A response pinged one minute later.

> At Village Spice Café now. Happy to talk.

A sense of relief washed over her. He hadn't gone into self imposed lockdown as expected. She replied immediately.

> Awesome. C U in 15 min.

Paisley couldn't believe how easy this was achieved. Adam was waiting to talk to her over lunch. Maybe her luck was changing after all.

Chapter Eleven

Monday morning Paisley cruised to the new job at Convict Crust. This early there were plenty of parks along the kerb. Paisley brought Rolla to a stop opposite the bakery with a rumbling muffler farting black smoke into the dewy grass verge. Wanting to impress Monique on day one, she'd dressed conservatively in a 'bakery uniform': pleated black skirt and white t-shirt, tucked in with a wide buckled corset. The harlequin tights with ankle boots were a last minute addition, not wanting to look boring. Checking her makeup in the mirror, she flattened curling strands of a wayward fringe, smoothed the cherry braid across her shoulder, and rubbed a streak of burgundy lipstick off her chin, satisfied all was work-ready.

She felt better after a long talk with Adam last week. Although he thought she was looney taking any notice of Auntie Sheryl's gossip, as a favour he agreed to ask one of his mates at the police department about Tobin to see if there was some history showing up on the system. She knew he was humouring her from the cheesy smile he flashed when saying it.

Not one to go behind someone's back normally, she felt reassured that Tobin was in the UK and therefore not directly approachable. Bad idea to ask Monique who was bound to get offside before the job even started. Adam would have an answer by end of week. This would put her mind at ease. And prove Bernie wrong. That would be worth it.

With jaunty strides, she made her way across the road to the bakery to be confronted by Anita at the front door waving a billowing dishcloth. A black cloud smelling of burnt almonds wafted out through the fly screen. Anita put an index finger to her lips and then smiled. "First day on the job and MM has already burned the almond croissants," she whispered. "They're everyone's favourite. Don't say a word. She's in a filthy mood," she laughed gleefully. "Come in. I'll show you where to dump your handbag and then you can help me set up tables."

The first customer arrived at eight on the dot of opening wanting a take-away cappuccino, putting the pressure on. Anita demonstrated how to operate the coffee machine to steam the milk at the exact temperature and measure and pat down coffee grounds for the perfect strength, and most important, the precise method of swirling the milk froth to make the bakery's signature emblem on the surface – a rose that was then dusted with pink vanilla sugar. This was much fancier than the pub's cappuccinos where she pushed a button and a machine drizzled instant foamy coffee into a paper cup. It was going to take a bit of practice to get the bakery's coffees to the perfection required by Monique.

When the customer asked for his favourite croissant, Anita was quick to think on her feet. "Sorry, we already sold the whole first batch to the Shire council for an office breakfast," she fibbed. "They're very popular."

Overhearing the conversation, Monique appeared in the kitchen doorway looking flushed and sweaty, wiping flour from her forehead. "The next lot won't be ready for another half an hour," she explained in a harried tone.

"Would you like us to put one aside to pick up later?" Paisley asked, smoothing the situation with professional aplomb. This thoughtfulness seemed to appease him and he left muttering about coming back.

Monique appraised the retreating figure and as the door swung shut smiled lasciviously. "On my sliding scale, I'd rate him a two."

Anita turned to Paisley to clarify. "She means 'worth a poke'."

Monique explained. "One is 'Hot as – he can poke me any time'. Two is "Yeah so so – worth poking but only if I'm horny'. And three is "Wouldn't touch him with a hot poker". She and Anita laughed.

"MM rates all her male customers," Anita said. "It's a game she plays. Keeps her from getting bored."

When Paisley remained quiet, Monique said with a wink, "Don't look so worried. Our rule here is: *What's said in the bakery …*"

"*… stays in the bakery.*" Anita finished the sentence, sharing a giggle.

A tinkling bell announced a new customer entering. A young woman wanted coffee and a pastry to take to work. *Marianne.* Exactly the person Paisley didn't need to see when flustered and in learning mode. Marianne was dressed in a corporate uniform, the crest of Quamby Bluff Shire Council on her jacket pocket. Admittedly, with her hair tied up in a severe chignon and wearing a suit instead of the Alice in Wonderland Steampunk costume, the girl looked much more mature this morning.

"Hi, Paisley. Are you working here now?" Marianne asked, making polite conversation.

Blushing, Paisley said in a chirpy tone, "Just helping out temporarily."

Anita handed over the order to Paisley while Monique observed and assessed her new recruit. Nerves caused Paisley to fumble putting an apricot Danish into a paper bag but she did a passable job making the coffee with a fuzzy rose motif. After Marianne waved goodbye with a *see you later*, Paisley cautiously cast a glance towards Monique, seeking approval. The boss rubbed her chin, a serious look on her face.

"I've been thinking. If anyone asks about Tobin, it's ok to tell them he's in the UK looking after his sick mother. You can say, it's up in the air when he'll be back. I don't want people to think he's left me."

At the forlorn tone in Monique's voice, Paisley was overcome with sympathy. "There's no way people are going to think that. I'll put them straight, be sure of that."

Monique's smile was thin and fleeting. "I know I can depend on you. You're a good friend."

Standing close, Paisley sensed Anita's flinch. "I'll do the same MM," she said, as if asking for recognition. Leaning across to hug Monique, the girl received a cold shoulder instead.

In contrast, Paisley received a touching moment of mournful gazing from Monique before an abrupt shift back into boss mode. "I'd better start another lot of croissants. Anita, show Paisley how to clean the coffee machine and where to dump the grounds," she ordered before disappearing into the kitchen."

Anita brushed off the hurt and saluted the back of her mother with feigned bravado; then obediently followed orders, continuing Paisley's training in all the quirks of the job.

"All the food scraps, coffee grounds, tea bags and paper waste have to go out the back into the compost," Anita explained, picking up a pail and showing Paisley through the back door of the kitchen and around the corner to an enclosure with dirt and weeds. "Tobin had a thing about being eco-friendly and he started digging all these compost holes in the backyard. Missy liked to help but we have to tie her up otherwise she'd eat all the compost and get sick."

Paisley laughed, picturing it.

Encouraged, Anita continued. "Bernie and I share a side bet that Tobin was digging for Old Man Chugg's gold coins. Did you hear the story? As Auntie Sheryl tells it, the coach house back in the day was prone to highway robbers. Old Chugg took to burying his profits in tea tins behind the stables throughout this half acre block. It's an urban myth that when he died his heirs couldn't find all the tins."

"Bedamned. Maybe we'll find gold amongst the compost," Paisley enthused, taking the piss.

"Various owners have looked and failed to find any. Bernie says it's a marketing ploy for unsuspecting mainlanders buying the property. Who doesn't love a buried treasure story? If true, it would be worth more than the value of the property," Anita said, pausing to ponder. "Could be why Monique's been pulling up all the floorboards in the bargain, hoping Old Chugg hid some of his stash under the coach house. Unlikely as that is."

"You never know. *Good fortune favours the foolhardy*. Isn't that a saying?" Paisley laughed.

"I think it *favours the brave*, but I like your version better." Anita dumped the contents of the pail into a deep trench. "MM used to go crazy about Tobin filling all those holes with muck littering the paddock, but now that he's gone, it seems she's taken to digging even bigger ones." She studied the six foot long trench with curiosity.

"I guess it saves on rubbish collection," Paisley said, screwing up her nose at the smell. A yelp in the corner of the yard drew her attention. "Missy!" she shouted, running over to the whippet with delight and giving it a hug. "The best part of the compost run is going to be visiting Missy during work hours," she told Anita.

"Yeah, but don't let MM catch you."

"We'll have to walk Missy after closing from now on, if Monique isn't too tired," Paisley mused.

"Yeah, I guess. Over by the stables there's a tap where you can wash the pail." Anita walked over and demonstrated the procedure. "On Fridays, after closing we throw some dirt over the top of the heap. It helps with the smell." She waved a hand in front of her nose. "Phew, that's rank."

By the end of the week, Paisley's confidence grew enough to do the job without tutelage. Anita apologised for absconding to go to university lectures but promised she'd be in and out during the week to help out in the café. Paisley couldn't complain. Anita was already getting up at dawn to make sandwiches and slices, while Monique baked loaves of artisan bread.

Eventually Monique spent more time out of the kitchen and in the café, having adjusted to the early morning routine and getting the hang of the woodfired oven. She served customers and kept Paisley company. Although she often complained of headaches and would disappear late morning for a doze, leaving Paisley to manage the café single handed.

Noelle helped out after school, clearing and wiping tables after first sitting down with a hot chocolate and a piece of cake. Arising from a nap around this stage, Monique was once again the life of the party, sharing gossip and stories with customers, making suggestive innuendos about each of the male patrons, and convincing Paisley to join in her secret rating system. During quiet periods, they'd debate the merits of tight butts and firm thighs, broad shoulders and long thumbs.

Paisley had never spent much time considering any bits of the male anatomy in such extreme detail and it proved to be educational given Monique's mature outlook and superior experience. It was fun sharing fantasies with a girlfriend. The job hardly felt like work, much to Paisley's delight. This made up for the fact that her cash in hand wages were much less than working at the pub. She understood Monique couldn't afford to pay more, struggling as she was with Tobin away and the bills piling up.

They hadn't walked Missy together all week because Monique was too exhausted, but she promised they'd start soon. Paisley had no complaints. She was happy to walk her best beastie alone enjoying their quality togetherness.

Friday night after work, Paisley felt energised and happy. A whole week at the bakery with Monique, her new girlfriend, and walking Missy every night, and it was all perfect. She squirted tomato sauce over a Cornish pasty purchased from the leftover basket at the bakery and ate it with relish. The fantasy pirate instrumentals of Abney Park, her favourite Steampunk band, played in the background. Perfect music to inspire retrofuturism fashion.

Clearing the table of dirty dishes and sauce bottles, she turned it into a craft table. There was a lot of work to do to meet her promise to Bernie, creating hats and waist coats for Light Up's shop window. As she pinned a vest pattern to a black and gold brocade material, she decided this was going to be an awesome Steampunk design. With a sigh of contentment, she thought, *life was going well*.

A few minutes before bed, her phone pinged with a text from Adam. News about Tobin.

She read his text.

Nothing's shown up.

Vindicated, Paisley smiled. She replied.

It's all good then.

I mean, Tobin Swan doesn't even have a driver's licence on record.

85

Are you sure his last name is Swan?

Chapter Twelve

Monique thought back to the day's event while dumping a garbage bag full of compostable paper plates and other organic material into the backyard trench, making sure it was evenly distributed to fill in any gaps. The stink was god awful. That was Tobin – Mr Do Good with his save the planet ideology and a cavalier notion that luck would prevail against all the odds. In the end, where did it get him?

Where did it get her? Buried treasure. Gold coins. They'd been fools; taken in by the oldest con in history. With time running out, exhausted, pouring muck on a sinking business venture. She was the one who wanted out. Tobin beat her to it, the bastard.

If only the damn dog hadn't run off. If only that young man hadn't posted his selfie on the Shire's Lost & Found Facebook page with Tobin's face in the frame. Life was the pits. Oh god, now that was ironic.

The biker club had shown up on Sunday as per their usual routine. Anita was too busy making up for lost study time to help out, useless, selfish girl. As tired as Monique was, it didn't make good business sense to say *no* to the trade; the bakery needed the money. It was a good way of using up the leftover slices and meat pies. With enough barbeque sauce, no hungry biker noticed the reheated pies were stale or the fact they were served on throw away paper plates. Or if they did, they didn't care.

Of course, they all wanted to know *where was Tobin*? If she had to explain one more time about his sick mother in the UK and see their knowing smirks, she would become hysterical. What was so wonderful about Tobin that everyone missed him? She was the one working her ass off while he'd gone to a better place.

The only good coming from the weekend was toying with delicious Lance. Picturing how her breasts brushed against his upper arm when leaning over to place his steaming hot coffee on the table made her instantly hot. She imagined sitting on that table facing him with legs wrapped around his torso, straddling him, her dress riding up exposing bare thighs and lace panties, bending forward to take his tongue in her willing mouth. Decadent. Wild. Next occasion she saw him, she'd whisper in his ear, seed this fantasy, get him panting for her sex.

In the meantime, she couldn't wait to share the gossip. Paisley would be so envious to hear the news. After a deep and meaningful, up close and personal discussion, she and Lance agreed on a unique design for a Special Ops tattoo as an anniversary present for Tobin. At least he pretended Tobin would return, not like his older, more cynical mates. Lance promised to work on the design and get back with a finished colour drawing for final approval. She was looking forward to another one on one encounter with the raunchy dreamboat.

On the downside, Lance kept asking about Paisley. *Did she see much of her? Does she go on walks with you and Missy?* His obsession with the Steampunk girl was boring her to death.

It was easy to shake her head, look sympathetic and evade answering directly. *I guess the girl lost interest; you know foster kids. No stickability.* Fair enough, it was a lie. But the look of defeat on his face was priceless. Toying with the boy had its fun moments.

Chapter Thirteen

The next morning in preparation for opening in half an hour, Monique studied Anita artfully arranging fruit mince tarts alongside iced Christmas cakes and plum puddings wrapped in calico with plastic holly leaf ties. When satisfied, she went on to place kitsch Santa decorations around the shelves in the cabinet. The girl had way too much time on her hands.

Four am starts were getting too much for Monique's fragile constitution. Anita, the lazy girl, helped out with sandwiches but it wasn't enough with Christmas around the corner. Watching Paisley place a glittery gold candle on each table with efficient if somewhat carefree abandon, she came to a decision. Her casual employee could start earlier and pull more of the baking load.

"That looks super special," she gushed, piling on the praise. Anita looked up with a smile that faded quickly when realising the compliment was directed elsewhere.

Paisley stood back to assess the final presentation; a satisfied grin lit up her face.

Best to keep her sweet. Monique wrapped her arms around Paisley in a friendly hug. "You've been the best. It's been so difficult with Tobin away. I appreciate the good job you've been doing, helping me, making the coffees and serving customers."

Paisley wiggled out of the hug, uncomfortable with physical affection. "That's what friends are for."

"Well, I reckon it's prudent to promote you." In the background, Anita's face registered jealous shellshock.

"Bedamned. It's only been a few weeks. But hey, I can always use extra money," Paisley joked. "What's involved?"

Monique had no intention of paying more but kept quiet, letting the quip hang in the air. "I've been thinking with your creative flair, as a fellow artist, you could easily learn more of the bakery business. Who needs Tobin? The two of us together – we're all that's needed to make this a success. What do you say?" Monique didn't give the girl a moment to consider either way. "Come into the kitchen. I want to share my secret recipe for Convict Crust's famous Cornish pasties," she said, pleased at Paisley's delighted expression.

✿ ✿ ✿

Paisley stood next to an industrial mixer watching Monique breaking up day-old loaves of sourdough bread and throwing in chunks to be pulverised by its spinning blades. On the long wooden table next to her, Anita grated carrots to stuff in salad rolls.

All business, Monique demonstrated how to pour in bags of defrosted frozen mixed vegetables and then minced meat in precise proportions – to turn the mixture into stodge. Not exactly the gourmet ingredients Paisley had been expecting. To add to the disappointment, Monique rolled out pre-bought pastry sheets across the kitchen table; the pastry was not even hand made. Then she gave exact instructions on how to fill, fold and edge each pasty with a bespoke crimp pattern, making a point of inspecting each of Paisley's crimped pasties and giving a rating out of ten as if judging a contestant on the Chef's Crown.

Paisley soon realised that crimping was the only skill that needed any practice in order to achieve Monique's fussy standards. It wasn't hard to seal the dough, only tedious trying to perfect a uniform braiding. After the first dozen stuff-ups, Anita lost patience and reluctantly demonstrated a trick to make crimping easier. Looking across for her mother's approval, MM returned a frown, as if it was Anita's fault and not Paisley's that so many pasty edges looked like lumpy knots instead of a neat, woke weave.

Unconcerned, Paisley continued to 'help', without achieving the perfection required.

"Presentation is the secret ingredient," Anita whispered. *"If it looks boutique and costs more it will magically taste gourmet. The key is what people believe."* She winked at Paisley with a wicked glint and continued to stuff salad ingredients into chicken rolls.

Paisley relaxed at being taken into Anita's confidence; maybe their relationship was turning around for the better. Even so, she wasn't convinced that Monique's formula was good business logic. It felt a bit deceptive after discovering the true ingredients. So much for secret recipes and all organic, local produce and the snobbery that went with Convict Crust's artisan reputation. It would never again hold the same mystique when she drove past on the way to Steampunk meetings.

But then she remembered the bakery's financial position. If dealing in perceptions helped with the bakery's bottom line, then who was she to criticise this business strategy?

With her face itchy from flour dust and hands sticky from tucking stodge into pastry, Paisley wanted to get the job done before opening and for once couldn't have cared less about perfect crimping, never having enjoyed cooking especially and not having any ambitions towards becoming a baker. She was happy to help out, but all of Monique's talk of them working well as a team and not needing Tobin was a worry. Paisley was only doing this job temporarily as a friend. She hoped Monique respected this boundary and wasn't planning on using her as a replacement baker for too long a run.

After scrubbing the muck off her hands, throwing the baker's apron in the laundry bag, and checking her face and hair for white streaks of flour, Paisley was relieved to return to the familiar café side of the business on the first ring of the customers' bell. For now, at least, Monique didn't trust her with baking the pasties in the wood fired oven. Better to let Monique burn the whole tray rather than Paisley. That would be a responsibility she could do without.

Anita followed with a tray of salad rolls, sliding it onto a shelf in the display cabinet. After instructing Paisley on the precise measurements for cutting up hazelnut slices cooling in the refrigerator, Anita hung up her apron and then raced out the door, shouting a belated apology about being late for a guest lecture and promising Monique she'd return before closing to balance the till and take the day's proceeds to the bank.

Chapter Fourteen

Wednesday eight am. An hour had passed. Paisley rubbed dough from her hands on to the apron tied around her middle and gazed at the dozens of Cornish pasties lined up on the kitchen table ready for baking. Monique cast a quick look over them, assessing the crimping technique before approving the lot with a nod and proceeding to shovel half a dozen at once into the glowing woodfired oven.

It was the third week helping with the baking and Paisley was finding the early morning starts too much, especially after night shifts at the Pub. Not to mention Monique disappearing for a nap before lunch every day complaining of headaches, leaving Paisley to manage the whole affair on her own for several hours. So far, despite being *promoted*, Monique paid the same *under the counter* rate and Paisley never found the right moment to mention this oversight to her frazzled friend, not wanting to sound ungrateful for the job but starting to feel like a dogs' body nonetheless.

"What are your plans for Christmas?" Anita asked casually while continuing to fill wraps with meat and salad.

Taken by surprise, Paisley decided the nosiness was really about Bernie and his family's Christmas plans, naturally assuming she'd be included in them. That wasn't going to happen. It was too painful watching a large, normal loving family spend time together, enjoying each other's company, laughing, telling stories, handing out presents, including her in the fold with easy grace as if she belonged – all that she ever wished for. Except, they weren't her family; she didn't fit in; and she stuck out like a wart on a perfect family portrait.

"I could go to Bernie's; he has this massive family get together every year. But, I don't," she answered, abrupt and sounding rude and hoping this would shut up Anita before having to offer lame explanations. Like how she shunned her parents and their boozy family fights each year. Not that they'd even consider inviting her or celebrating the season with anything more than a cask of red, a case of bitter brew, roll your own dope, and packets of barbeque chips in stoned stupor. At least, they saved her saying 'no' without feeling a flicker of guilt or regret. "It's just another day of the year for me."

"We can't have that," Monique joined the conversation. "You must come to our family lunch. With Tobin away, there'll be an empty chair needing to be filled. I can't bear it. We need you!"

"MM cooks a traditional English feast – roast pork with crackling, apple sauce, plum pudding with brandy custard. Way too much food. She puts coins in the pudding for luck. It's so good." Anita looked wistful, caught up in the dream. "What are your special family traditions?"

Paisley never had enough continuity in her childhood to establish any sort of traditions (perhaps her parents' drunk and disorderly habit counted as a 'tradition' but not one she admitted to). Each of her many foster families had their own way of doing Christmas. Most celebrated on the day with a lunch that included a wide circle of family and friends that were strangers to her, making the event uncomfortable and lonely. The venue would change from family to family. One year it would be a barbeque with roast meat and veg in the garden; the next the beach with seafood and salads. On one placement, they celebrated the night before Christmas with a dinner of cranberry stuffed turkey, pineapple ham, and pumpkin pie topped with marshmallows. Yuck.

The last wish on her Santa list was to participate in yet another happy family's tradition. Ignoring Anita's well intentioned question, she replied, "Thanks, but I always work over the holiday period. The double and triple loading is all the Christmas cheer I need. Baby Jesus is my hero." She didn't mention the extra pay also included Christmas dinner each night she worked – the pub's famous roasts and all the trimmings. That was all she required to fill-up on the season's greetings.

"Well, I'm not ready to take 'no' for an answer. It's an open invitation. Decide on the day," Monique pushed. Paisley wasn't sure why but it was annoying. Not to mention the dark looks Anita was sending her way.

"Hellfire. Is that wall clockwork true?" Paisley shrieked, changing the subject. She had just enough minutes to tidy up and race back to the café to finish filling the display cabinet with slices of fruit cake and turkey salad wraps. She barely managed to adjust the multi-coloured hair extensions in her ponytail, splaying them to look wild and feral, to match her newest, handmade skirt made out of flounced tulle, black velvet and panelled strips from a deconstructed Highland jumper, before customers began arriving.

A tinkling bell announced their first customer, *Mr Two Score*, the same chap every day wanting a cappuccino and a croissant. He asked for takeaway in his usual manner – polite – unless Monique burned the batches. This was a rare event now that she had the hang of stoking the coals to the correct temperature and the baking time right. Paisley labelled him one of the harmless.

She braced for the next several hours of serving customers seated within the confines of the cosy café, anticipating all the ways to fend off amorous patrons as she carried trays of coffee and wound her way between the crowded tables. A few male customers missing their weekly flirtations with Monique decided Paisley presented a good substitute for playful gropes. Pinched backsides and suggestive comments did not come with the job description as far as she was concerned, but it was condoned by Monique, encouraged even. Paisley was caught in a dilemma, not sure how assertive she could be about the unwanted attention without driving away most of the bakery's male customers. The whole point of helping Monique was to improve the business's bottom line – even if that meant Paisley's *bottom* was unwittingly part of that equation.

She gritted her teeth and hung in there until mid afternoon when the bus dropped off Noelle after school. Male patrons were less likely to verbalise crass jokes and lewd innuendos with a ten year old wandering around the café. Lower Teasel residents still held some old fashioned values.

Monique had trained her youngest daughter well to be useful. Noelle helped Paisley string fairy lights across the windows and decorate a plastic Christmas tree in the corner with a box of antique angels Monique had found in the shed. The kid was a trooper and especially helpful with clearing the picnic tables from the outdoor barbeque area that were often overlooked during busy periods. They worked well together as a team and the extra support was enough for Paisley's stress levels to subside.

Eventually Monique came out of seclusion and made a point of heaping praise on Noelle's decorating skills. Her presence took the heat off by entertaining the guests in her unique style. After all, it was her business and therefore, her rules.

It was after four o'clock before Anita returned from shopping and could relieve Paisley at the front counter, giving her a chance to sit down for a bite to eat. Her favourite spot was hiding in a shadowed corner of the barbeque area, her back to the street. The roar of a motorcycle in the distance sent shivers through her along with images of Lance's crooked smile and form fitting leathers. Unlikely, but if she ever saw him again, she vowed to take Monique's advice and not play it safe. Taking a chomp out of the chicken Caesar wrap, she allowed her imagination to skip away into dream territory.

"Paisley?" A husky male voice aroused her from miles away daydreaming. Turning around with the sun in her eyes, all she could see was a dark figure. "I saw the scarlet braid and the Doc Martins and thought it must be the elusive Steampunk girl!" Slowly adjusting to the bright light, Lance's form began to materialise and come into focus. Paisley chewed and swallowed and tried not to choke.

"Lance? What are you doing here?" was the best she could come up with on the spot, partially covering her mouth with a hand, hoping lettuce wasn't stuck in her teeth.

He marched across the brick patio and sat down straddling the bench so close she could hardly breathe. "Monique wanted a tattoo for Tobin. Thought I'd bring a design for final approval."

"She never mentioned ..." Paisley's voice trailed off, unable to form a coherent sentence, locked on Lance's happy gaze.

"I can't believe you're here. Have you seen Missy? Monique said you hadn't been around for ages, that you lost interest in walking Missy. She didn't have your number ... It doesn't matter. You're here now. I've found you again."

Paisley wanted to call *timeout* to process Lance's comments. He'd been looking for her? Asked Monique who hadn't mentioned a word? Told Lance she wasn't interested! What was that about? Even worse, Monique claimed to not know where to find her! What else had she said that wasn't true?

Lance was too busy pulling out his drawings from a leather satchel and spreading them across the picnic table to notice Paisley's bewilderment. "What do you think? Is that a badass Special Ops design or what!"

Pulling herself together, she critiqued the design. It was beautifully drawn, intricate, dark, edgy – the dude was seriously talented. She told him as much in so many words.

"Thought you'd like it." Lance grinned. "This has inspired me. What if I design a tattoo specially for you? A Christmas gift. Something fantastical and Steampunk. I'll make it awesome."

No one did something for nothing.

"A gift? For what?" The words were out of her mouth before her brain registered how ungrateful they sounded. She was still smarting from Monique's betrayal, her heart warring with all kinds of muddled feelings of suspicions and distrust and justifications about Monique and Lance misinterpreting things. All the same, she wondered what Lance and his family did for Christmas. A bizarre image of them exchanging tattoos instead of presents crossed her mind.

Lance paused to consider her knee jerk comment, not seeming to take offence. "No reason except I want to. It would be so cool. I promise, you'll love it." To emphasise the point, he placed both hands across his heart.

"Yeah, well no. I can't imagine loving anything that much I'd want it stuck to me forever," she said.

"I was hoping to change your mind on that," he said under his breath.

The hurt look on Lance's face said it all. What was wrong with her? She'd totally missed the point of their conversation. The guy was trying to impress her with his skills as an artist and she'd gone all cantankerous on him. Even if the idea of a tattoo was terrible – okay trendy – but nonetheless terrifying, her lame comment hurt his feelings which hadn't been the intention.

So much for Monique's advice on how to wow a guy. Paisley was hopeless at playing the game.

As if on cue, Monique tittered in the background. "Then, Paisley, you're totally lacking imagination," she purred, gliding across the patio, the backdoor of the kitchen left open. The woman must have been watching and waiting for the worst possible moment to intrude. Inwardly, Paisley groaned knowing the opportunity to correct Lance's opinion of her was lost.

"Lance, I'm hurt. Shouldn't I have been first to view your etchings? After all, I'm the one paying for your services," she said with a pout. She placed both hands on Lance's shoulders as she bent over to study the drawing. "Perfection," she gushed. "You totally met my expectations." Coming from her, the words sounded sexy, suggestive, and mature. A woman confident in her appeal and not shy about taking risks. The type of woman Paisley wanted to be but kept falling short. Suddenly, she hated Monique.

"Paisley, have you finished your snack? Lance and I have things to discuss privately," Monique said.

Dismissed and put in her place, Paisley scrunched up the remains of her lunch and slunk through the back door to join Anita behind the café counter.

Sometime later, Lance came over to order an extra large cappuccino to take away. "Since when do you work here?" he asked. "Weird that Monique never said. It's like you're a different girl every time I see you. I can't figure you out."

It felt like an apology to Paisley. Another chance.

Except Anita answered instead. "She's been here a few weeks helping out, since Tobin pissed off."

If left at that, all would have been fine. Stupidly, Paisley added, "It's only temporary – not permanent." *Eeech, that word again.*

"Yeah, I get that. Nothing permanent. That's your thing." Lance handed over a ten dollar note to Anita while Paisley focused on steaming milk for his coffee.

Monique shouted from the kitchen. "She's the bakery's own will-o-the-wisp. Foster kids are like chameleons; they want to fit in but can't be tied down. They have to keep changing their colours like camouflage and moving on." Her laugh echoed across the room.

If meant to sound frivolous, to Paisley it sounded mean. Her face fell. All she'd ever wanted her whole life was to settle down and belong. The one sore point in her armour and Monique had zeroed in and turned it into a joke.

Sensing the hurt, Lance tried to rescue the moment. "I'm told you need to dress like a flight attendant to fit in around here," he said in a droll voice aiming a dig at Monique's fashion sense.

The rescue came too late and was misconstrued. Paisley abandoned the coffee machine and fled to the ladies' room in humiliation. On the way she heard Anita explain, "She doesn't take jokes well." The warning referred to Monique but he took it to mean Paisley.

"I meant it as a compliment," he said apologetically watching Paisley flee. "I love the way she dresses."

Monique preened in the background thinking he meant her. "Keep that up and I'll let you join my loyalty club to earn extra mileage," she shouted loud enough for Paisley to hear. Lance frowned but kept his mouth shut and didn't correct all the misunderstandings. It was getting too complicated and he kept making things worse.

Paisley hid in the ladies' room for as long as possible. Looking in the mirror, she applied even blacker lines of kohl around her eyes and bolder smears of burgundy lipstick. As a final touch, she pulled out strands of wiry, fake hair to stick out as if electrocuted. An act of defiance. She didn't care about looking different, not fitting in. She did not care.

Coming out of hiding, to her dismay Lance was still at the counter waiting. She stood back, pale and as lost as an orphan, before plastering on a blank, distant expression and strutting past him to clear tables.

Lance shook his head with a wistful look as if coming to a decision. Pocketing his change and grabbing the take away cardboard cup in one hand, with the other he gave her a military salute with two fingers pressed to the side of his forehead. "See you around, Steampunk girl. Take care." He was out the door and gunning his Harley before she could say farewell and Godspeed.

Emerging from the kitchen, Monique joined Anita at the counter in order to stare at his retreating rear like a quality meat inspector. "Definitely a one," she stated, licking her lips. "Anytime, anywhere."

Stricken at the insensitivity towards Paisley's feelings, Anita nudged Monique.

"Come on – it's all a bit of fun." Monique addressed a stone faced Paisley with an innocent expression. "Didn't you like the way I made you sound mysterious and hard to get?"

"No, not really. Don't do me any favours in the future," she grumbled.

"Trust me. He'll be back. Men love women to be puzzles. The harder it takes to work you out, the wilder their imaginations get to work."

Anita glared at Monique. "Yeah, what are friends for? Try to be more grateful, Paisley."

"Who needs to be some guy's project. I don't like playing games with people. It's either real or – forget it." Paisley piled a used tea cup onto a chocolate-smeared plate. She added the dishes to the next table's stack with a clang, picked up the rickety lot and headed towards the next table.

"Too right. Fuck and forget them, that's what I say," Monique agreed with enthusiasm before disappearing into the kitchen.

Paisley considered the advice and wondered if it applied equally to Tobin, but she bit her lips and kept the thought to herself.

On the way to dump the dishes in the kitchen sink, Anita grabbed her to whisper, "MM's doing her best to deal with the hurt of Tobin's absence, especially since he didn't come home for Christmas. Underneath that tough exterior, she's lonely and grieving. We need to cut her some slack."

Paisley shrugged. Right at the moment, she cared less about a girlfriend's heart being as soft as a Santa marshmallow. What about her own heart for a change? It could use some Christmas cheer for once.

Chapter Fifteen

Paisley's *best boss ever*, Mel, had scheduled her for three late shifts behind the bar during the week leading up to Christmas. Generous and meant this week's rent would be paid in full and on deadline. No need to sneak happy hour peanuts as a substitute for dinner. Paisley rushed from one end of the counter to the other answering finger signals for *one more of the same*. The Draught Horse Pub's Friday night bar was packed with boisterous locals celebrating the end of year break with office parties. No one was drunk yet, only merry and loud.

As much as she enjoyed being run off her feet, showing off her competence and efficiency at pulling pints, tonight she was anxious to have a minute's break to talk to Bernie and Anita. Immersed in each other's company, they didn't seem to mind waiting as they sipped Stout and Pagan cider, respectively.

Finally, getting a break, Paisley grabbed a mineral water, took a replenishing gulp and leaned elbows on the counter across from her friends. "Salutations, how are you two going?" she asked.

"Good," Bernie said, summing up his contentment.

Anita put her hand up. "I wanted to apologise for MM interfering yesterday with you and Lance. Best intentions aside, she has no sense of boundaries. I hope she didn't ruin anything."

Paisley shrugged. "Can't ruin something that never got off the ground. But I am having second thoughts about continuing at the bakery. The early mornings plus my late shifts here are starting to get to me."

"You can't quit on me," Anita shrieked in fake horror. "You can't leave me alone with MM. She'll have me doing all the work and I'll have no chance to finish my summer school classes. I'll fail my studies and never be able to leave! I'll be doomed."

"Take a compass bearing, Anita. She's not going to leave you in a lurch," Bernie said, glaring at Paisley to agree.

"It will ease up after the holidays. We shut the café in the first week of the new year to give ourselves a rest," Anita reassured.

"Is it possible for Monique to hire another temporary baker to help out until Tobin returns?" Bernie asked.

"Like an apprentice?" Anita looked doubtful.

"Hellfire, when is Tobin coming back?" Paisley asked. "I mean, is he? Monique sometimes acts as if he's gone for good."

Anita shook her head. "Don't worry. He'll be back. Tobin left his Harley in the stables. He loves that bike as much as he loves Missy. Unless something out of the ordinary happened, he wouldn't abandon the love of his life." She laughed but then became serious. "I've looked at the bakery's accounts. It's breaking even with the help of Tobin's army pension going into the business bank account, but there's no way Monique could afford to hire someone properly and pay Award wages at this juncture."

Paisley waved her hands in the air. "I didn't sign up for forever! I'm being a good friend."

Bernie, the pacifist, intervened. "What Anita is saying, when the bakery starts making a profit again, Monique can hire extra help and let you off the hook."

"If Tobin is away for much longer, which he won't be," Anita added reassuringly.

"Right, so in the meantime, how can we help make this happen as quickly as possible? Who has any ideas for improving the bakery's profits?" Bernie asked.

Paisley was called away by a bearded patron in a flannelette shirt gesturing with an empty pint glass in the air. After sorting him out, along with a few others wanting refills, she returned to her friends aware of Mel's scrutiny at the other end of the bar.

"I've had a Thomas Edison light globe moment. What do you think about offering the Steam Festival's catering contract to the bakery?" Bernie asked.

Anita gushed, "That would be awesome."

"Monique would need to put in a competitive tender for due process. But the bakery fits the criteria of us supporting local businesses. I think that's a seriously good suggestion," Paisley said to be encouraging but was thinking surely Tobin would be back well before then.

"I can write the tender proposal first up. MM doesn't need to know just yet. She can get all Moaning Mona about new ideas at first," Anita said.

Paisley wasn't convinced she could hang out at the bakery until March. "The Steam Festival is only a couple months away. We need to come up with other suggestions before that."

"I need a project for my final paper in marketing. As reluctant as I am to do too much for Monique, I could look into setting up a social media page for the bakery and Instagram —"

"— approach Isle Tourism for an article," Bernie suggested.

"Make up a story about Old Man Chugg's hidden gold, or a highwayman's ghost, or something like that to make the bakery stand out," Paisley said with building enthusiasm.

Lost in thought, Anita didn't say anything for a few minutes. "It's doable. I can do it, for Tobin. He deserves to return to a viable business," she answered confidently. The three of them high fived.

Hopeful they had a plan. Paisley returned to serving drinks worried if she didn't return to work asap Mel would give her the sack for slacking off.

Chapter Sixteen

Towards the end of the lunch rush, Paisley cut up a tray of White Christmas into even squares and layered them on an antique china plate to top up the display case which ran low on sweets this stage of the day. In the café, Monique sat with a few regular customers entertaining them with a heartrending account of Tobin's phone call the night before. It started with his mercy dash to the UK to visit his dying mum and moved on to how his mother was in and out of hospital for medical treatments; how Tobin went shopping and cooked for his dad who was useless around the home; ending with an embellishment about Tobin signing with British Special Ops once again in order to help pay medical bills that were adding up.

She artfully tugged on the audience's heart strings by extrapolating on how awful it was for Tobin losing his beloved mama, the centre of his world. Mama was a fighter and was holding on contrary to doctors' predictions, but alas, Tobin was not expected home soon. At least not before the New Year, unfortunately.

As any good narrator, Monique paused for effect, letting this statement hover in the air as if already seeing the shadow of his mother's ghost. Everyone knew Tobin would not be home for Christmas.

Satisfied at her audience's sad nods of understanding, she continued with more enthusiasm. Amidst all this chaos and grief, he missed her and the kids and found a spare moment to call at least once a week. Last night he had a long chat to Noelle, remembering it was her birthday in a few days.

Credit where it was due: Monique was a brilliant teller of tales. Her purpose was to explain the reason Tobin was nowhere to be seen. The effect was to render the crowd spellbound with sympathy for Tobin, as well as to impress the patrons with her stalwart efforts to hold the bakery business together while he was away.

It all made perfect sense in the first telling, but over the course of the day, as Paisley digested the facts of the matter, some weren't adding up. Didn't the UK have universal health services? So why did Tobin have to get a job to pay the bills? Would the SAS hire him again, seeing as he was pensioned out with PTSD a few years ago? That was not a medical condition that simply vanished into thin air. And, if he planned to return soon, why take on a new job?

The bell rang and a tradie stomped in, his boots covered in grass clippings and his overalls streaked with dirt. After ordering and paying for a long black to take away, he grunted that he'd be sitting outside. Paisley brought out his coffee and began to clear paper cups and leftover food from the outdoor tables. Noelle turned up and plonked a school bag on the patio's brick pavers. She'd stepped off the school bus and didn't see Paisley in the café, so she'd come looking to say 'hi'.

Paisley never quite found it easy talking to a ten year old. To start a conversation, she decided to go with, "It must have been cool talking to your dad and getting birthday wishes all the way from the UK."

Noelle screwed up her face with a look that indicated she must be crazy. "The UK? You're joking! I haven't spoken to my dad in ages and he's always been in Western Australia."

Not the reaction Paisley expected. She was positive Monique told customers Tobin had spoken to Noelle recently. *Ages* must be an exaggeration. Kids experience time differently from adults. But why was the kid under the impression her father was in Western Australia? Had she been told something different from the rest – or was Monique covering up for Tobin for some reason? Maybe he'd forgotten the kid's special day. This made it awkward.

Paisley tried again to make conversation. "I've been told it's your birthday in a few days. Is it the pits celebrating on the same day as Christmas?" Noelle shrugged. "What do you want for presents?"

"Anything Minecraft. Books, games, a t-shirt or a hat – anything." Noelle's eyes lit up with excitement. "I've asked for Mum to make me a Minecraft cake."

"Hellfire. Sounds like it's Minecraft or nothing!" Paisley teased.

"Pretty much," Noelle said, picking up her school bag and heading back inside the café. "I wonder if Mum's up by now."

"I'm finished here. I'll come in a minute. I want to send a quick text message to a friend first," Paisley said. She waited for the door to close behind Noelle. The discrepancies in Monique's story were starting to niggle despite Paisley's allegiance to her friend.

Something wasn't right in all this. What was going on with Tobin? She began to question a lot of what Monique was saying.

Paisley pulled out a phone from a deep pocket hidden among the folds of her skirt. She keyed a quick message to Adam.

Is it possible to find out Tobin's army record? He's re-joined the SAS in UK.

A minute later her phone pinged with a reply.

No and I'd still need his last name.

Der. U R right. Any suggestions how?

The phone went dead. Paisley was anxious to return to the café before Monique noticed she was gone. "Come on. Come on," she whispered. Adam didn't reply.

Noelle yelled from the back door, "There're customers to serve."

Finding answers would have to wait.

✿ ✿ ✿

Later that afternoon, a half hour before closing, Paisley was busy wiping down tables when her phone pinged with an incoming text message. She called out to Noelle to watch the few remaining customers in the café. As an excuse to escape outdoors for some private space, she grabbed the compost pail from the kitchen to give the impression it was a chore requiring immediate attention.

Reading the text message from Adam, it was his reply to her earlier question.

> Could trace name of owner thru car rego number.

Of course. It was so obvious. Except the Land Cruiser might be registered in Monique's name only. She didn't want to waste Adam's time on another wild goose chase.

What about Tobin's Harley? That would most certainly be registered in his name only. She recalled Anita saying he kept it in the stables.

Paisley emptied the pail into the compost trench and casually walked over to the tap by the stables, taking it slow to rinse it clean. She peered through the wooden slats, adjusting to the shadowed gloom inside, trying to locate the Harley to check out its license plate number. There were rusted tools draped in cobwebs hanging from the ceiling and the walls. There was a patch of oil on the dirt floor. A lot of empty space. But no motorcycle.

Missy began to whine and chafe at the tether wanting attention. Paisley dropped the pail and ran over to give her a thorough tummy rub. "Yes, my beautiful girl. We'll go for a walk soon, I promise," she cooed. At the back of her mind, she was thinking *Where was Tobin's Harley?* Weird it was missing. Anita said he loved that bike more than anything else, including Monique apparently.

Back inside the café, Paisley ruminated about this new development.

"Is everything all right?" Monique appeared from the kitchen, picking up on her sombre mood. "I was thinking we could walk Missy together after work. We haven't done that for a while. Noelle might want to join us."

"Yeah, sure," Paisley said, surprised at the sudden offer. "I was wondering. How did Tobin travel to the airport again? I can't remember what you said." Noelle stopped sweeping and looked across, paying attention to the conversation.

Monique frowned. "That's a question from left field. Why the sudden interest?" With a guilty glance towards Noelle, she didn't wait for an answer, saying rather cautiously, "I called him a taxi. It was the middle of the night and I didn't want to wake my daughter."

"Oh, I thought he might have taken his motorcycle. I noticed it's not in the stables." Paisley tried to sound casual and simultaneously study Monique's face to determine by her reaction if she was being honest.

Monique's eyes went dark. "Why is that any of your business? How dare you give me the third degree, prying into things you know nothing about?" she hissed, sending a wave of animosity through the peaceful café. Two customers finished sipping the last dregs of tea from their cups, picking up on the disturbance. They craned their necks around to eavesdrop.

Paisley blanched at the intensity of her public display of fury. "Hellfire. You're right. My bad. I'm sorry, it's your business, not mine," she said, finding a sudden interest in the cappuccino machine and giving a polish to its already sparkling surface. "I thought maybe it was stolen. Anita told me Tobin loves his bike," she mumbled in an undertone, aware of the customers' scrutiny.

A forced laugh erupted from Monique. "Stolen? Don't put ideas into people's heads. The last thing I need is more gossip about Tobin," she stated loudly to the room. The customers looked away quickly. Giving a quick glance to check if Noelle was listening in and satisfied with the girl's head down immersed in sweeping, she whispered to Paisley, "I don't want to upset the kid. Can you keep this quiet for now?"

"Sure," replied Paisley, wondering why secrecy was so important.

"I didn't want to make a big deal about it but the truth is Tobin asked me to sell it. He needed the money to stay on."

Paisley didn't believe this for one minute, but for the sake of ending the row on a harmonious note, replied, "Bedamned. I take it he's not returning to the bakery for a while. That's too bad."

Monique hesitated as if there was more to be said. But instead, she hugged her enthusiastically indicating all was forgiven. "Lucky, I have you. I couldn't cope without you helping."

The hug, if not the words, felt insincere, like a calculated diversion of her attention. Was Monique telling the truth about any of it? Paisley wasn't convinced but why would she lie? There was no point in pursuing this further with her girlfriend already so touchy about the subject. Another door closed to finding out about Tobin's past.

And opened up further questions about where he was and why he was taking so long to come home. There was something curious about this whole thing especially with Monique being so touchy and tight lipped about it. Paisley could feel in her gut something was not right. Wild imaginings spilled over like an overfed, spongy sourdough starter in her mind. Maybe his mother wasn't dying and he wasn't in the UK at all. Leaving in the middle of the night after a fight – maybe something else had happened to him. That long compost trench turning up in the backyard at the same point he disappeared was suspicious … Suddenly, shivers rippled through her body. Where was Tobin?

Feeling repulsed at a picture in her head of Tobin amongst the vegetable peelings and a sudden need for space, Paisley wriggled out of Monique's grasp. "No worries," she blurted, unsure what else to say and not wanting Monique to glean the direction her thoughts were heading. "I'll check to see if Noelle wants to walk Missy with us after we close the café," she said, pulling away out of reach. For once, she would have preferred going directly home rather than spend more minutes in Monique's company.

She needed to put the questions roaming around her head to Adam to get his take on the goings on at Convict Crust Bakery. He was sensible. Maybe he could talk her out of believing there was a mystery to be solved around Tobin's disappearance. She wanted to trust Monique again. She was the only girlfriend Paisley had.

Chapter Seventeen

Paisley shuffled and pushed papers on the table into one pile for Bernie to file away in his Festival folder. This first meeting of the Steampunk Club for the New Year was going well. The Steam Fest organising committee had tasked the club with arranging the festival's catering. Bernie put forward the preferred top three proposals: Village Spice Café for cappuccinos, salads, soups and curries; Country Women's Association for drinks, cakes and cheap sandwiches; and Convict Crust Bakery for boutique pies and pasties. No one appeared suspicious at the bakery's inclusion. In previous years, CWA always won the contract, but this year, Village Spice was the running favourite. Anita argued on behalf of the bakery. A robust discussion was taking place. A bright spark dressed as a jungle explorer in a pith helmet and khakis with an elaborately decorated arm guard suggested the catering be shared amongst all three candidates.

During the debate, Paisley leaned towards Bernie. This was their first proper catch up since Christmas. She avoided happy family scenes during the 'festive' season and Bernie, being a normal person with normal relatives, had been involved in plenty of happy family gatherings over the past few weeks. So, she hadn't seen much of him lately. In a hushed voice, she began to fill him in on her talk with Adam concerning all the developments regarding Tobin – Monique selling his Harley, Noelle unaware her dad was in the UK and Monique lying about him speaking to the kid for her birthday. It was all highly suspicious.

To give the guy credit, he didn't laugh outright to her face. Instead, he listened with a sober expression and then added his own fuel to the fire. "A few days ago, Auntie Sheryl told me a package arrived at the Post Office for Noelle from a Mr. T. Swan. But get this – it was postmarked Perth, Western Australia."

"Not the UK," Paisley reaffirmed. "Noelle is right. Her dad is in WA like she said. So why is Monique lying about Tobin?"

Bernie shook his head. "No idea." Then his eyes lit up. "Maybe Tobin isn't her actual father."

Paisley gasped. "Bedamned! If Tobin's not her biological father then his last name won't be Swan. Of course!"

"I was joking," Bernie said.

Paisley grabbed his arm. "Think about it. He disappears and there's no sick mother in the UK. Why is Monique lying, as if anyone cares? Then, suddenly there's a massive trench behind the bakery. That's got to be suspicious." She went quiet, contemplating possibilities.

"I'll bet she's buried his body in the compost!" she mumbled, off and running on a rollercoaster ride of preposterous imaginings. "He's out of the way and she gets to keep his army pension."

Bernie chuckled, used to Paisley's exaggerations. Humouring her, he fanned the flames. "Killed him and stuffed the meat pies with his liver and kidneys," he stage-whispered in mock horror.

Paisley gasped and then realised he was taking the piss. Of course, if a package arrived in the post from Tobin, from Western Australia, then he had to be alive. She was being an idiot. She punched his arm in good fun. "A new take on Convict Crust's artisan pasties – they contain the actual convict," she joked, joining in the gross game.

Bernie started to say something about the bakery's specialty, artisan blood sausages, enjoying the horror narrative, but they were interrupted by Jungle Explorer offering closing remarks in the debate leading to a vote. This required their attention.

Jungle Explorer was saying if they attracted a big enough crowd, why not contract all three caterers? All they needed was for tourists from the Mainland to pump up attendance numbers. Anita responded by volunteering to look into how much a tourist campaign would cost, suggesting there might be grants available from the Shire Council.

Mad Hatter asked for a vote on this suggestion that catering contracts be awarded to all three applicants. Before Paisley could stop him, Bernie went all official and seconded it. She was still imagining what put the *gourmet* into Convict Crust pasties and felt grossed out.

However, there was no point continuing to fantasise. Duty reasserted common sense. As the club secretary, she recorded in the minutes a unanimous vote and noted the Chair would send a letter to the Steam Fest organising committee explaining the decision, and then, if they approved the decision, a letter would be sent to each applicant.

Following the meeting, as usual, members disbursed to the pub's lounge for meals. The Pocket Watch Fiddlers played a brooding cover of 'Underneath the Radar' adding foghorns and sirens to their version.

Paisley was itching to ask Anita about Tobin's Harley for a second opinion. While they waited in line to place a counter meal order, she tapped Anita on the shoulder. "Do you know what happened to Tobin's motorbike?" she asked, attempting to be heard over the band and the noisy laughter of Steampunkers in the Draught Horse Pub's packed dining room. She gave Bernie a triumphant smile. He raised his eyes to the heavens.

"Oh, no, was there some sort of mishap? Noelle better not have tried to sit on it again. Last time, while pretending to ride it, she knocked it over. Tobin loves that bike. If she scratched it, there'll be hell to pay," Anita laughed.

"Um, no, it seems to be missing. Didn't you say he kept it in the stables? I thought you might know where it's gone." As soon as the words were out, seeing Anita's frown, Paisley regretted sounding like a busybody. How would she explain this sudden curiosity?

She was saved by Adam gate crashing their small party. "Mind if I join you?" he asked. "Marianne couldn't stay; she's got a work function on tonight. And I thought I'd follow up to see how your enquiries were going regarding—" he stopped short at the look of horror on Paisley's face.

The band finished its song and re-arranged its musicians to give their cellist centre stage. 'Another Cog in the Machine' began to play. The audience cheered, this being a favourite.

"Adam, let me introduce you to our newest member. This is Tobin and Monique's daughter, Anita Swan," Paisley said loudly and slowly as if talking to a small child.

"Right, from Convict Crust Bakery." Adam got the message to not say another word.

Anita picked up on the awkwardness of the moment. "Actually, my last name isn't Swan. It's Howard. There are occasions when I'd like to distance myself from the 'Swans'," she joked. Hearing Paisley's surprised gasp, she prattled on. "The truth is Monique is my step mum. My dad's in Queensland – he pays the uni fees. When I decided to go to Eden Isle's university, MM offered room and board in exchange for helping at the bakery. MM likes to give the impression we are one happy family. She says perceptions are everything in small towns. I'm made to go along with it."

"There's so much more about you I need to find out," Bernie gushed with awe.

Paisley's curiosity got the better. "If Monique's your step mother, does that mean Noelle is—"

"—Right, my half sister."

"And Tobin?"

"Well, not an actual step dad in the legal sense. He and MM never officially tied the knot."

Paisley was dying to ask Tobin's last name, but couldn't quite segue into that line of discussion without appearing even nosier. She and Adam shared a look. Things were getting complicated.

"So, Tobin's not a Swan, I take it?" Adam prompted, not realising how much he sounded like a cop. Anita narrowed her eyes but ignored the question.

The line had moved and Adam was asked to place his order. All conversation ceased, except for the practical matter of what to have for dinner.

Mischievously, Bernie looked knowingly at Paisley and declared, "I feel like a steak and *kidney* pie with *organic* garden vegetables."

Falling in line with his humour, she asked with all innocence, "Is that the house special? I've heard they're sourced from a local bakery which uses an artisan recipe using the ba ... bake ... baker," she stuttered deliberately, "baker's own secret ingredient, the kidneys."

Anita, not in on the joke, joined in. "I'm partial to the savory tomato sausages." She looked puzzled when they doubled over with laughter.

Bernie recovered first. "On second thought, it's safer to stick to the parma," he said with a straight face, smiling at Anita.

"Okay, if you say so," she replied doubtfully. Bernie and Paisley shared a few more chuckles.

Adam was invited to share their table. Generously, Paisley shouted the first round of drinks knowing Mel would give her a staff discount.

Once settled into their meals, Anita brought up the topic of Tobin's motorbike.

Paisley had been hoping she'd forgotten the earlier blunder; instead she was forced to explain. "I was rinsing the compost bucket by the stables and happened to glance inside. Tobin's bike was missing and I asked Monique about it." Bernie made eye contact as if trying to signal *'what are you doing'* but it was too late. She was committed to the story. "It's just that Monique told me

Tobin asked her to sell it, but if he loved the bike as much as you say, I wasn't sure he'd let her do it," Paisley explained.

Anita went quiet and thoughtful. "No. You're right. Something's wrong. I need to talk to MM."

After finishing their parma and chip meals, Paisley stacked everyone's plates in the middle of the table out of habit. Anita announced a trip to the ladies' room before heading home. Once out of ear shot, Bernie turned to Paisley in fury.

"Hellfire. It's gone beyond a joke, giving my girlfriend the third degree, all this conspiracy nonsense. It's not funny anymore. Drop it, Paisley. All that stuff about Tobin's motorbike, last names, the whole family tree? I'm surprised she was polite and didn't tell you to piss off."

"That's not fair. You started it!" Paisley spluttered. "Remember our conversation about Auntie Sheryl accusing Tobin of being an ex-con? I've been trying to prove her wrong." She turned to Adam for support.

He cleared his throat. "Paisley asked for my help – having been a cop – to find out if Tobin had any priors on record."

"But he couldn't find out because we don't know Tobin's last name. We thought it was Swan but it's not. Despite what Auntie Sheryl said about Noelle's package coming from T. Swan. And I had this idea about tracing his real name through the Harley's registration number, but the bike went missing." Paisley was whispering. Trying to be heard above the background hum in the pub, it came out as hissing.

Bernie looked frustrated. "Hellfire. Aren't you getting a bit obsessed about Tobin? Just drop it. Who really cares if he was an ex-con, except for Lower Teasel gossips – which you are sounding more like every minute."

Paisley was devastated at Bernie's disapproval. Calling her a gossip hit a sore point. "But, I'm fairly sure Monique has been lying about Tobin and I want to know why. It's not only about who Tobin is really. It's about what's happened to him." In the pub's dim light, her eyes glowed like some crazy woman.

"For the Eternal's sake, nothing's happened to him. And how hard can it be to simply ask Anita: *What's Tobin's last name?* Put an end to this ridiculous conspiracy theory of yours."

"And when she asks me why I want to know – what do I say?"

Bernie smirked. "How about, I'm a nosy busybody who's heard Tobin has a prison record and I've decided to go behind your back and—"

"Okay. I get you. I'll drop it," Paisley conceded. She looked to see if Adam was inclined to contradict. He shrugged.

"Can't do much more anyway. Not without a last name," he said, not invested in any of it.

Anita arrived back at the table with a smile on her face. "Ready to go?" she asked Bernie.

"Can I grab a lift with one of you? Saves me walking." Adam looked at each of them. Paisley quickly put up her hand.

Driving Adam home did not provide an opportunity for flirting as Paisley usually longed for. Not his fault. She was preoccupied with the earlier argument with Bernie, concerned that the mystery behind Tobin's disappearance was becoming an obsession instead of a way to prove Auntie Sheryl wrong. Bernie was calling her a gossip. She couldn't bear it if he began to think less of her. He was starting to go all protective of Anita, as if Paisley was crazy or something. That hurt. Any hint she was unstable hit a sore point.

When Adam leaned across the seat to kiss her goodnight, she absently turned to gaze out the window, lost in thought about another man for very different reasons. His lips brushed her cheek in a chaste peck. He was out of the car before she registered a missed opportunity to wow him. Monique, her friend and mentor, would laugh with glee. Paisley watched Adam stiffly march to his front door with a looming sense of self pity. When it came to guys, she could be hopeless sometimes.

Chapter Eighteen

Their first customer for the morning, Mr Two Score left the bakery with his take away coffee, a perfectly baked chocolate croissant and a smile on his face. This should have boded well for the rest of the day. However, since falling out with Monique over the disappearance of Tobin's motorbike, Paisley tiptoed on eggshells around the café feeling guilty about doubting her girlfriend's honesty and casting aspersions about her character, even if only between herself and Bernie.

From the sidelines she felt a sulky gaze on her back. Tension in the air hung like smoke from early morning burnt pasties. Mentioning the missing motorbike had been a tactical error but she wasn't exactly sure what hurt Monique the most. Was she disappointed in Paisley being a small town busybody? Or worse, was it construed as disloyalty – enough to end their friendship?

Judged as unworthy was not a new experience for Paisley. When it came to relationships, she managed to screw up most of them. But fair go. Monique was a notorious gossip, too. When the shoe was on the other foot, *hello, double standard*! It wasn't fair.

Hellfire. When was Monique going to forgive her?

It was difficult to work out how to make amends, except by making coffees and handing out sweets with efficient competence. And smiling at Monique now and then, to reassure her there was nothing to worry about. If that didn't soften her mood, a gentle reminder she was helping out from the goodness of her heart as a friend might serve as a wake up call. Paisley may be clueless but she was not the enemy here.

After Bernie's comments at the pub, she decided not to care about where Tobin was or why his beloved Harley was missing from the barn. Bernie and Monique were right. It was none of her business and a tendency towards obsessiveness had gotten way out of control. Best to drop the issue. The problem was how to let Monique know without opening the wound even more.

If she lost a girlfriend over this, it would be her own stupid fault. And all too familiar. Losing close relationships was her modus operandi. History repeating itself. When was she going to learn to keep out of trouble by keeping her mouth shut?

To rub salt into wounds, Marianne turned up for a café latte in the middle of Paisley's maudlin ruminations. "Seen Adam lately?" she asked, handing across a tenner with casual grace.

Paisley recognised female competitiveness in the nonchalant sweep of the hand and pitied the girl. The guy was gorgeous but it would be years before he was ready to commit to a steady relationship. It was a marvel of female hormones that women kept pursuing the unavailable. "Not since last meeting. I expect he's man caving again." She shrugged to indicate familiarity without possessiveness to protect Marianne's feelings. Fighting over a guy was the last thing on her mind this morning. She'd had her chance and blown it with Adam the other night after driving him home. Who was a loser nowadays? At least she and Adam shared something in common.

The tactic worked. Marianne clutched her take away cup and swept through the café with a wistful smile on her face. Dream on, Paisley smirked while wiping down the cappuccino machine with a wet cloth.

Mid-morning during a lull in customers, Monique came from the kitchen to stand behind the counter closing the space between them. "I'm not mad at you," she whispered.

Paisley cast a guilty look and began to mutter apologies, but Monique put a finger to her lips. "Hush. Anita and I had a talk about Tobin and his Harley. It was responsible to own up to what's happened. No more secrets. You deserve an explanation as well, but I've been too upset." Seeing Paisley's face crumple, she added, "Not with you, sweetheart. With Tobin."

Relief washed through her like a hot shower after getting chilled in the rain. "It's not fair that he's left you to run the bakery for all these weeks even if his mother's been ill," Paisley said keen to get back in her good books. "How's his mother doing anyway?"

Temporarily thrown off topic, Monique hesitated in delivering what was going to be a prepared speech. "His mother? God only knows." She stumbled over the right words to cover the blunder. "A sick mother was a lie, his excuse. He needed a break to think. How many women have heard that one before? The truth is he came back from the UK – but only long enough to claim his precious motorcycle and then piss off again." She waited for Paisley's show of sympathy. "Good riddance to the jerk."

That explained the parcel from WA But why construct a tale about selling the bike? She decided to overlook the small white lie and focus on the larger issue. "Bedamned. You mean he's gone for good? What will you do?" She couldn't imagine Monique continuing with the bakery without extra help and with finances tight, this would not be possible for a while. It wasn't as if she could help out for much longer. Night shifts at the pub and early morning starts at the café were exhausting. Now was not the spot for this to be mentioned, however. Monique had enough to worry about.

"It's going to be tough. Luckily all he took was his precious Harley. It could have been a lot worse," she mused. "Angry and ashamed as I've been feeling about his abandonment, I'm also relieved. He had what you'd call a shady past."

Paisley received a sideways glance, as if Monique was checking her reaction for early signs of disbelief. Her first thought was Bernie gloating about being right. She'd never live it down. "I suspected as much," she said.

Satisfied, Monique resumed. "We came to Lower Teasel through something similar to a witness protection program – due to Tobin's involvement with ..." She stopped as if catching herself in over sharing. "There's no need to bore you with the details."

"That's okay. I want to know."

Just as things started to make sense to Paisley, Monique changed tact, which was quite disappointing. It appeared to be true that Tobin had been an ex-con after all. Bernie would be satisfied with that explanation but she wanted details. She wasn't totally sure about trusting Monique. Instinctively, something wasn't quite right, but she couldn't pinpoint the source of her unease. She needed to learn more about her friend's past. Fortunately, Monique seemed happy to continue confiding.

"Our relationship was passionate but stormy. He could be emotionally abusive at times." She caught Paisley's eyes seeking understanding. "His nickname for me, *Moaning Mona*, for instance. I tried not to let it get to me, but over the years it wears a person down being critical of everything I did or said. We argued a lot about money. He could be controlling."

Paisley nodded, uncertain about how to respond to Monique's confession. Inside, she felt a twinge of disappointment about Bernie being proved right about the 'Tobin mystery'; it had turned out to be rather vanilla. After growing up in foster care, she was no stranger to domestic discord. Monique's experience was not story worthy. Disillusioned about her friend's original charisma now tarnished, she saw Monique like herself – rather dysfunctional – no different or more special than anyone else. It shouldn't have made a difference to their friendship, but she couldn't be sure if it did.

"I'm sorry. I had no idea," she offered, attempting to sound sympathetic.

Monique's lips thinned. "No one did, not even my daughters. They adored Tobin. He exposed all of us at a point when we needed to keep a low profile. I needed to protect my daughter, no matter the cost." Lost in a memory, her awareness came back to the room with a sudden, rude awakening. She looked shocked at what she'd divulged.

"You've been a victim of domestic abuse," Paisley affirmed, hoping she'd keep talking and explaining more of the details.

"Coercive control." She nodded with sadness. "I can't face telling my customers what's happened when they ask about Tobin. Could you do this for me? Pass on the truth so they sympathise instead of judge me? I'll love you forever."

Paisley was deeply moved, although a bit disappointed that the sharing had come to an end. However, Monique trusted her with this important mission. She gushed reassurance. "Of course. We're like sisters. I'll say he was abusive and you kicked him out. Now you're a single mum battling against the odds to keep this business going and you need their support. Don't worry. After I'm through, the town folk will back you one hundred percent." The previous lies Monique had asked her to convey to customers, about Tobin being in the UK visiting a sick mother, were conveniently put aside. Spontaneously, Paisley reached over and gave a quick comforting hug.

A bell tinkled in the background indicating a customer entering the café. Paisley stepped away from Monique and plastered on a customer service smile. A young mother struggled to pull a stroller through the doorway.

Monique sniffled into a serviette. "Thanks. You're a champion. I'm going to take a Panadol and lie down for a couple hours." She squeezed Paisley's shoulder. "Mind the café for me, darl."

Monique disappeared out the back to her residence. Paisley was left running the café again. Alone. But capable. That was a sure sign of trust, meaning they were back to being best girlfriends. All was forgiven about being a nosey busybody. There was no mystery about Tobin disappearing. Of course, it was obvious. Like most men, the guy had pissed off for greener pastures. Tobin may have been on the run from a 'criminal past' and been rehabilitated through a witness protection program, but he hadn't been transformed into a good guy either. Monique had been too ashamed to admit they'd separated, but she was better off without the abusive jerk. Girlfriends needed to stick together. Anyone enquiring about the health of Tobin's mother would cop an earful.

Now the truth was out in the open, there was nothing to worry about. She could stop obsessing. No more secrets. So there, Auntie Sheryl – you were right! Once Paisley explained the story to Bernie, her good character would be redeemed.

The task now was a righteous mission to tell the world about Tobin's true nature. She'd win the townsfolk's sympathy to Monique's side. It was the least she could do after doubting the woman's honesty. Paisley could be too cynical for her own good. This had been a lesson in learning to trust people instead of being so suspicious. What did she think happened to Tobin? She'd been an idiot.

A flustered young woman stood at the counter and jiggled a stroller while a newborn's loud wails echoed throughout the empty café totally out of proportion to its size and strength.

"What would you like to order?" Paisley asked bright and chirpy, full of good will to the world.

"A mega coffee, double shot, three sugars and a cream bun. I'll eat outside," she said, apologetically, digging into her purse and handing across a twenty dollar note. In a droll voice, she said, "I tell people she was planned."

Paisley chuckled. "It's the pits when they don't come with a one hundred percent guarantee so you can return them for a refund if not totally satisfied. Consumer Protection should investigate this business of parenthood. It should come with warnings – buyer beware."

"I love her best when she's asleep. No, actually, I love her best when I've had a good night's sleep." She stopped to think. "Remind me what that feels like. I've forgotten."

"A form of bliss I obviously take too much for granted," Paisley laughed while stuffing a cream bun into a paper bag.

Encouraged, the young customer became chatty. "It wasn't until I had a baby that I realised it's not possible to die from lack of sleep. After weeks of no sleep, you get so tired you think '*I should be dead*' but you're not. You can't die! It's a super woman freak of nature thing. Instead you stumble on in a half dead state." She rocked the stroller back and forth on automatic while Paisley steamed milk in a jug. The wails toned down a few decibels.

"A strong coffee is what the doctor ordered," Paisley said.

"I'll take it as an infusion straight to the vein, thanks. These bossy creatures have the ability to magically turn you into the walking dead. Just so you know, it's not contagious, but I'm officially a zombie. In case you want to shoot me on sight with a tranquiliser gun. Put me out of my misery. I would be grateful."

"Sorry but we're not allowed to discriminate based on zombie disability," Paisley replied in a serious and official tone while fixing a lid to the take away coffee mug and handing it across. She received a wan smile.

"Trust me to find the one politically correct café in all of Eden Isle."

"Here, let me help manoeuvre the stroller through the doorway while you grab the coffee, Ms Super Woman. I know just the spot where you can have privacy to drink, eat and doze."

The café went quiet. "OMG. She's fallen asleep at last. This café must be charmed."

"Sleep spells are the Thursday special. We do love potions on Fridays, if you're interested."

"God no. If it's all the same to you, I'll avoid Fridays, at least until she's a few years older."

"Good decision. Love can complicate your life if you're not careful." Paisley gazed at the adorable sleeping bundle. "She looks all cuddly like a doll." Young mum grunted, too tired to be impressed.

Getting the message not to go mushy, Paisley maneuvered the stroller across the café, careful to miss bumping chair legs and table edges, out the door and around the corner to Convict Crust's shaded courtyard. "There you go," she said, leaving the silent stroller next to a picnic table after securing the brakes.

The mum collapsed onto the bench with a sigh. "Wake me in a couple hours."

"I think your little mite will do that for you. Sweet dreams."

On days like these Paisley loved her job and all her customers – even the walking dead and the screaming mites. Life was looking good.

Maybe she could last at the bakery for a bit longer, until Monique got back on her feet.

✿ ✿ ✿

A few hours later, Monique emerged but only to announce she was leaving for a hair stylist appointment. "I've got a hot date on Friday," she bragged. "I want to look like a new woman."

Paisley thought it was too soon for Monique to move into the dating scene after ending a long term relationship. Dating had changed a lot over the years. Being in a vulnerable state, her girlfriend could end up badly burned. "Is this wise when you are still hurting from Tobin?" she cautioned.

"Got to get back on the horse at some point," she said off hand, dismissing Paisley's concern. "Sweetie, I'm not out for commitment. Just dinner and a quick shag." She patted Paisley's hand. "It's with Simon, Mr Two Score," she whispered. "He's safe and steady. And his girlfriend's away for the weekend. See, no complications."

Not sure how to respond but certain dating a customer – and a local – would amount to lots of town gossip, Paisley plastered on a fake smile. "Is that his name? Simon. I'll have to stop referring to him as a number," she joked. "Just don't get caught." She hoped their sneaking around was worth it for both of them. The last thing the bakery needed was to lose a regular given its precarious financial position.

"I'm always careful." Monique preened with self confidence. "That's why I picked Mr Discretion himself as my first. It's like taking candy from a baby. Watch and weep."

"Personally, I think you are worth more than someone's one night stand." Paisley was getting all sanctimonious on behalf of her friend.

Monique gave her a friendly hug. "I get off on secrets and the fear of discovery. Makes for awesome orgasms," she winked, grinning at the bright blush that crept up Paisley's neck. Glancing at her watch, she declared, "Sorry but there's no time to chat or I'll be late. You should be right minding the shop." It was a statement, not a question, leaving Paisley no choice but to agree.

Chapter Nineteen

The scents of cured tobacco and leather wafted into Paisley's nostrils when she pushed the kraken knob on the heavy door to Light Up. This never failed to instill a familiar sense of safety. All was right in the world when she stepped into Bernie's shop. She carried a woven plastic shopping bag containing handmade Steampunk vests and a few Alice in Wonderland hats with a sense of satisfaction. Bursting with excitement, she couldn't wait to hear what Bernie would say about them. Personally, she knew they were her best work yet. They'd make the shopfront window display look amazing.

Bernie hunched over the front counter staring at a laptop, Anita brushed up by his side. They barely looked up to acknowledge her presence. Whatever displayed on the screen transfixed their attention.

Curious and curiouser, Paisley dumped the bag on the floor behind the cash register and peered over their shoulders. "What are we looking at?" she asked, naturally assuming inclusion into their clique.

Anita moved aside to let her in. "Tell me what you think. I've created a social media page for Convict Crust. We're hoping, it might help the bakery become more profitable."

Paisley leaned in, bumping Bernie good naturedly in the process. "Salutations from the Guild of the Artificers."

"Oh, right. Greetings from the Laudator Temporis Acti," he said at last, still distracted. "I think it's awesome, Anita. Can I hire you to design a page for Light Up at some stage?" He turned to his girlfriend, all gushy smiles. Grumpily, Paisley noted her BFF ignored her contribution to his business success, the bundle of Steampunk garments she'd slaved over, on the floor behind his legs.

Paisley raised her brows in disgust and decided to be more discerning. "Let's have a look." Taking control of the mouse, she scrolled through the screen shots. The title page showed a street view of the bakery, angled to compliment the Federation style building with its white bricks and tall chimney stack. The Convict Crust sign hung in clear view. Underneath the title were several photos: the rustic wood fired oven dating from the turn of the century and baskets of artisan bread spread across the long wood table, scrubbed clean of flour, Monique with a white baker's apron in the kitchen; a blown up shot of the café's display case filled with delectable cakes and slices, and several close ups of Noelle's smiling face, posing with a mug of hot chocolate or munching on a blueberry muffin under the oak trees in the patio area. Each photo came with a pithy caption, drawing the audience into the Swan family like old friends. A sideboard listed a dozen customer comments, all flattering in the extreme. An arrow invited visitors to click on a video that walked them through a crowded café with customers locked in conversations, lots of laughter, good food, exceptional coffee, the best in pleasure and indulgence. Paisley was impressed. Anita had created more than a screenshot of the bakery. This was a three-dimensional experience where one could almost taste the coffee and smell freshly baked bread.

"Hmm. I guess it will do," she said in a droll voice before grinning at Anita. "By the Grand Mechanism, Bernie's right. It's damn awesome. But you knew that already."

"I hope my university tutor feels the same way. It started as a project for Media PR," Anita said with a touch of pride.

"Smart, killing two birds at the same time,' Paisley agreed. "You're bound to get a distinction."

"The big question is what will MM think about it?" Anita winced, mimicking Bernie's expression.

Paisley picked up on the body language. "She doesn't know about it, I take it?" Anita shook her head slowly.

Bernie filled in the gap. "She will soon enough. There's a loyalty program advertised, so when people start asking for their free coffees, I think the cat will be out of the bag."

Paisley gasped. "You haven't activated it before getting her permission?" She could only imagine Monique's reaction. Anita would be in so much trouble.

Anita wasn't receptive to criticism from Bernie's BFF. "Not yet but we want to do it very soon," she replied somewhat testily. "I'm working on massaging the Loyalty Scheme so it adds value rather than cost. Once that's done ..."

Bernie offered reassurance. "We're hoping after it's activated and the bakery draws in more customers, it will start making good profits before she finds out. Then she can't be mad, can she?" The awkward silence that followed meant no one knew the answer to that.

All Paisley could do was shake her head in disbelief.

"I was careful not to post any photos of Tobin. I know he hates being photographed," Anita said in an attempt to justify their plan.

"That's something, at least, with his shady past and being in witness protection," Paisley said.

Anita looked confused. "What are you talking about?" Then it dawned on her. "What's MM been saying? You realise she's a compulsive liar? Tobin doesn't have a criminal past. He's the one trying to get away from *them*." Trying for patience, she explained. "He was on a police rehabilitation program in Queensland to get him out of a dangerous biker's gang he joined straight out of the Army. Once he learned of their illegal activities and refused to be part of it, he knew they would kill him if he tried to leave. The government scheme provided him with a vocation and a chance to start a new life. He met MM around the same period and they decided to move as far away as they could get, which turned out to be Eden Isle."

Bernie shot Paisley a glance that could have split a log in two. To cover for her blunder, he said, "I guess that explains why he loved his motorcycle."

"And came back for it," Paisley said.

Anita shook her head. "He loved that bike. I can't figure out why he would have agreed for MM to sell it; something must have spooked him … unless his gang found him somehow and he was in trouble." She looked across the shop, lost in thought.

A contrite Paisley murmured, "Sorry. I got the wrong end of the periscope. Of course, he never would have allowed Monique to sell it. Once he's done with whatever business he has in Western Australia, I'm sure he'll be back." Nervous and guilty at being caught out gossiping, she continued to over explain and contradict herself. "But maybe it would be better if he didn't return. If he was abusive, Monique is better off without him, right?" She refused to look at Bernie knowing he was fuming at her interference in Anita's private life.

"He didn't even wait long enough to say goodbye to us … it's not like him," Anita said, talking to herself. Then as if jerking awake, she registered Paisley's comment. "Tobin abusive? He's as gentle as a lamb. What made you think he's in WA?"

Digging herself into a deeper hole, she mumbled, "Um, Noelle's birthday present from Tobin." Seeing Anita's blank expression, she added, "Stamped from Western Australia."

"I don't know where you're getting your information but it's total shit," Anita bridled. "Noelle never got a present from Tobin. Why would she get something from Western Australia?" She may as well have added, *dummy*, from the tone of her voice. "What I do know, however, is that Tobin sold his motorcycle because the bakery's bank account had a windfall deposited into it not long after the bike went missing. There's no other explanation. For once, I believe MM. It's got the bakery out of financial difficulties for the next few months, which is what Tobin would have wanted."

An awkward silence followed this revelation. None of this explained where Tobin was, if he wasn't in WA. Who was *Mr T. Swan* then? It appeared Tobin had returned from the UK long enough to sell his motorcycle and then vanished once again. For some reason Monique was protecting Tobin. It seemed impossible to get a straight answer from the woman. An image of the compost trench flashed across her mind, quickly suppressed; her imagination running wild. It was sensible to forget the whole thing.

Changing the subject and trying to get back into Bernie's good books, Paisley grabbed her shopping bag off the floor and began unloading its contents. "I've got Steampunk braces, waistcoats and plumed hats, as ordered. Have a look."

Bernie began sorting through them while Anita held each one up for an inspection. Retail therapy was working as a distraction to calm her prickly mood much to Paisley's relief.

Confident that the previous misunderstandings were resolved for now, Paisley flourished an invoice in Bernie's direction. Opening the till, he counted out the cash and handed it over without hesitation. "Thanks, Paisley. They're perfect. In fact, I think we already have a sale," he said looking across at Anita with puppy adoration.

"I can't decide which one I like the best," she moaned, continuing to view each one with an eye for its suitability.

Leaving her to decide, Bernie turned back to Paisley. "I almost forgot. Your biker friend, Lance, stopped by a few days ago. Asked if he could leave business cards." He reached under the counter and pulled out a card to show her.

Paisley's heart began a drum run. Acting nonchalant, she studied the card. Lance's business address, email, and phone number stood out like a road sign. *Turn right in one hundred meters.*

"He said you should check out his body art studio, if you ever fancy a road trip all the way to Whaler's Cove. Mentioned he'd be good for a fisherman's platter. Sounds like a good deal." Bernie prodded her arm to get a reaction.

"The Steampunk design is a clever touch," Paisley said, injecting a neutral tone to her voice. She pocketed the card.

"I think the guy likes you," Bernie said. Without further prying, he changed the subject. "Would you mind if Anita came with us on Sunday when we check out the Showground facilities for the Steampunk Challenge? She's wanting to design posters for the event and take some photos for the bakery's social media page seeing as they're one of the sponsors."

"No worries. We could use her help with publicity." Paisley appreciated Bernie's respect for her feelings. His parents raised him to have good manners. She punched his arm. "No need to ask. She's your girlfriend, so she's always welcome, dude." Anita overheard and gave her a grateful smile.

As if Anita needed her permission to be with Bernie. Paisley was flattered but knew in matters of the heart, Bernie had already made his choice. She was happy for him, if only a bit lonely. She knew soon the tables would turn and Bernie would be asking Anita's permission before Paisley tagged along.

Rolla would never make the journey to Whaler's Cove.

Monique could end up her only friend.

✿ ✿ ✿

Back at her unit, Paisley sat at the kitchen table under a yellow fluorescent bulb picking out stitches from a second hand, burgundy velvet jacket. From her laptop playlist, The Clockwork Quartet sang a folk story about the watchmaker's apprentice. The song acted like a lullaby, making her heavy-eyed. It was impossible to focus on the job at hand. She had plans to use the material for something special, but wasn't sure how it would end up. Her mind wandered to snatches of conversation held earlier in the day at Light Up.

The tip of the stitch picker stabbed her middle finger as it pushed through a tough seam. A drop of blood seeped through the hole. She dropped the bundled fabric onto the table top and sucked the finger. The folk song with its ticking clocks took on a gothic, horror atmosphere.

It was odd that Lance had travelled all the way to Bernie's shop but didn't bother to stop in at the bakery. Monique must have scared him off with those innuendos she throws around at every male with a heartbeat. She was way too old for him. Why then, when it came to Monique and men, did everything end up flirtatious like it was a competition between them?

To be fair, it wasn't all Monique's fault. On those few occasions, Paisley's mood hadn't offered encouragement to Lance. That last wave he gave meant goodbye for good, she'd thought. But now he told Bernie if she ever visited Whaler's Cove, he was good for lunch. That could mean ... something. Did she dare hope?

Picturing Rolla, her old faithful bomb of a car, chugging up the narrow, steep road through Bramley Ranges, she seriously doubted it would make the trip. Her heart flipped. Could she chance it?

There were too many uncertainties. Out of habit, she imagined her mixed up feelings jammed into a glass bell jar and sealed from her fragile heart, now safe and protected. Confusingly, the laptop blared Lindsey Stirling's violin melodies while a singer pleaded 'Shatter Me' in direct opposition to Paisley's resolve. Bedamned. The song tugged on heartstrings. She brushed tears from her cheeks convinced safe was better than rejected and hurt.

Willing a switch to a less heart wrenching topic, she mulled over Anita's comments about Monique. The accusation of her being a 'compulsive liar' rubbed the most. It was clear that Anita and Monique held differing views about Tobin's character but who was to say which ones were closest to reality. If the guy was abusive, there were many reasons Monique would try to cover for him.

Having experienced many and varied forms of domestic abuse in foster care, Paisley learned that telling the truth was not always the best course of action. How a man appeared to others did not always equate to his actual behaviour in private situations; however, pointing out this discrepancy to authorities had not protected her. As a matter of fact, usually speaking out backfired and placed her in new and different perils. It was better to keep silent, and even lie when required, as a means of survival. Over time, given enough danger, lying became one's default position. Her friend, Monique was demonstrating the same instinct for survival for good reasons.

As a loyal friend, Paisley respected her silence.

As a naturally curious, small town busybody, she wanted to find out what those reasons might be.

Chapter Twenty

In the Convict Crust courtyard, Paisley piled tomato sauce soiled paper plates and used coffee cups onto a tray wearing rubber gloves, and swept dust and fallen leaves off picnic tables and chairs with a dishcloth. On hot summer days, customers preferred to sit outside under the shade of the oak trees rather than indoors where it got crowded and stuffy. She entered the bakery kitchen through the back door, pushed the heavy paneled wood with one foot and shouldered it open. Dumping the tray contents into a bin, she pulled off the gloves, threw them on top and then removed a spotty apron to the laundry basket. From the dining area, Monique's trilling laugh floated through to the kitchen. Flirting with a male customer, as usual. Paisley scanned her short sleeve tee shirt and flounced skirt for signs of food stains, brushing off a few crumbs from the giant red heart decal across her chest. Out of the corner of her eye, she noted a small child waiting at the counter.

It was Heath, her little brother.

"Hellfire. What are you doing here, dude?" Paisley gushed in surprise. "Your dad hasn't arranged for our weekend, has he? Don't tell me I forgot."

Heath giggled. "It's only Thursday, silly. We came to surprise you. I wanted a hot chocolate and a brownie, so Dad decided we could check out your bakery. *Fi-nal-ly*. It's cool."

"I'm glad you approve." Paisley glanced across the packed room to see Eddy and Monique at a table locked in conversation. Two mugs of cappuccino were going cold – Monique must have made them. He was bragging about fly fishing at Sapphire Creek where he had this awesome cabin tucked away in the mountains. More like a fishing shack, she silently corrected with a smile. Definitely flirting. She hadn't seen Eddy so animated for ages. Monique had that effect on men.

"Can I have a marshmallow with my hot chocolate," Heath asked, breaking her absorption.

"Of course, dude. I'll make it right this minute. Do you want to go out back to see Missy? I'll bring your order to the courtyard, if you like." She pointed through the archway to the kitchen door. Heath disappeared out the back fast as a thrown dart.

Out of the corner of her eye, as she frothed milk, Paisley watched Eddy with Monique feeling a sense of disquiet. Bedamned. What was that foreboding all about? Seriously, she couldn't be jealous, not over Eddy. If she was being possessive, she had no claim on him. By rights of their previous relationship, he was like family, that was all. He couldn't be classed as a friend in the true sense of the word. He was simply her *ex boyfriend*. Paisley had no hold on him. Good luck to her girlfriend. She deserved a nice guy.

That's how she *should* be feeling – but wasn't.

Paisley tried. Logic wasn't working. Her heart clenched with worry. Eddy was up against a pro and he could be clueless with women. When pitted against Monique, he was way over his head. Should she intervene, break up their intimate moment? A sense of family responsibility warred with Paisley's weary worldly wisdom telling her to stay out of it.

Monique was a friend, too. Where did the balance of her loyalties rest?

Remembering the job at hand, she checked the thermometer attached to the milk jug and immediately stopped frothing before the milk burned. Pouring a small amount of hot milk in a paper cup, she mixed it with cocoa powder and stirred to smooth out lumps. Then she added the remaining milk and topped it with scoops of foam, marshmallows, and candy sprinkles. Heath would love it. Tearing her attention away from the love birds, she packed a fudge brownie in a paper bag and along with his hot chocolate carried Heath's order out to the courtyard.

Calling his name twice, he emerged reluctantly from the back yard where he'd been patting Missy. As he grabbed for the brownie, Paisley pulled it away. "Do I need to remind you that dogs aren't allowed chocolate?" Before handing it over, she waited until Heath's expression changed from woebegone pleading to acquiescence. "Good," she said with a mock frown. "I'll leave your drink here; don't let it go cold."

Returning to the café counter, she couldn't help but glance at Eddy, who appeared dazed at being caught in Monique's intimate gaze – as if she provided his oxygen and he, a drowning man, was desperate to suck in her breath.

Continuing to watch and judge, Paisley saw Monique attend to Eddy's every word; to giggle at random as if he were so clever. Eddy puffed up in a bumptious pose, basking in the adoration. As if they were the only two people in the room. As if they were special.

But this was her ex, plain old Eddy. What game was Monique playing?

Paisley felt an envious stab to her gut. Eddy was as hooked as a trout on a fly-fishing line. Credit where it was due; the woman had a winning allure. His glazed eyes shone with a religious, life-saving fervor. Monique was his Madonna; he was a sinner thirsting for holy water.

A jeer echoed in her head, *Watch and weep little girl at an expert at work.*

Eddy had never gazed with such longing like that at her, not even when they'd first started dating. Most of the time when they lived together, she'd felt invisible, a ghost that cooked, cleaned and entertained Heath; useful but not an object of desire. There had been a sense of security in their easy, albeit passionless, relationship. When the inevitable decision came to move on, it was Paisley who initiated the separation, never considering it would break his heart. As far as she knew, he'd dated but never entered into another serious relationship since then. Hence, a residue of guilt about hurting Eddy lingered to this day. He was a good guy and deserved better than what Paisley offered.

But that didn't explain why Monique targeted Eddy. She was way too sophisticated for him. Was it some game she was playing, messing with him to mess with Paisley in the process? Her girlfriend admitted to enjoying competition when it came to romance. Was she trying to make Paisley jealous?

Or, maybe Monique was sincerely attracted to Eddy. No accounting for hormones. Paisley shouldn't be so mean and judgmental. Give her friend the benefit of the doubt. From objective analysis, Eddy had a certain rugged charm with his beard and plaid flannelette shirt, workman's boots, and a husky baritone smoker's voice. The attraction of opposites.

More customers arrived all at once and she became too busy seeing to their orders to spare a moment to dwell on the mysteries of romance. Before she knew it, the cogs of the great clockwork had shifted; Eddy and Heath headed out the door with a wave from Monique who generously also waived their bill. What's more, Heath went home with a bag full of free peppermint chip cookies. The lad was stoked, won over by his dad's new friend. Paisley watched from afar, hurt that Eddy and Heath had forgotten to say goodbye, and thinking her friend's generosity was a first for a woman whose business was tottering on financial brink.

Monique sauntered over to the counter with a misty smile. Paisley cringed, waiting for the routine number to be appointed, wondering if Eddy would be a one or a two.

"He seemed like a decent guy," Monique said. "Quite interesting actually."

"He's my ex," Paisley blurted, surprised at Monique's dreamy tone.

"I know, he mentioned it," Monique said. "Tell me all about him, the movies he watches, music, sports – more importantly, what's he like in bed?"

There it was, the anticipated rating question. This was getting too personal. Paisley blushed. "We've discussed this before. You remember, when we first met and you gave me advice about how to attract Adam. I told you Eddy was more interested in gaming until midnight."

Monique went thoughtful. "I remember. Eddy was your first long term relationship. You lacked experience, am I correct?"

Grudgingly, Paisley admitted this was true. Changing the subject, she decided to throw some crumbs. "He supports Hawthorn and goes to the occasional home game, but isn't fanatical about anything but gaming. He drinks red wine. What else do you want to know?"

"Don't tell me anything more. It will be fun finding out – and working out ways to lure him away from his laptop and into bed at midnight." She giggled suggestively. "By the way, I like the sound of his cabin hide-away. Do you suppose he'd take me there?"

A mean-spirited Paisley so wanted to clarify for the record that the *cabin* was more a fishing *shack* and it was owned by Eddy's *mate*, not Eddy, but she bit her tongue and held back. Suspicious about Monique making future plans and moving in on Eddy so early in the piece, she aimed to discourage her girlfriend. "I don't know. Eddy's shy; he's not dated much. He a lonely bachelor ... safe but lacks experience ..." She didn't finish the sentence.

"I'd be good for him, is that what you're trying to say? Get him back on the horse?" Monique grinned. "Put in an endorsement for me, darl. My womanhood is wet with anticipation. Sometimes you just know when it's right. You know what I mean?"

Knowing Eddy as intimately as Paisley did, she was sure Monique would be in for a huge disappointment. But who was she to impose her experience on another? By the Grand Mechanism, Eddy might become a changed man under a mature and skillful woman's tutelage. She tried to expunge that image from her mind.

Whatever.

The last thing she was going to do was act as a go between and set up a date for Monique with Eddy. Even if that was what girlfriends were for.

Monique disappeared out the back to her bedroom and returned wearing an orange neon and black sports bra, matching jogger's tights, and top of the range running shoes. "Need to lose a few kilos and get in shape for the sexual marathons on the horizon," she said to Paisley. It was a joke, of course. She felt and looked fabulous; no need to diet. The Lycra outfit pulled in her body to accentuate curves in all the right places.

"Don't tell me; I don't want to know," Paisley groaned. "I guess this means, we won't be walking Missy together tonight?"

Monique raced out the door and didn't bother to answer. Her thoughts were on more sizzling matters. Such as meeting Simon at The Common's barbeque pavilion. They'd been doing it there twice a week since their first date. When her habitual disappearances began to arouse suspicions, taking up jogging simplified explanations. No one questioned a healthy exercise routine. Jogger leggings quickly slid down the legs, freed her sex and stretched as she opened her legs. No need to fuss with buttons or zippers. A perfect solution.

Jumping into the Land Cruiser, she turned the key and sped off. If losing weight was the point, she probably should have jogged to The Common. But there was no point arriving exhausted and out of breath. Getting her hot and sweaty was Simon's job.

She smirked. If one believed science, then vigorous shagging consumed a lot of calories. Coincidentally, it also served a bonus purpose. Afterwards, she had a burst of energy that powered the run around The Common like she was some turbo chook, burning up more than calories.

A pity Simon was only good for a quick shag across a picnic table. His girlfriend resisted going away for another weekend to see her parents, despite Monique pushing him to arrange it every time they met. No luck. This resulted in a delay in doing prolonged lovemaking on a comfortable, cushioned bed, which would have demonstrated they were in a more committed relationship. She wondered if he was up for that or if his girlfriend's stubbornness was used as an excuse.

No matter. The fantasy of a secret tryst and the risk of getting caught in the act by an innocent passerby aroused and satisfied in the short term.

Pulling into the carpark, she smiled at a memory from a few weeks ago. When Simon couldn't make their rendezvous, knowing her powerful sex drive, he worried so much about disappointing her that he'd sent a mate as a surprise stand in. That was thrilling, to find a stranger waiting in the shadows of the pavilion, taking her in a rough, doggie style with silent command; never knowing his name; never getting a good look at his face hidden within a black hoodie. The anonymous nature of his brute penetration sent her spiraling into violent multiple orgasms, even causing her to briefly faint from ecstasy. It was like nothing she'd ever experienced with Simon. She wanted more.

She sent out a fevered wish to the universe. *Please god increase Simon's workload so he can't make it today.*

Re-living the memory sent a burst of wet heat direct to her crotch, making her ready without the need for Simon's hungry tongue. If he only knew the reason. She grinned. Maybe they could share this fantasy together. A threesome. That was an idea. She would talk to Simon about her predilections, ask him to arrange more surprises with his mates. If he'd done it once, there shouldn't be any reason he couldn't arrange it again. That was something to look forward to. Unexpected shocks fired up the mundane, fed the imagination. Maybe today was the day ....

No, not today then. As she descended from the Land Cruiser, Simon poked his head out from behind a treated pine support, his hiding spot that was part of the pavilion structure, checking if it was her. He gave a weak wave and shuffled his feet, looking furtive. A couple strolled past the barbeque area with a West Highland Terrier prancing on a lead. Typical locals, bad luck, they stopped to chat with him.

Monique hesitated, wondering whether to approach or wait until they left. Fortunately, their little dog pulled on his lead and they didn't stay long. This made things interesting. She and Simon would have to calculate their fuck to finish before the olds finished walking around the meandering oval path of The

Common. Hopefully, Simon was up to the challenge. She began to jog over to him, eager and ready to go.

A picture of the old couple catching them in the act crossed her mind and made her laugh. They'd probably have heart attacks. Slowing the pace, she strolled casually towards Simon, keeping him waiting, drawing out the minutes, deliberately building tension to accentuate the risks they were taking.

Next meeting, she'd convince Simon to bring a mate to stand guard while they went at it. And change places afterwards where he could watch.

Chapter Twenty-One

Paisley wandered through Light Up's aisles, picking up quirky teapots and examining mugs with captions appealing to masculine humor. With no intention to purchase anything, she was on a mission of another kind. Casually, while Bernie rang up totals on the cash register, she happened to mention Monique's interest in Eddy, hoping a male friend's objective point of view might sort out her warring emotions.

Bernie sounded surprised but not concerned particularly. "Wonders never cease. I can't see their relationship working, but then I've never understood women's attraction to Adam either. The buffoon," he added for good measure. "What would I know about how Monique's attraction meter works?" He was being flippant until he noticed Paisley's worried look.

"It feels wrong, but I can't say why," she said. "I don't want Eddy to get hurt. I like Monique and we're friends but she can be rather forceful and he's sort of a nerd." Bernie gave her 'the look'. Too late, she realised the faux paus.

"Hey, nerds deserve love, too!" His tone was jovial but the sentiment was a pointed reminder that Anita was sophisticated and she liked him, a self-proclaimed nerd. Paisley had the grace to look sheepish.

"It may be nothing but … she's just met him and is pushing to go to 'his hide-away in the mountains'. Does that seem suspicious to you?" Paisley whined, seeking Bernie's complicity.

"Suspicious of what? By the Leagues, you're doing it again – being a boffin – inventing mysteries and creating airships out of thin air. First Tobin. Now Eddy. Cease and desist being so overprotective of Eddy. Give the guy some credit; he's old enough to look out for himself." Bernie pushed a tab on the cash register and it began to spit out a print out of the day's operations. He studied it intensely, an indication their conversation about Monique and Eddy had reached a conclusion.

After a long drawn out silence, Eddy looked up to see Paisley's puckered lips. "My suggestion is to worry about your own love life for a change. For instance, have you phoned Lance to arrange lunch yet?" Paisley shrugged. "The dude's really into you. Take some time off – treat yourself to a seafood platter and some harmless flirting."

"You make it sound easy," she replied.

"It could be, if you let it." Bernie looked smug but Paisley remained unconvinced. "It's just a date – not a forever thing."

That was the problem when it came to Lance – and her heart. He was simply gorgeous and nice and *normal.* Everything that forever was about. This was not her usual experience with people. She screwed up every relationship she'd ever had, except for Bernie, so far. Reading way into the future, her heart knew *forever* was the only story she wanted to contemplate with Lance. And failure was too scary to face. Better to play it safe and not go there.

For Bernie, another *normal* person, it was all simple. "This is what you do: start off easy, text him to touch base. Then ask him to phone you. Talk and get to know each other, then take it from there. See. No worries."

"Right. Nothing to lose," she said under her breath, "except my life." Louder, she said, "If I make an idiot of myself, you'll be blamed."

In a droll voice, Bernie said, "When have you ever made an idiot of yourself? Except all the time! Just do it already and put me out of my misery."

On the drive home, Paisley cogitated about what to text to Lance that sounded awesome and intriguing; came up blank on clever and pithy remarks; then talked herself out of it, deciding instead that Bernie had probably got the wrong message. How could Lance possibly be truly interested in her? The last few instances they'd met, she pushed him away due to that chip on her shoulder. He'd have to be deaf and dumb to ignore those unspoken brushoffs. What was his deal? He must want something from her; the same as everyone else. Was it worth a free lunch to find out the truth? It was easier to not bother.

She couldn't see Eddy working out with Monique either. Eddy was too shy to make the first move, and was probably too shy to accept Monique's. And if he did, she was too sophisticated and experienced when it came to men. He'd be a lamb to the slaughter for sure.

But then again, Bernie hooked up with Anita as if it was the most natural thing in the world for two people to find each other and start dating without all the push and pull and conflict associated with romance. And Bernie was definitely a nerd of the first order. Maybe, Eddy had a chance with Monique. They'd be an odd couple. But who was she to judge when it came to relationships? Bedamned. Did that mean she and Lance had a chance?

Chapter Twenty-Two

A week had gone by since Eddy and Heath had visited Convict Crust Bakery. Monique knew Paisley had avoided discussing Eddy with her but the issue wasn't over by a long shot. She needed to make a move on that front asap.

The bakery was slowly sucking all her savings into a black hole. She relied on Tobin's army pension deposited into the bakery's bank account but knew that could stop any day now that he wasn't coming back. Their reasons may be different, but he wasn't the only one who needed to disappear. Overly cautious, he got spooked first and left her holding the fort and all the responsibility. Curses to that kid Anita started dating. Posting a happy shot online about a missing dog reunited with its family was one of those stories that travelled more widely than anyone could have expected. Curse Missy for being so adorable. Convict Crust Bakery's sign displayed in the background, easy to read. Tobin's face wasn't the only one in-frame. It wouldn't take a genius to find out where the Swan's lived these days. It was a matter of days, weeks at best. Returning Noelle's package from Western Australia 'Address Unknown' forestalled the inevitable – but not for long.

In the kitchen surrounded by crimped pasties and half-made sandwiches, Paisley and Anita were deep in conversation about boyfriends. Ready to chastise them for slacking off, Monique held back. When had Anita taken over her role as confidante? She'd been careless and let her friendship with the girl fall away, right at the moment when she needed Paisley. It was vital to take control back.

"What's this about Lance?" she asked as an excuse to join in.

Anita answered. "Lance wants Paisley to visit his tattoo parlour at Whaler's Cover but she's not sure what to do."

"It's a long drive," Paisley said.

"Poor kid. I had to let him down gently about not needing his tattoo design, after all that effort he put into it. I need to make it up to him somehow," Monique replied.

Paisley squirmed, uncomfortable with any suggestion of sexual innuendo regarding Lance. "It was a cosmic contrivance," she muttered in praise of the design.

Monique pressed her advantage. "The guy's talented, no question about it. I wonder if his creativity flows over into other aspects of his life?" She winked. Then changing the subject, she wondered out loud. "If I explored Eddy's bod thoroughly, would I expose any hidden body art?" Seeing Paisley shake her head, she smiled suggestively. "Tattoos make me hot. A special ops design would be perfect on his butt."

Paisley blushed. "I'm not sure a Special Forces tattoo would be his thing."

"I'm going to ask him while I explore where to place it on his body." She looked wistful. Paisley picked up on the broad hint.

"About Eddy ...," Paisley stammered.

Monique couldn't help showing excitement. "Have you spoken to him? What did he say?"

Paisley winced. "I only see him occasionally when I babysit Heath on a weekend. It's not a regular event. I'm sorry but I haven't had a chance yet ... if you still want me to?"

A shrewd look crossed Monique's face. "Don't put yourself out on my account. I see what's going on. He's not into you anymore, you know."

Anita decided to intervene before the conversation turned catty. "MM, this isn't a competition."

Paisley looked huffy. "By the Eternal, Eddy is like family but nothing more. He's a free man to go out with whoever. I'm happy to help things along but I can't say how soon it will be. That's all."

Monique appeared satisfied with her answer. "Since that day you returned Missy to us, I've felt our connection; more than a friend, like being your older sister. We've grown even closer by working together, seeing each other almost every day, sharing secrets, helping each other out. If Eddy and I did get together more or less permanently, we'd become one big family – Heath, Anita and Noelle, you, me and Eddy. And Missy. How wonderful would that be?"

Anita placed two fingers in her mouth and pretended to vomit. Paisley punched her in the shoulder good naturedly. "By the gods of the Grand Mechanism, I believe that would be the most wonderful outcome in my whole life," she replied with feeling.

"Good. Then it's settled. About Lance, if you're asking my opinion, if it was me, I'd jump his bones in an instant. Long drive or not."

Anita burst out laughing. "As if we couldn't see that coming."

Monique checked Paisley's reaction – a vexed look quickly covered up. "Of course, I've met Eddy so my heart is taken," she said in a sing-song voice, acting cute. But the message was clear. This was the deal: if Paisley set her up with Eddy, she'd leave Lance alone.

Chapter Twenty-Three

Paisley was getting impatient with Eddy. Fine, he didn't want to take fashion advice from someone who dressed as a goth character from the nineteenth century but today wasn't about her. It was about fixing him up to go on a date with stylish, elegant Monique. She'd traveled all the way to Plover Point with him on her day off, so he could shop at Albert's Lair, an exclusive men's boutique recommended by Adam – when she could have taken him to K-Mart or Target at Gorse Plains for all Eddy cared.

He had to trust her judgment because he didn't have any when it came to coordinating a 'look'. Paisley had a thousand times more dress sense, particularly when dressing men. Faded, short sleeved Hawaiian shirts and khaki cotton drill shorts were not going to cut it when it came to making a first impression. She'd based her masculine style cues on Adam's look; it was impossible to go wrong.

"I don't know," Eddy grumbled, studying the summer weave, long sleeved top with a designer emblem on the front Paisley held up for his inspection. If he wore it with a light weight jacket, a tie wouldn't be necessary. "It's not me."

"By the Eternal Clockmaker. That's the point," she said, exasperated at his stubbornness. This was the tenth top she'd picked out; with his tall, slim frame each one would have made him look spectacular.

"I don't feel comfortable pretending to be someone I'm not."

"Hellfire. No one is *comfortable* on a first date, Eddy." Paisley took pity. She'd been totally surprised when Eddy got up the courage to phone Monique and ask her out, even if he'd been assured a rejection was out of the question. Perhaps her ex wasn't so lame when it came to women after all. Or, he really liked Monique.

Nonetheless, Paisley offered reassurance automatically. "You can still be yourself. Monique likes you already, so you don't have to worry about that. However, you don't want to embarrass her by looking like a redneck from the backwoods."

After another ten minutes of deliberation, he agreed to the 'fancy' top. Choosing neutral coloured pants and a loose linen jacket to go with were much quicker decisions helped along by a male shop assistant who apparently conveyed a more credible air of trustworthiness when it came to male fashion. Eddy allowed the shop assistant to talk him into a second top, a lemon polo shirt, hinting it would be needed for his 'second date'. Why hadn't Paisley thought to appeal to the man's ego like that? Life would have been much easier.

The next frustrating debate occurred at the barbers. Paisley wanted Eddy to cut his shoulder length hair into a short, layered style and shave off the beard altogether. She lost that argument. He remained stubbornly attached to the pony tail and allowed the barber to tidy the split ends but nothing more. Coloured highlights were out of the question. *Did she think he was a girl?* Thankfully, the beard was trimmed back from a bushy feral nest to something a pipe smoking English gentleman would approve of. She hoped Monique didn't mind kissing prickly fur.

Altogether, Paisley was satisfied with the day's efforts. Eddy was as prepared and presentable as he'd ever be for his date.

On the drive back, before dropping her home, he eventually came around to thanking her. "You've been a real mate today. Sorry if I drove you crazy."

"By the Eternal. I hope for your sake it will have been worth it. Where are you going to take Monique?" she asked.

"I haven't decided, but Stubblefield's got a good Chinese restaurant," he said, darting her a quick look as if expecting disapproval. She didn't disappoint.

"No, no, no. That's not fancy enough. You want to impress her, Eddy." Paisley began to scroll through her phone after googling Eden Isle restaurants. "It may be a long drive but there's a wine bar and bistro at the Imperial Casino at Whaler's Cove. That would be the perfect atmosphere – casual but tasteful. Monique could have a flutter on the pokies or the roulette wheel. It would be a memorable evening. If all goes well, you might decide to book a room and stay overnight." She brought the phone to her nose to peer at the screen to hide a grimace. The thought of Monique and Eddy doing it ... she did not want to go there.

"Let's not get ahead of ourselves," Eddy said with a sober expression. After a long pause, he agreed to the bistro idea.

Paisley had done all she could. Now it was up to Eddy to take it from there.

Chapter Twenty-Four

Paisley strolled into the bakery kitchen, hung a favourite handbag – black leather decorated with chains and an old fob watch – on a hook in the cloak closet, and donned a white apron over her lace blouse and bustled skirt. Outside, this early in the morning of late summer, it was pleasantly cool but inside with the wood oven stoked with red hot coals, the room was tolerably hot. Anita gave her a wide smile and continued to cut sandwiches into quarters and stand them in plastic triangle containers. A stack of a dozen sat on the benchtop ready to be transferred to the café display counter. Monique wiped damp strands of hair from her forehead looking as if she hadn't slept all weekend. She tested the oven temperature and commented it would be ready in ten minutes. Paisley quickly got to work rolling out dough for the day's pasties. Busy with their jobs, no one said anything.

Finally, Paisley had to ask. "How did your date with Eddy go?" From Monique's stony silence, it was a flop. What had Eddy done?

Anita sniggered. "She's in a shitty mood because she didn't get laid – up all night, lots of hokey pokey, but the earth did not shake, rattle and roll before the music stopped."

Upset for Eddy, Paisley felt a need to defend the guy. "It was his first date after a very long drought. I suspect nerves got the better of him."

Monique looked piqued. "I have to say, that was a first for me, too. Never has a guy gone soft on me before getting off. Most often they're so eager it's over before I can blink. He really made me work for it, and in the end, my jaws locked and I couldn't keep going." Seeing Paisley's stricken face, and mistaking it for sympathy rather than horror at hearing about her and Eddy's private sex life, she added, "Not to worry. I'm not one to give up easily. I like the guy; he's a sweetie."

"Take it slow, give him a chance to gain his confidence," Paisley suggested in a meek voice.

"I'll cope," Monique winked knowingly. "There are other ways to—"

Anita interrupted. "It could be that he's a smoker. I've read that smoking can affect a man's libido, especially in older men." Anita, keen to be part of the gossip, offered her unhelpful opinion.

"Hellfire. He's younger than Monique." Paisley bristled, clearly uncomfortable with the topic of her ex and sex. Using a tablespoon, she splatted filling onto pastry rounds and began crimping with frenetic concentration.

Anita didn't pick up on the change in mood. "A friend of mine is a natural therapist. I know she's recommended a specific herbal remedy for couples experiencing this situation with excellent results. Horny Goat Weed." She smiled in delight. "Cool name, by the way."

"Never heard of it," Monique retorted. "But I've never needed to, until now."

"It's for Eddy, not you." Anita grinned, enjoying teasing her.

Monique huffed. "Why would I need it? I'm so horny I have half a mind to pull Mr Two Score into the broom closet and have my way with him when he arrives any minute now."

"Why wait for him. Just use the broom handle!" Anita snorted. "But close the door. We don't want to hear you grunting."

It all got too much for Paisley. Throwing off her apron in disgust, she escaped the banter and marched to the bathroom to compose herself.

Momentarily surprised, Monique and Anita watched her leave.

"Was I too much?" Anita asked.

"She's a bit of a prude, I fear," Monique whispered with a mean grin. "Now, about that Horny Goat Weed. Can you get me some for Eddy?"

"Sure, no worries. But how are you going to convince him to use it? Rather a sensitive topic, don't you think?"

"That's where Paisley comes in." Monique gave her a look of triumph finding a clever solution. "What are friends for?"

Anita scoffed. "Miss Prude? How are you going to pull that off?"

"She'll come round. Trust me."

Anita stared trying to read her motives. "Why are you going after Eddy with such determination? You're not spoiled for choice. What's so special about him?"

Monique looked wistful. "Once I've got certain things sorted, I believe he's the one who can give me what I've been needing since

Tobin left: safety and security. And that's more than special – he's the key to my future happiness."

"This is Eddy we're talking about?" Anita rolled her eyes, not believing it for one moment. Apparently, she shared Paisley's doubts about Eddy as a potential lover and partner for Monique. "Whatever," she said finally, ending the conversation.

Monique shovelled hot coals to the back of the oven and slid uncooked pasties into the cavernous void, a secret smile on her face.

Chapter Twenty-Five

Pounding knocks on the door to the flat reminded Paisley of the clock. Quickly, she added a sprinkle of Italian herbs to the pot of bubbling tomato sauce on the stove, gave it a stir, and ran to answer.

Eddy stood in the stairwell dressed to impress in a lemon polo shirt and clean, newly pressed khaki drill pants. A wafting of a supermarket brand aftershave tickled her nostrils. She suppressed a sneeze. Heath pushed past carrying a bulging brown paper bag filled with something greasy from the looks of the marks on it.

"Hi, come in," she said, opening the door wide and stepping back.

Eddy shook his head and handed her a lead. Missy's head poked out from behind his legs. "Monique said you wouldn't mind taking her for a walk. She's okay with you keeping the dog overnight. I can return her tomorrow when I pick up Heath."

"Missy!" Paisley shouted in surprise. "Of course, we don't mind." She bent down on her knees and gave the dog a hug. Missy rolled on her back for tummy rubs which she obliged with big smiles of happiness.

From the kitchen, Heath shouted, "She's not been fed."

Eddy shuffled his feet with impatience. "Look, I've got to get going; Monique awaits. Don't want to give another wrong impression, you know, being late."

Paisley stood up to talk. "I'm glad you asked her for a second date. That took a lot of courage so soon after the first." She studied his face, hoping she hadn't overstepped the mark and given away too much but she wanted to sound encouraging.

"Actually, Monique asked me out," he said, looking mystified rather than smug. "She's going to pay, said it was only fair."

Paisley was speechless wondering what game Monique was playing, chasing the guy as if she were desperately in love – or just desperate. Recovering, she managed to splutter, "By all the magic of the Alchemists. You're going out for drinks then?"

"For drinks, dinner, dessert – the works, apparently. Go figure. Anyway, I'll see you tomorrow when I pick up Heath around noon." Eddy peered around Paisley's shoulders looking for Heath.

Curious, Paisley couldn't stop asking, "Where are you going?" It had to be somewhere exclusive, knowing Monique's tastes. If she ever asked Lance out, where would she take him? She couldn't imagine anywhere special enough.

"The Chinese at Stubblefield," he replied with an *I told you so* look on his face. "She loves sweet and sour pork."

Paisley returned a contrite glance. Chinese had been his first choice before she'd talked him into going to the Casino. That would be the last time he trusted her judgment. It was necessary to bow out.

Heath emerged to give his father a dutiful hug. "Bye, dad," he said and then without further fuss, grabbed Missy's lead and pulled her away to disappear inside the flat. Eddy shrugged theatrically as if to indicate the brush off was a fact of life. He turned to leave, and, without a further goodbye, took the stairs two at a go. She watched his cocky descent and decided if he had that much energy, he wouldn't need to take Horny Goat Weed, a bottle of which Anita had placed in her apron pocket earlier in the week. She had no idea how to introduce the herbal remedy to Eddy without an awkward explanation of what it was meant to cure and, worse, how she knew he needed it or why she was interested in his sex life at all. Come Monday, she was going to hand back the bottle to Monique with a definitive 'no' to helping out. There was a limit to what friends were for.

Closing the door firmly, she wandered into the kitchen. Heath sat on a stool with a greasy bag of cold Cornish pasties open on the benchtop. She recognised the distinctive crimp from Convict Crust Bakery. Heath poured ketchup on the lot with one hand and fed Missy one pasty with the other. The dog chomped it firmly in her jaws, just missing his fingers, and dashed off to a corner to eat before Paisley could intervene. Heath licked greasy fingers and stuffed a sticky, tomato sauced pasty in his mouth with such contentment, she decided the lad ate like he hadn't eaten a decent meal in days. As if that stodge was *a decent meal.* She bit back a sarcastic remark but couldn't quite let go of the hurt of betrayal.

"Hellfire. What's this? You never have to bring your own food on sleepovers. I was making my special spag bog for us because I know you love it. I have garlic bread and gelato for dessert. You'll ruin your appetite eating those."

With a mouthful of unchewed mush, Heath replied, "MM gave them to me for my dinner. They're the best."

What he meant was *she's the best*. So much for Paisley's overnight with Heath being exclusive, just the two of them spending quality time together. Monique had managed to inject an invisible but nonetheless dominant presence in the flat through a cunning bag of leftovers. Appealing to a little boy's appetite and his delight in receiving free gifts.

Worse, with one sweep of her magic bakery hand, Monique had rendered Paisley's favourite family dinner ritual insignificant, unimportant, feeble. It felt as if Paisley couldn't offer anything more when the kid's tummy was already filled and satisfied. When it came to relationships, why did everything end up a competition with Monique in the middle?

"Hey, did you save one for me?" she said, pulling out a stool and sitting down. Heath pushed the bag across and she studied the squashed mess before making a selection. "You know I could have heated these up in the microwave, if you'd waited." She took a delicate bite resigned to this being dinner.

"I know," he said, not seeming to care one way or the other. Missy sat next to him, tail wagging, obediently waiting for the next offering. He broke a pasty in two and gave her one half. "Can I have a cola, please?" Eddy didn't approve of sugary soft drinks, so this was their big secret, the exception to the rule only on sleepover nights.

With a sigh, she went to the fridge and pulled out two cans. At least, some of their special ritual could be recovered. Popping the lids, she passed one to Heath and took a gulp from the other.

"After eating all this stodge, we are definitely going to need to walk Missy," she announced. It came out sounding a lot meaner than intended, but it was how she felt. To soften the tone, she added, "When we come back, there's a tub of mango gelato in the freezer with your name on it."

With a mouth full of mush, Heath gave her a thumbs up sign.

Chapter Twenty-Six

Paisley worked her way through the room crowded with Steampunk Club members bunched into small groups, giving each other mystical handshakes and discussing time machines and the merits of retro futuristic mechanical devices found in movies such as Sherlock Holmes and The League of Extraordinary Gentlemen. She plonked onto a seat next to Bernie who was organised and waiting for the meeting to begin. "Salutations from the Guild of Artificers," she mumbled.

She dropped a shopping bag holding a notepad and pen with a dramatic flourish onto the table. She *so* needed to complain about the disastrous weekend with Heath, how she felt unappreciated and designated to the role of babysitter, not family, all of a sudden, since Eddy started dating Monique. She anticipated Bernie would listen in his usual fashion and, in a few words, talk sense into her. He was her touchstone for normality. She depended on him to make her feel better about herself and life in general.

However, this was not to be.

After a rote response to her salutation, her BFF turned a shoulder towards Anita sitting on his other side and listened intently to the monologue going on there. Paisley's complaints had to wait in second place to the new girlfriend. It took a moment to recall the reason Anita held pride of place at the committee table. Tonight's meeting was about putting forward her poster designs concerning the Steam Fest Challenge for the members' approval. She was the designated PR star responsible for the challenge's success. It was her night to shine.

Paisley was as useless as a barnacle on a steamer's hull. She sat back and stared out into the room, resigned to remaining undistinguished during the meeting. Bored, she searched for Adam's long army coat and not seeing him, scanned for Alice in Wonderland, Marianne's signature costume. Usually, where one was, she'd find the other. Mad Hatter was in the crowd locked in a heated debate with Jungle Explorer. They were surrounded by men in top hats with monocles, herringbone frock coats, and sweeping black capes; and women dressed in long gowns with bustles, their faces obscured with sequined masks and feathered plumes. A feeling of warmth and belonging arose in her chest. *Hail to the Grand Mechanism.* At these meetings, she fit in. Within this room, she felt at home.

Conan beat his sword on a Viking shield to call the meeting to order. Groups dispersed and the room quietened with all eyes focused towards the Chair. A stranger entered the room looking around as if lost. His brown hair was shoulder length and he wore a leather bomber jacket and leather pants cinched into knee high boots crisscrossed with buckles. He took a position at the back wall, arms crossed, and waited.

Recognising Lance, Paisley gasped and then blushed. Next to her, Bernie gave the guy a thumbs up sign. Now it made sense. Her

BFF had set this up. She cast a double whammy his way. So, Bernie knew about this and didn't tell her.

Lance smiled. She wasn't sure if it was meant for her but couldn't stop a grin lighting up her face. Suddenly feeling shy, she shuffled her notes and tried to look important. Except, up at the front, with no role except to jot down notes, she felt exposed as if on display like a shop dummy. She hadn't even bothered to dress up for the meeting, wearing her go-to, old faithful jodhpurs and brown bomber jacket instead of a tartan skirt and sexy corset. Her cherry red hair was tucked into a pilot cap with goggles – not her feminine best. Bernie could have warned her.

The meeting with its discussions and motions and votes zoomed past in a blur of self-consciousness. Every time she looked up, there he was, leaning against the wall, with those smouldering eyes. Not sure what to think or do, Paisley wanted to disappear under the table.

The heated discussion finally ended with a vote and a round of applause for Anita's winning advertising poster, everyone was happy.

As members exited for the bar and dining area, Lance fought against the traffic, making a line for the committee table. With a wildly beating heart, Paisley tried to stuff the notebook with its scribbled minutes into her plastic bag pretending not to notice Lance's tall frame looming over her.

Bernie, ever polite, was the first to offer a welcome. "Hail, Lance. By the Gods of the Grand Mechanism, I'm glad you could make it."

"Hi, guys." Lance looked at Paisley with a twinkle in his eyes, noting her shy response. He tapped her shoulder. "Steampunk Girl, it's awesome to see you again."

His touch had the effect of an electric current buzzing through her system. Her arm jolted. The notepad fell out of the bag, crashed onto the table and sent pens scattering. "Salutations," she said, grabbing at the pens as they rolled to the edge.

Ever the gentleman, Lance caught a couple pens and handed them over with the flourish of a knight gifting her roses. She accepted as gracefully as one could with a face so flushed it matched her cherry coloured hair.

Lance turned his attention to Anita. "Congratulations on your poster designs. They were all awesome. You have real talent for graphic design."

"Hope so. It's what I'm studying at uni with the aim to make it my career," Anita quipped, accepting the compliment with aplomb. Paisley felt like a klutz in that moment and envied – but also sort of hated – Anita's easy confidence with guys.

Bernie ignored his BFF's nervous fluster. He stood and clasped Anita's hand. "We're going to grab victuals in the sanctum of the provender. I've reserved us a table. Kindly follow your navigator of the behemoths. This way."

For one awkward moment, Lance looked at her and hesitated. She wondered if he would hold her hand, too. Noting the panic crossing her face, he followed Bernie and Anita. Paisley tagged behind, quickly pulling off the pilot cap and goggles to uncover a more feminine, cherry red braid. Not that she cared what Lance thought.

They arrived at their table to find Adam and Marianne settled in. Anita and Bernie claimed their seats, leaving two spaces together. Paisley half smiled seeing it was so obviously a set up for her and Lance to sit next to each other, secretly pleased but horribly nervous. After introductions were made, Bernie announced he'd buy the first round. "Sparkling white to celebrate Anita's success," he announced.

Anita jumped up with him. "Tell us what you want and we'll place the order all at once," she offered. Each gave her their preference and she skipped off. Marianne leaned in close to Adam whispering something only he could hear. Paisley was left frozen in her chair unable to start a conversation with the gorgeous guy next to her.

A relaxed Lance turned to a stiff Paisley, breaking the ice. "I've stopped in to Light Up a few times to see Bernie and Anita, hoping you'd be there. Anita's thinking of getting a tattoo; she's going to design it." He waited for one of her acerbic remarks about tattoos but she remained silent. "They suggested I come along to a Steampunk meeting to check it out. I'm glad I did. It was really cool. Tell me more about the Steam Fest Challenge you've been organising," he said trying to coax a conversation out of her.

This was safe ground. With an easy topic that covered a more rational sort of passion than the one she'd been avoiding, Paisley's racing heart calmed. Taking a deep breath, she told him about their plans to raise money for the Street Kids of Lower Teasel by going for a Guinness Book of Records for the largest gathering of Steampunk costumes at one event. She talked about event sponsors and the catering and what it would mean to Lower Teasel businesses to have a load of tourists turn up, spending money in the village. Continuing to monopolise the conversation, she talked about her hobby, making Steampunk jewellery, vests and hats to sell at Light Up, and her dream to one day make this a full time occupation.

Lance listened and asked intelligent questions and appeared impressed. Paisley's confidence grew with each passing minute. When their meals arrived, it felt like they were good, old friends. Paisley was blushing with excitement rather than embarrassment. Bernie and Anita watched the budding romance and looked pleased with themselves. Adam glanced across the table with a puppy dog longing before Marianne pulled his full focus back to her.

With meals finished, they sat back and listened to The Pocket Watch Fiddlers strike up a manic version of 'Shatter Me' with an Irish violin competing with clocks chiming, cogs cranking, and the sounds of glass shattering. Lance tapped his fingers in beat to the music. Soon enough he leaned into Paisley. "Radical band. We have to dance." Before she could respond, he'd pulled her up out of her chair towards the dance floor. She shrieked with mock resistance and then laughed with delight. Marianne jumped up and dragged Adam along. Bernie and Anita eagerly followed. Before long, all of them were prancing and leaping like elves around a fire, grabbing elbows and twirling each other in circles, bumping hips, laughing and having the revelry of their lives. The band revved up the music after each song, encouraging more patrons to join the dance floor. The dining room filled with wild and rowdy cheering and slapping of tables.

The band called a break. Lance, Paisley, Marianne, Adam, Bernie and Anita slunk back to their table, breathless, wired and thirsty. Bernie volunteered to get a round of drinks.

Lance announced it was getting late; he had to travel back to Whaler's Cover. He stood to go. The evening ended too soon. Wanting to prolong her company with Lance, Paisley decided to walk with him to his motorbike. On the way, he offered to hold her hand. She gladly complied. Under a half moon, in the shadows of the Draught Horse Pub, they stood together, holding hands, savouring their new found connection, hearts beating in unison with a quiet knowing. To articulate their feelings would have spoiled the moment.

Lance broke the silence first. "I better get going." Dropping on one knee, with a fist to his heart, he said as solemn as a Celtic warrior, "I promise to see you again soon, Steampunk Girl." He kissed the top of her hand reverently as if she were a princess in a fairy tale.

Much too soon, he jumped up, swung a leg over his motorbike, blew a kiss and murmured 'call me'. Then he donned a helmet, kick started the motor and zoomed off.

Breathless, with her heart pounding in her throat, Paisley watched as he disappeared into the distance. It was all too perfect. Was she ready to believe? *By the Eternal. Maybe this time I will.*

Chapter Twenty-Seven

Despite it being late in the day and the bakery filled to capacity with coffee orders banked up, Paisley hummed along to the tune of the espresso machine frothing milk with a dreamy smile on her face. Lance had texted every night for the past week like she was his girlfriend. He wanted to get involved in the Steampunk Club and offered to plaster Anita's Steam Fest posters around Whaler's Cover. He promised to come to the next meeting to see her. She crossed her fingers, not quite believing her good luck. She dared to hope but didn't want to get too excited. It was early days and a lot could go wrong. Recalling Monique's previous advice on how to win a guy, which Paisley tried with Adam, it was clear she lacked the necessary nous to convey the *wow factor* when flirting. She'd never be like Monique or Marianne when it came to men. But Lance didn't seem to mind. So far.

Noelle tugged on her sleeve, breaking into Paisley's reverie. "Can Heath and I go play in my room?"

Annoyed at being pulled away from dreaming about Lance, she didn't want to bother with childish concerns. She wasn't a parent to either of them so the decision wasn't hers to make. However, gazing at Noelle's expectant face, with Heath hopping up and down impatiently behind her back, Paisley acted with authority – and passed the decision on. "Maybe you should ask your mum?"

"I tried but she's busy." Noelle expelled an exasperated sigh to make the point.

"Yeah, dad, too," Heath said to support his friend and pile on the pressure to Paisley.

She looked over at Monique locked in an intimate tete-a-tete with Eddy and understood Noelle's predicament. They'd been like that for at least half an hour. This was becoming a regular thing for Eddy, stopping in for a coffee once or twice a week as an excuse to chat to Monique, ignoring Heath and everyone else in the room. She smiled at the pair of love birds. It was so cute watching love blossom. As the saying went, *everyone loves lovers*. With a slight jolt, she realised all the previous angst about Eddy dating Monique had dissipated. Somehow, with Lance more or less a new boyfriend in her life, she felt magnanimous about other people's relationships.

Lucky Noelle was around to play with, otherwise Heath would be bored out of his brain during his dad's assignations. Although Paisley could have used the girl's help cleaning tables, she felt generous today.

"It's okay. Go and play in your room."

Noelle grabbed a couple jam tarts from the display before they skipped off. Paisley watched them through the archway to the kitchen as Noelle keyed in the security code to the residence. The door opened with a click and they went through. She waited until the lock snapped back into place before resuming duties at the coffee machine. The kids would be safe behind all the security and, being only ten years old, couldn't get into too much trouble in

Noelle's bedroom. Probably better than wandering the bakery, not being watched by their parents. If she could gain Eddy's attention, she'd mention where Heath had gone, otherwise when eventually coming up for air he'd notice his son was missing and begin to worry.

A frowning customer weaved through the crowded aisles between tables and puffed up at the counter. The man challenged her about a strawberry tart he'd ordered and hadn't received. She paused milk frothing to look contrite. Inside, however, she refused to take any blame. It wasn't her fault Monique, Anita and Noelle had deserted their posts at the busiest stage of the day, leaving all the work to her. She plated the pastry and passed it across the counter, ensuring it came with a bright smile and effusive apologies.

He walked away grumbling, without saying thank you. Her thoughts returned to dreaming about Lance. Nothing could dampen her high spirits, not even grumpy customers.

It was almost closing time and only a couple tables were occupied with diners draining the last few sips from cups of tea. Silently, Paisley wished they'd hurry up so she could lock up and head home. Fingering the metallic phone case in her pocket with its gold scrollwork, clockwork gears and cogs, she debated whether to sneak a peek inside for any recent text updates from Lance. Succumbing to curiosity, the message screen on the phone remained disappointedly inactive.

The door to the bakery opened with a soft jingle. A hint of trouble like an invisible breath whispered in her ear. Inwardly, she kicked herself for not hanging out the closed sign sooner to discourage new customers entering this late on a Friday. Ignoring intuition and aiming to remain positive, she told herself the man probably would be satisfied with a take away coffee or a bag of leftover croissants. That wouldn't be so bad. Nonetheless, like a hit of impending turmoil getting up her nose, she felt an urge to oust the irritant. *Not quite the right customer service focus required for the job.*

That was before recognition dawned. She must be tired. Clearly, her intuition was off. It was only Mr Two Score. No, she meant *Simon*. She must remember to refer to him by his real name. Unusual that he would show up so late in the afternoon when his normal routine was to patronise the café first thing in the morning.

Paisley's friendly smile faded as quickly as it appeared. The man didn't look very happy. Somewhat alarmed, she saw him stalk across to Eddy's table and stand over Monique like a towering blaze of fury. Before she could blink, Simon began to cause a scene.

"Where have you been? I've been waiting all week, getting more and more frustrated, and you haven't showed!" He yelled and then pointed a stiff finger at Eddy. "Is *this* the reason you've been avoiding me? I get it – one man is never enough to satisfy your voracious appetite. That's okay; I don't mind; bring him in to the ménage a trois. But don't stop coming." He began to hyperventilate, his face turning purple.

The room went quiet. The remaining customers – an elderly couple and a single middle aged woman – sat perfectly still, unsure whether to leave quickly, or stay and not draw attention. Paisley froze, wondering if she should call the police. But this was Simon, one of their regulars, and he wasn't being violent, just rude and belligerent so far. At the same instant, she had a passing thought, grateful the kids were locked behind a security door and not witnesses to the embarrassing scene. If things escalated out of control, they'd be safe.

Simon wasn't finished. Taking in a deep breath, he began to plead. "I've worked my guts out to gratify your cravings – to go along with your indecent fantasies, to please you," he spluttered. "Against all I know to be good and wholesome under the eyes of god. You've cast a spell on me, you *Jezebel*. I constantly dream about fucking you; I imagine new positions, new places, any means to keep you from getting bored. I can't stop! I'm obsessed with you." His face creased into a vicious sneer but his tone of voice was pleading like a spurned, lovesick teenager.

Paisley slid behind the bulk of the cappuccino machine, peering around it and feeling sick to her stomach. Hellfire. She gasped at Simon's crudity and vile accusation. Before this, he'd seemed such a mild mannered man. Harmless. A good guy like Eddy. When had he turned into this vulgar psychopath? She'd warned Monique dating a regular customer was bound to end badly, but was reassured that after one *mind-numbingly uneventful* date, any notion of continuing their relationship died a dreary death. That had been ages ago. Paisley wondered if Monique had lied to her and kept seeing the guy secretly. She recalled Simon had a girlfriend; cheating was never a good idea.

Paisley never considered a break up could become so public and so loud. Monique must be mortified. Her girlfriend detested gossip when it was about her.

However, Monique refused to engage. She looked bored and unimpressed at Simon's rantings and managed to convey a relaxed demeanour throughout. Paisley wondered how she kept cool under such a barrage. It was impressive.

Another surprise. Bedamned. By the Grand Mechanism, Eddy, the pacifist, pushed back his chair and stood up to eyeball Simon, man to man. "That's enough from you, mate. I won't have you disrespecting my girlfriend." Paisley was taken aback at Eddy coming to the rescue. It was so out of character. He must really like her.

Simon turned away from Eddy and addressed Monique, lowering his voice. "Has the novelty worn off? Am I no longer worthy to service you? You turned me into a sinner and then broke my heart into a thousand shards of glass." This came out as a hiss of bile from a mad man. He pivoted and jabbed an open palm at Eddy's chest. "Do you know the nasty games she plays? Are you one of her minions now?"

"Shut it – or I will," Eddy growled. He put a hand on Simon's shoulder as a warning.

Simon shrugged him off and opened his arms as if to envelop Monique in a hug. She pulled back in disgust. "You can't stop doing it with me. You can't." Simon crumpled to his knees at Monique's feet in the manner of prayer. "Joan's left me – because of you. I love you. Spank me. Whip me. Whatever I've done, punish me but come back. I'm yours for eternity, now damned to the fiery depths of hell," he entreated, his words and manner making less and less sense, and indicating a rapid decline into a lovesick psychosis.

It was pitiful to watch. Before their eyes, the man deflated into a sobbing mess. All the vitriol dissipated. Monique looked upon him with disdain as if he were a cockroach deserving to be squashed under foot.

Eddy helped lift the guy by the shoulders, saying it was time to go. "Don't embarrass yourself any further, mate. We've all been there," he said with compassion. Simon held his head down and allowed Eddy to steer him out the door of the bakery. The poor guy stood looking lost for a few minutes before wandering off down the street. Eddy closed the door firmly.

There was an awkward moment in which no one knew what to say or do. Quick on her feet, Paisley filled in the hiatus. "Hellfire. I imagine that's the last we'll see him as a customer," she remarked, affecting a droll voice. The middle aged customer snorted, probably more from relief than humour. The elderly couple were too shocked to express a reaction. All three customers raced out the door. Paisley obliged by locking it behind them and remembering to put up the closed sign.

Monique had some explaining to do.

"Are you okay?" Eddy asked all soothing and concerned, racing back to Monique. Bedamned. Paisley expected his first question would have been *what the hell was all that about?* Clearly, he wasn't buying any of the accusations Simon had thrown at her. Monique had the grace to look pale. Lifting a tea cup for a bracing sip of brew, her hands shook. Simon must have triggered memories of Tobin's abuse, Paisley thought with sympathy.

"The guy's been stalking me. We had only one date and I thought I made it clear I wasn't interested in furthering a relationship," she began. "Obviously, he's been fantasising about me. Too late, I see he's a religious fanatic, out of touch with reality."

Eddy bent down and hugged her. "Anyone can see the guy was a whack job. There's no need to explain."

"No, full disclosure. I want you to know the whole picture. Everything. No secrets." She sniffled into a tissue. "I started jogging around the Town Common recently. Simon turned up occasionally. I thought it was all innocent, running into him like that. Naturally, because I knew him, we conversed, but nothing too serious or personal." She blew her nose. "He must have read more into it, got the wrong message. Poor man. I feel sorry for him."

"If he gives you any more grief, tell me. I'll put him right," Eddy blustered.

By the Eternal. Paisley wondered what he planned to do; it wasn't as if he had martial arts training or any street fighting cred. The dude was an IT nerd who sat at a computer all day. From the smile of gratitude on Monique's face, she didn't seem to care. That's true love for you.

After a few more murmurings of endearments and reassurances, Eddy's attention returned to the room; he noticed the bakery had emptied of customers. He looked at his watch. "Is that the hour? We'd better get home for dinner and let you do the same. Will you be alright?"

Monique returned a wan smile, brave and heart wrenching. Overcome, Eddy supplied more reassuring hugs.

Full of largesse, she made him wait while packing a bag full of leftover sandwiches, pasties and cakes. "No need to cook tonight, love," she cooed.

Eddy accepted the bag with a kiss. Only then did he scan the room in parent mode, checking for his son's whereabouts for the first time since their arrival. "Paisley, have you seen Heath?" he asked, sounding worried.

Paisley clenched her teeth. Now he noticed her existence. As if he assumed it was her job to have watched over Heath while she was working her ass off. His tone implied she'd let the team down because from all appearances the kid had disappeared from the bakery. You know what – *not her problem*. Heath was her spirit bro but she wasn't the kid's parent, guardian, or a full time babysitter. It wasn't her fault Eddy had been in lah lah land for the last hour gazing into his girlfriend's eyes and during this interlude had neglected his role as a father.

Paisley pulled herself up short. Where did that bitchiness come from all of a sudden? The stress from Simon's meltdown must have affected her more than she realised. For some reason, watching Monique handover all that food to Eddy and Heath for their dinner triggered this suppressed anger. It felt like Monique crossed a boundary, from being a new girlfriend to being more like a mother to Heath. Like she could do more of the family stuff with them than Paisley could. Like she was taking over, leaving Paisley relegated to nothing more than a babysitter when required. No longer Heath's family.

She shook her head to loosen the cobwebs of paranoia. It had been a long, exhausting day. Monique had been put through the ringer with Simon. Paisley needed to cut the woman some slack. She and Eddy deserved to be happy, without people like Simon – and herself – getting in the way. If she could help out, support their budding relationship in any way, she should do it without complaint like a good friend.

"He and Noelle were in her room playing. I meant to tell you but things got a bit hectic." Paisley was busy closing up the cash register, anxious to finish up. All cosy, dreamy thoughts about Lance well and truly dishevelled, she longed to return to the safe confines of her flat in order to conjure up that romantic fantasy again. Forget Eddy and Monique and their dramas.

"Would you mind getting him, tell him I'm about to leave." Eddy was busy taking hold of Monique's care package.

"No can do. I don't have the security code. See ya!" she raced from the kitchen, reached for her handbag, ready to walk out the back door.

"Security code?" Eddy sounded puzzled.

She overheard Monique explaining. "Not to worry; I'll get him. I'm big on safety and protection, especially since being on my own. After today's episode, I don't need to elaborate as to why. There are a lot of nut cases out there. Eddy, you were magnificent today, *my mountain man*. Who knows what Simon might have done if you hadn't stepped in to rescue me?"

Paisley didn't wait to hear Eddy's reply but she could picture the pleased look on his face after receiving such praise from his girlfriend. Monique had a way with men, wrapping them around her pinkie. Although it got her into trouble just as much, if the Simon incident was anything to go on. Why else would she be so obsessed with an expensive, up market security system? Perhaps after today, she'd listen to her advice about being more careful with men in the future, particularly ones that were regular customers.

In the driver's seat, she turned over Rolla's ignition ready to head off home. At least Eddy was a safe choice. He would never hurt a fly, let alone a defenceless woman. He was one of the good guys. Thinking about it, she felt more reassured about Monique's judgment. After all, she picked Eddy over Simon. That was smart.

Chapter Twenty-Eight

"Please, ple-ee-ze, Paisley, you have to do it for me!" Heath leaned forward with hands clasped as if in prayer. "It's so Noelle can see the floors underneath all the stuff," he explained. "It's their first sleepover." Seeing the skeptical look on her face, he added persuasively, "I tidied my room – you have to see, it's awesome. It took me all day. I ran out of steam for all the rest."

This was one of the first Saturday's Paisley was not required to work at the bakery – not due to generosity on Monique's part but rather owing to a local holiday celebrated in the northern regions of Eden Isle which closed all businesses for the day despite it being the height of the tourist season. Wanting to make the most of the weekend and impress her little bro after a night of babysitting, she flipped pancakes in a hot frypan, more interested in a big breakfast with eggs, bacon, and blueberry pancakes doused with butter and maple syrup than the outrageous idea of cleaning Eddy's unit to impress the Swan family. What was her little bro thinking? Cleaning outranked baking on the list of the top ten things she hated doing, especially when it wasn't even her home.

"I get it. You want to make a good impression for Noelle and Monique, not put them off for life. Trust me, I know your dad is not the most wonderful housekeeper." She paused to think.

Eddy could use some help when it came to impressing Monique. She was a perfectionist and impressions counted with her. *Nothing but the best*, Tobin had said.

Paisley winced. Hellfire. There was some truth about Monique being put off for life if she saw how he really lived, like a hoarder never throwing a thing away. It was early days in their relationship, that brief period when they were lost in romantic clouds exaggerating good qualities and ignoring the less desirable characteristics. Such as calling Eddy *her mountain man*. What was going to happen when she realised the only mountainous thing about him was the ever-growing pile of junk in his unit?

Paisley sighed loudly. "Hellfire. It's a big ask. You'd owe me big time."

"Yes!" Heath shouted, raising a palm for a high five. "I knew you'd do it."

"Bedamned. Only for you, little brother," she laughed, wondering what possessed her to agree for any reason. If she were honest, the underlying truth was not very charitable: it was to win Heath's heart back from Monique who was increasingly taking over in a pre-emptive role as his new step mother.

✿ ✿ ✿

The next day, Paisley parked Rolla on the street outside Eddy's unit. It had just gone midday, so she thought it would be safe to sneak into his place undetected. Heath said they were leaving for the beach at Sea Glass Bluff first thing in the morning and would be spending the day there. There was plenty of time to get the job done, so she thought.

She wore men's dark navy overalls (usually reserved for painting) and scrunched her hair into a cap to keep it off her face. Any nosy neighbor watching her pull out a bucket, brush and pan, a roll of green garden bags, a duster, and a mop from Rolla's boot would believe, rightly so, that she was the cleaning lady.

Heath remembered to leave a key under the front door mat. First step of their plan ticked. Paisley closed her eyes as she opened the door, delaying the inevitable. The heavy odor of old cigarette smoke and the prickle from dust in an unaired hallway rushed up her nose. Staring into the gloom of a dark corridor, a shamble confronted her. Books were piled shoulder high in uneven stacks against the hallway walls, with a cricket bat, a ladder, creased jackets, garden tools, and other stuff thrown on top and up against the stacks. The floor was littered with torn envelopes, junk mail, muddy boots, boxes, bags of rubbish, crunched up wrapping paper from Christmas. Heath was right – there were no wooden floorboards to be seen beneath the debris. She hated to think what the kitchen dining area looked like. But a promise was a promise. Snapping rubber gloves over her hands, she got to work.

The job took longer than expected. It was dusk when she finished finally, exhausted but satisfied, having washed a week's worth of dishes, sanitised the kitchen counters and sink, likewise the bathroom sink and shower, made up Eddy's bed with freshly laundered sheets dried in the sun, and hefted garden tools, a ladder and a dozen garden bags filled with rubbish into the shed in the backyard. Proud of her efforts, his unit looked more than simply a place fit for human habitation – it smelled of fresh linen and vanilla cleaning spray, exuding an aura of a home cared for with pride. Heath really owed her one for this effort. Eddy better appreciate it.

Surveying the finished result, she decided to pick a mix of flowers from the garden and place them in a vase on the dining table, unnecessary but nonetheless a pretty gesture.

Her phone rang as the last of the cleaning paraphernalia packed into Rolla's boot. Heath's name lit up the screen. "Hi, bro. I've just finished up. By the Eternal, everything is sparkling. You've got nothing to worry about. I left the key under the mat."

Heath's response was distorted from background noise, the beeping of machines and names being paged through an intercom system. "Noelle and MM have gone home. They're not staying over now." He sounded out of breath and miserable. This was Paisley's first concern.

"You sound like you've got asthma? Do you need to take your puffer?"

"Dad forgot to pack it. I'm at the hospital with sunstroke. The doctor says that can happen with bad sunburns. I didn't drink enough during the day."

"Sunburn?" Paisley was thinking it must be a serious sunburn to have caused sunstroke. "Did you forget to put on sunscreen?"

"Dad forgot to pack it. I forgot my hat. Me and Noelle were paddling on her kayak for hours; it was awesome fun. I didn't wear a tee shirt over my bathers; it was too hot. Noelle did and she got sunburned anyway. But they didn't stay in Emergency. MM didn't want the doctor to look at her."

Paisley cringed at the notion Heath was in the sun for hours. He'd be fried to a crisp. She was furious at Eddy for forgetting to pack sunscreen and for not watching him properly. "What was your dad doing all the while you were in the water with Noelle? How could he let you get so burned?"

The questions were rhetorical. She knew the reason Eddy had become so distracted he neglected his son – but for hours? This was so not like him. Monique had him completely bewitched living in some fantasy world while the kids played on their own unsupervised. Anything could have happened to Heath, or Noelle for that matter.

"Actually, kiddo, could you put your dad on the phone. I'd like to talk to him."

Heath called out to his dad and there was some rustling and clanking before Eddy said, "Yeah, what is it?"

Without preamble, Paisley leapt into a confrontation. "Hellfire! What's got into you, Eddy, letting Heath get so badly burned? Were you so engrossed in rolling around on the grass with Monique, you forgot you're a father first and foremost?"

Instead of sounding apologetic, Eddy launched into defence mode. "Keep your voice down." She could hear footsteps and a curtain pulled, sounding as if he left the ER cubicle for more privacy. "Monique firmly believes Noelle and Heath are too young to know we are in a sexual relationship," he whispered.

"Ha, so you were off shagging for hours while the kids were playing in the ocean unsupervised! I knew it," she shrieked. "You shouldn't lie to Heath. He should know why you've got your head in the clouds and lost all common sense. By the Eternal, you have to take responsibility and apologise. My bro needs reassurance it won't happen again."

"How I handle this is none of your business, Paisley. You're my ex-girlfriend, nothing else. Even if you think of Heath as your brother, he's not. Stop assuming you're more important in our lives than you are. Just – butt – out. Give Monique a chance to become his step mum; you've got to back off and give us room."

"What? Are you saying I'm not supposed to care about my bro getting neglected and hurt anymore because you've started dating again? That's not fair."

"If you want to keep seeing Heath, I am going to insist you respect Monique's wishes in this matter and not mention that we are having sex – until she decides the timing is right."

Eddy's edict rendered her speechless. He was allowing Monique to dictate what she did and didn't say to Heath; to insist, in fact, that she lie to the kid. What right did anyone have to order her around, prescribe the boundaries of her relationship with Heath? Threaten to stop him seeing her if she didn't do as she was told!

"Can I speak to Heath again, please," she asked with a chill to her voice. To say she regretted all the cleaning she'd done earlier was only half of the picture. The fact was she felt abject embarrassment, that she'd been so stupid as to believe helping Eddy with his relationship with Monique would in any way benefit Heath or be appreciated. In reality, she was superfluous, not considered family or in any way special; she was a stray that did not belong. That hurt. She'd been an idiot. But never again.

"Hiya." Heath came on the line, sounding tired.

"Dude, I'm upset you've got badly sunburned and I'm mad with your dad and Monique about it. Your dad doesn't want me saying things to you about his relationship with Monique ... so we can't see each other for a while. Sorry."

"Oh, okay. Bye" Heath sounded less than okay about it but that was it. The line went dead.

Paisley hopped into her car, slammed the door and drove off dodging traffic like a rally car driver. There was no way she could forgive Eddy or Monique after this.

In one afternoon, she'd lost Eddy and Heath – her family – and Monique, her only girlfriend. All people eventually disappoint.

Let go and move on. She repeated the mantra over and over again. It was the motto she lived by. Self-reliance may hurt but it never disappointed.

Chapter Twenty-Nine

Half listening, Monique struggled to remain focused, but managed to nod encouragement now and then pretending to be impressed, as her step daughter took her through the pages of a social media site she'd created. This was the last thing she wanted, coming to the bakery on a Monday morning exhausted after a day at the beach with Eddy and compelled into expending energy concentrating on a boring university project. All she longed for was to return to the normal, mindless routine, rolling, crimping and baking.

Always eager for approval, Anita expected verbal accolades and Monique wasn't in the mood to hand them out on something she couldn't care less about. The girl's timing was off. This presentation at seven in the morning could have waited.

Noelle was home from school complaining about suffering from sunburn and laying on the guilt. Monique's mind churned over the relationship implications for her and Eddy. She should have felt bad about what happened to the boy, but sometimes small stuff ups happened, especially when one's attention diverted to more gripping activities than watching kids play in the sand.

Whether it was a placebo effect, or the real deal, the Horny Goat Weed pills she insisted Eddy take worked like an aphrodisiac. She and Eddy went at it for hours like feral cats, first rolling around on towels under the beach umbrella, and then when the sand started to lodge in and scour intimate places most uncomfortably, they moved to the back seat of her SUV to continue groping and probing, tasting and biting, slapping and tickling, building into a frenzy where he pounded and pumped her like a train's piston. For a guy lacking serious skills in the sex department, he rose to the occasion rather well, showing promise for the future. If he was willing to let her teach him a thing or two, he'd make an okay sexual partner.

Heath's and her daughter's sunburns were mostly their own stupid faults; they were old enough to know better. Chalk it up to bad luck – one of those accidents along the road towards a longer term goal. Although this was hard for a daughter in pain to understand, Noelle had to learn to suck it up.

Luckily, Eddy was too filled with his own brand of remorse to lay any blame on her. His late night, make up fuck call provided an extra, unexpected benefit. He defended her views against Paisley's on how to raise Heath. So soon after he'd shown his machismo protecting her from Simon, he went further proving her honour was once again irreproachable. The bloke was smitten. As an act of righteousness, he'd cut Paisley down to size at the hospital which, in Monique's view, made the sunburn fiasco worth it. His apology was priceless. All it took was a good fuck with an element of novelty thrown in for good measure and, like all men, the bloke was putty in her hands.

She cast a sly glance across the table at Paisley crimping pasties, her head down, uncommunicative, looking sullen, not the least interested in Anita's demo. Monique hadn't expected her to show up for work ever again, not after Eddy boasted that he'd laid down *the law according to Monique*. Was it possible the girl would remain a loyal friend even after that? What a joke.

No. More likely, the girl needed the money. Credit to a solid work ethic. The bakery could use the extra help for a little while longer. It would look better if business continued as usual for the immediate future.

Shame she couldn't use Paisley for babysitting Heath again. Anita would do it with the right incentives. Such as, if she played her cards right and handed out enough compliments about this boring university project.

Monique leaned forward and started to pay more attention to the presentation.

A forced smile of encouragement froze on Monique's face as comprehension dawned. The subject matter was not a fake site as she assumed. It was Convict Crust Bakery.

Anita played the video clip where the camera walked through the bakery filming happy customers, including a close up of Noelle with a hot chocolate smile, panning to an outrageously dressed Paisley at the cappuccino machine, and slowly working its way behind the scenes to the kitchen with its wood fired oven. A full frontal of Monique tipping a paddle of freshly baked croissants onto the table top followed, with the final shot a panoramic view of the outside of Convict Crust Bakery with its white bricks and chimney stack.

Gaining more confidence as the demo continued, Anita advocated the importance of customer feedback. Pointing to a sidebar for streaming posts, there were half a dozen showing in what Anita called 'real time'. "Of course, the administrator – that will be me, I expect – can delete any uncomplimentary posts or any that are fake or abusive. There's nothing to worry about." She continued to scroll through the screen.

All Monique registered in her panicked state were the Swan family's smiling faces, the address and contact details of the bakery, the opening hours – it was all there to see, out in the open. Nowhere to hide. What had the foolish girl done? Maybe it wasn't too late to mitigate the damage. If Anita hadn't handed in the assignment yet, there was a chance she could confiscate it and delete the lot. But there was no need to alert Anita ahead of the game plan. She needed to play it cool and pretend everything was fine.

"The quality of the photos is superb. You are very talented," Monique murmured through clenched jaws, trying to smooth the spiky edge off her voice. At least, Tobin had been left out. Not that he'd be coming back. But that was one more connection to her, a complication she didn't need.

Sponsorship of Steam Fest was a pain in the proverbial she didn't need at this point. If only that could be deactivated along with the site. Another one of Anita's initiatives. The girl was out of control.

Anita continued with the demo clicking more tabs, heartened by the compliment and not picking up on Monique's actual emotional state.

Monique's mind wandered off topic to flip through viable options to let the girl down gently. What needed to be emphasised was it was impossible for this site to *ever* go live. Because clearly, that had to be Anita's intention – too much work had gone into it for it to be left on a shelf once it was graded. In her panicked state of mind, Monique decided it needed to be stopped even before the assignment was handed in.

Clueless at Monique's escalating apprehension, Anita missed the hot and humid fumes of stress emanating from her step mother, gathering around the kitchen like acrid ghosts in a horror film. She continued to explain the public relations logic behind each post, seeking feedback and collaboration on any aspects Monique might think required improvements or additional detail that would make the site even more attractive.

Monique's mind was tracking on a single trajectory. The work had to be deleted as quickly as possible. No doubt about it.

The worst was yet to come.

"I know from looking through the accounts, that we're in trouble. That's why I've started a loyalty program. It was the most difficult to get right, if the bakery was to make money off it. That's why I waited before going live. The whole idea was to help Convict Crust's bottom line and I had this genius idea on how to entice customers back to the bakery on a more regular basis and to direct their own social media contacts to 'likes' on our site at the same time."

Anita was too absorbed in explaining the program she devised to notice Monique flinch as if hit with gunshot. "Did you mean to say the loyalty program has started already?" Monique asked in a choked voice.

"Umm, yes. The whole site went live this morning. I'm so excited. As of today, customers from around the valley should start flooding in." Anita puffed up with an air of self importance.

Monique straightened, stepped back, crossed her arms, and took in a deep breath, not able to say a word. A scream of frustration would have been an appropriate response, but she willed calm. There must be a way out of this.

Worried at Monique's body language signals, Anita began to ramble in defence of the project. "I know it takes a while for you to accept innovation but I wanted to surprise you, show you what was possible before you could say 'no' automatically. Contemporary businesses have to get on board all the social media platforms in order to stay relevant. This is the start of bigger things to come."

Paisley started to take notice of the direction of their conversation and gave Anita a look filled with sympathy. An "I told you so" look. Then she returned to crimping, not in the least concerned about the bakery's loyalty program or its bottom line. Her own loyalties had disengaged as of yesterday.

✿ ✿ ✿

Monique was lost in thought, her mind working overtime on the problem to hand. If the site had gone live, it was too late. The damage was done. He had unlimited resources. He'd sworn to find them no matter what it took. He'd never stop looking. The package he sent to Noelle was a test run. Returning it 'Address Unknown' was a short-lived subterfuge. After Anita's helpful initiative, his search algorithms would find them again – or would any day now. If luck was on their side, she figured on a grace period of a week, maybe two. A plan started building in her head, a list of what needed to happen in order to affect another escape.

Thank the stars Eddy was roped in so early. His fishing cabin would be a temporary solution to use as a hide-a-way until a more permanent arrangement could be implemented. The sooner she could look at it and assess its features for security purposes the better. She'd insist he take her fishing this weekend and stay overnight.

She was certain Eddy wouldn't put any obstacles in her way. The guy was into rescuing damsels in distress. He'd proved that the other day.

"So, what do you think?" Anita interrupted, anxious to know if she'd overstepped the mark.

Monique burst into laughter. "I think, this is quite an achievement. You have no comprehension of the monumental consequences that will result from what you've done here, Anita. This is a game changer of the first order."

In the background, Paisley snorted. Anita returned a wan smile, not sure if this was a compliment or ridicule. On balance, she was more used to the latter from her stepmother.

Chapter Thirty

From the backseat, Paisley stared out the window of Anita's Honda Civic observing forest gullies on the left side of the road so steep and dense they dropped into a dark oblivion. She'd tuned out about thirty minutes ago from listening to Anita's forensic breakdown regarding Monique's lukewarm response to the website she'd created for Convict Crust. Bernie kept up reassurances and praise. How much did one person need to be told she was awesome, talented, blah, blah, blah?

They were on route to Whaler's Cove where Anita had a special Sunday appointment with a certain ink artist. Paisley's stomach churned. She blamed the road rather than nerves, not wanting to admit tagging along with Anita and Bernie may not have been the smartest idea. Would Lance be pleasantly surprised, or annoyed with her? This visit was about his work, not about entertaining a girlfriend. She'd have nothing to do but stand around and get in the way. Hellfire. She should never have let Bernie talk her into coming. It was going to be another relationship disaster to add to an ever growing list.

Sitting in the backseat, left out of the conversation, she felt like a hanger on. This was the future now that her BFF had a sweetheart.

Paisley needed to debrief with Bernie about that last conversation with Eddy where he'd told her to butt out of his life.

Eddy and Heath had been her family and now they weren't. There was no way Monique could be a girlfriend after this. More relationships ruined. Bernie was the only normal person she knew who could explain things to her: where she'd gone wrong; help her understand people; make it easier to *let go and move on*. That had been his role for as long as they'd known each other. Except now Anita monopolised his attention with measly issues about how her step mum made her feel inadequate. Join the club, sister.

Paisley couldn't get a toehold into their one-to-one. All she could do was stew in her own misery. It was maddening.

Despite her wallowing, she watched the pair with envy. And was struck by a realisation. Her BFF had never looked so engaged and happy. Seeing him through Anita's eyes, he transformed from the kid who'd been her faithful schoolyard nerd into a grown man, a businessman who was interesting, creative, fun. He'd moved on and she'd missed the remake. She was the one stuck in place, resisting growth and change, with a chip on her shoulder. She remained that weird school girl defiantly refusing to fit in. Expecting rejection as if it was written into the structure of her particular DNA. An aberration from the norm.

Bernie had found Anita.

Eddy had found Monique.

Too easy – for them. They were normal.

The journey was taking forever. Anita's car was an old model – not as old as Rolla but heavy rounding the continuous curves of the mountain pass through the Bramley Ranges. Anita was a careful driver, braking before each bend.

Paisley was on a fool's journey, seeking out Lance like some stalker wannabe girlfriend. Embarrassing herself in the process. At the next curve in the road, she imagined opening her door and jumping out, rolling down the embankment and disappearing into the Man ferns. She doubted anyone would miss her. They'd probably be relieved the hanger on was gone at last.

Picturing the potential for getting spiked with Man fern fronds which would result in blood and gut injuries, and squeamish about pain, Paisley reconsidered acting like a drama queen. Other people caused you enough hurt and pain without the need to inflict self harm simply to make a point. Coming to her senses, she resisted enacting such drastic action.

Instead, when they arrived at Whaler's Cove, she'd go shopping. Rather than tagging along to watch Anita get inked. No need to stand there looking singularly alone and needy. She could show Lance she was independent and capable of doing her own thing.

Paisley rested her head against the cool glass of the window to ease the onset of nausea. The backseat was comfortable enough for her to fall asleep for the next hour or so. The monotony of the scenery dulled her mind into a meditative stupor.

Up front, the conversation took on a new direction. Anita was speculating as to why Monique seemed disinterested in the future financial growth of the bakery.

"Do you think she may be considering selling up?" she asked Bernie. "Her way out of situations has always been to latch onto a man and run away from her problems. Like she did with my dad. With Tobin gone, maybe she believes Eddy is the way out?"

Paisley perked up, paying more attention.

"Does Eddy earn good money? I think he's got a government job but I'm not sure what he does." Bernie twisted around from the passenger seat to seek Paisley's opinion.

She was chuffed at being included. "He's an IT technician with Forestry. Worked there forever. With shifts, I guess it would be good money." It had never crossed her mind to ask about his salary. If Monique was thinking of running away, Eddy was not the moving kind. His attraction had always been his dependable immovability.

"It's just that I can't see what she sees in him," Anita was saying. "Calling him her *Mountain Man* and wanting to go fishing. She hates the outdoors and camping. Not to mention her understanding about IT begins and ends with asking Noelle to fix a stuff up when she taps a wrong key. There's some other agenda going on, I'm sure of it."

Paisley was sure of it, too. Now was not the moment to add to the suspicions. With too much speculation and not enough evidence, Bernie would lose patience. Sure enough, he shrugged and changed the subject.

"Did you remember to put on an Emla patch to numb your lower back before we left?" he asked Anita. "We're fifteen minutes out from Whaler's Cove."

"Yes, dad," she joked. "Noelle helped stick it on. I also remembered to email my design for Lance to create a transfer. No need for him to draw freehand. It should save a lot of messing about. I know you want to do more at the Cove than watch me get inked."

"Only lunch. Maybe a walk along the beach."

"What's your design?" Paisley asked.

"Ah, that's a surprise – for Bernie's eyes only," she said teasingly. "All I'll say is it's going to be what's called a 'tramp stamp'."

"A tramp stamp?" Paisley asked. She didn't know anything about tattoos and couldn't understand the appeal. She wondered what Bernie thought about it. But she imagined anything Anita liked, he would too.

"You know because of its placement on my lower back, just above my butt crack and undies line. When I wear low cut jeans and a short summer top, it peeks out."

"Hellfire," Bernie sighed.

Paisley rolled her eyes. "Just to let you know. When we get there, I'm going to head off to the shops. Let me know where to meet for lunch."

"Oh, I thought you'd want to watch Lance at work," Anita said.

"No worries. I'll send a text about the lunch venue when we are ready to go," Bernie offered, reading Paisley's mood.

The car began its descent from the forested mountains to the gentle pastured hills below. The suburban outskirts of the Cove became visible and beyond that, the city buildings clumped together, with a blue streak in the far distance where the ocean met the horizon.

Too soon, they were driving across the city towards the harbor to end up at a small shopping area fronting the beach. The car pulled up and parked in front of 'Mandala Ink'.

Lance waited outside, pacing back and forth along the pavement anxiously checking his phone. His face lit up with a broad smile as soon as he recognised their car. He dashed across to open Paisley's door. Inwardly she cringed. No chance to do a runner.

"You came! I was afraid you'd talk yourself out of it," he was saying. He grabbed hold of her hand as if he expected her to flee like a flighty stray cat. "I'd like you to stay and see my work. But it's okay if you don't want to watch. Some people can't. Let me at least give you the grand tour so I can brag a bit."

Bernie and Anita stood outside the shop waiting to be acknowledged, wry grins on their faces.

"Welcome to my creative studio," Lance finally said with a flourish. "Everything is set up, ready to go. Come on in." He led them through the front door, pulling Paisley along.

She was taken by surprise. She'd imagined a tattoo parlour as some grungy, back alley sort of place with a slightly illegal feel to it. Not this brightly lit, poster paint coloured reception area with walls lined with huge photos of pop stars and movie actors sporting their body art. The place conveyed a Marvel comic book feel, although it was stamped with Lance's unique style. Four orange vinyl chairs in the shape of overstuffed hands were arranged in a half circle in front of a clear plastic table piled with fat books filled with designs. A fridge filled with bottles of still water, organic juices and fermented kefir drinks stood in a corner with a sign 'Help yourself while you decide'. The front of the reception counter was covered in coloured snap shots of his work.

"Come through to the studio. We can get started straight away."

They walked around the front counter through a doorway into a room that resembled a surgical suite. The smell of antiseptic hung in the air. His sterile tools rested on a clean towel – the hygiene in his studio was meticulously executed. Pots of pigment were ready for mixing. His inking gun was placed on a small table with a movable arm, within easy reach. Lance motioned Anita over to a lounger that looked as if it came from a nineteen fifties dental surgery. Positioning her on her stomach and propping pillows in various places, he ensured she was comfortable. Then he placed a modesty towel across her bottom and asked her to scrunch down the top of her pants. Only her lower back was exposed. In the background, Bernie sat on a plain metal chair keeping a watchful eye. He looked more concerned than Anita, who lay there with a huge grin, clearly excited. Paisley remained standing, waiting for an excuse to make her escape.

Lance rolled up his chair and pulled an overhead lamp across to light up the area. He was all serious professionalism. He'd donned work goggles and a mask. "Good. I see you remembered the Emla patch. You shouldn't feel a thing." Without further discussion, he began to transfer an outline of her design from a paper stencil. Then the buzzing began. And hundreds of tiny needle pricks. Anita was brave, but Paisley could see tears seeping from the corners of her eyes.

She could feel the buzz of each prick vibrate through her teeth. "Sorry, I need some fresh air." It was time to go.

Anita chuckled.

Making her way to the door, Lance called out. "Remember, I promised you a seafood platter. We should be ready by one."

"I'll send a text," Bernie reminded her.

She felt too sick to her stomach to contemplate food. All she could think of was cool sand and ocean waves. Stepping through the front door, she overhead Lance laughing in the background. *'Glad she's gone'.*

Quickly closing the door, feeling mortified, what she didn't hear was the rest of his sentiment. *'I couldn't concentrate with her watching. Look, my hands are shaking. I felt too self conscious wanting to impress her'.*

Nor did she hear Anita's warning. *'Stop thinking of your girlfriend and get your head back in the game. You'd better not mess up, dude'.*

The air smelled salty and sea weedy; gulls circled overhead squawking; crashing waves drowned out most of Paisley's morbid thoughts. It was a perfect Summer's day on Eden Isle, with a gentle sea breeze offsetting the piercing rays of the sun on her naked face. She'd risked coming today with scant makeup and a toned down look – jeans and a pirate shirt girded with a summer weight corset. Her ankle boots became wet from a surprise wave. She ended up taking them off and carrying them along the beach.

She walked along the beach crying. What was it with people? She didn't get them. Lance seemed pleased at first when she arrived but then expressed relief when she left. And then he wanted to meet for lunch like that was such a big deal. Talk about mixed messages. What was she to believe?

After meandering up and back along the Cove, she felt drained of emotion. Deciding to hide away from the world for a few moments, she found a sand dune suitable for shelter from the breeze. Snuggling her bum into the soft sand, she lay back safe and secure like a swaddled baby, and promptly fell asleep.

The beeping of her phone woke her. A text from Bernie asked *Where are u?* with a preceding text, thirty minutes before, spelling out the name of the seafood café they were heading off to.

Paisley wasn't hungry. No, actually she was but couldn't stomach the thought of seeing Lance and Anita and Bernie all smiles and happiness, when she didn't belong. She was the odd one out, as always. There was a problem if she didn't show up. From a practical point of view, she needed a lift home. She had to put on a brave front, face them and pretend all was fine.

Too easy. She'd been doing this all her life.

Arriving at The Claw and Fin Seafood Café, Paisley first saw Bernie and Anita chowing into a massive platter of prawns, oysters, crumbed scallops, calamari rings, and French fries with three kinds of dipping sauces. Her heart fell; she was very late. They'd started without her.

Anita waved her over to their table. "Sorry, I was starving and couldn't wait. After my inking travails, I needed to comfort eat." She waved a prawn in the air before dipping it in cocktail sauce and popping it into her mouth with sensual pleasure.

Bernie swallowed a mouthful of French fries. "She's joking. I reckon for most of it, she fell asleep, she was so relaxed. Her tattoo looks awesome." He raised a glass of sparkling water and toasted Lance.

"Let's celebrate! I am no longer an ink virgin." Anita announced. "Next, it's Paisley's turn."

"Hey, what about me?" Bernie exclaimed with mock outrage. "First, design something for me."

Lance stood up and ushered Paisley to a seat next to his. "Are you alright? We were getting a bit worried. I waited for you before ordering. Are you okay with the seafood platter?"

His solicitude confused Paisley, but also felt good. The dude had a way of redeeming himself. She sat down and decided not to bite the hand that was about to feed her. There was only so much *feel sorry for herself shit* she could do in one day. "Sure, no worries."

"And to drink?" he asked.

"I'm fine with cola, a pint glass. Thanks."

While waiting for the order, Anita persisted in teasing Paisley about getting a tattoo. "So, if you did, what would you choose? A feminine Steampunk symbol – say, like Amelia Earhart or Madame Curie? Or how about a Greek goddess like Athena Warrior Woman! Or, an angel like Mercury – the one with wings symbolising flight?" Paisley kept shaking her head, smiling but also annoyed at being badgered.

"Mercury is a god, not an angel," she corrected.

Lance watched carefully, gauging her reactions, noting the ones that made a small smile cross her lips and the ones that made her screw her face in disbelief. They shared a look. Silently, she was asking to be rescued from the onslaught of her friends taking the piss.

He held up his hand. "Enough, already. I can see Steampunk Girl remains unconvinced. May I remind you that Paisley once told me *'she'd never love anything that much that she'd want it stuck to her for good'.*" He paused for comedic effect. "I've been trying to

change her mind about that for months, but she's very stubborn."
Getting the innuendo, they all laughed, except for Paisley who
blushed the colour of her cherry red braid.

"I've spent many a night regretting that turn of phrase," she
mumbled. "It's just that a tattoo isn't like make-up you can wipe
off at night."

"My offer stands. When you are ready, it would give me immense
pleasure to design the perfect one for you. Representing your
deepest conviction, your inspiration, a symbol from your heart."

Paisley shook her head slowly.

Lance addressed Bernie and Anita. "I can see it may take many
years for my talents to be recognised and to gain her trust. I live in
hope. In the meantime, she remains a perfect canvas, requiring no
further embellishments." Lance raised his glass in the air and then
dramatically took a slug as if making a toast – or a pledge.

Much to Paisley's relief, the food arrived at the right moment to
save her from further embarrassment. Anita and Bernie finished
off the remaining food from their platter and ordered dessert.
Ignoring Paisley and Lance, they leaned into each other whispering
stuff that was of interest only to them.

While she ate, Lance picked at the food, more intent on sharing
details about himself and his family than eating.

It came as a pleasant surprise that they had much in common.
Such as, he supported a children's charity, too. He explained that
he would enter ink art competitions and donate any winnings to
Kids Asthma Foundation because his little brother was asthmatic.
"I'll show you my ribbons sometime. They're hanging on the wall
in my bedroom," he winked suggestively.

To cover her shyness, Paisley asked quickly, "How many have you won?"

"Only a couple so far. The best was a comp held on the Mainland, lots of competitors. I came in third which is good considering I'm new to the profession."

"How old is your little brother?" she asked, glad that Lance had a sibling. She tried not to think too much about missing Heath.

"The Bruiser's eight. My parents had Bruce late in life; he was their surprise baby. The story goes that Mum thought she was starting menopause. To make her feel better, Dad decided to take long service leave and was about to book an around the world tour for them. Then mum found out she was pregnant. Threw a spanner in their plans. Dad spent his days off work changing nappies at midnight." Lance chuckled. "It did him good. I'd never seen him so relaxed and satisfied with life. He and mum are closer than ever."

"Shame about having to cancel their trip," Paisley said.

"They'll go someday," he said. "Dad works in the government, a boring job in administration. He'll soon chalk up more leave. When you meet him, I have to warn you about his hobby which is a bit scary." He took in a deep breath before continuing. "He carves sculptures out of wood."

"What's scary about that?"

"He does it with a chainsaw." Lance watched her reaction.

"Bedamned. No way!"

"When he's had a bad day at the office, he goes out the back and starts carving. We stay out of his way." Lance grinned. "He demonstrates the technique at agricultural fairs across the island.

It's awesome to watch. Bruiser and I refuse to follow in his footsteps, much to dad's disappointment. No surprise, he hasn't found an apprentice yet to pass on his skills."

"By the Eternal. I'm not sure I could watch. It would be too scary. I mean, I couldn't even watch you ink Anita. I'm a big chicken when it comes to pain."

"Just as well. I couldn't work with you watching. My hands shook too much! My mum is an artist as well, but not so frightening. She works in scrap metal, welds big sculptures for parks and public spaces. Usually gets commissioned by local councils or corporations. You may have heard of her? Skye Mandala?"

"Hail the Grand Mechanism! Your mother is the *famous* Skye Mandala! I love her work. She's amazing and so supportive of all the Arts," Paisley gushed. "She's been my inspiration for some of my pieces of jewellery."

"Famous might be taking it a bit far; well known on Eden Isle would be more accurate. But yes, that's my mum." Lance looked pleased. "Mum's my biggest supporter of my art. I've loved drawing and colouring in since I was a toddler."

"And you are very good at it," Paisley enthused, feeling generous.

Lance gazed into her eyes with adoration. "I can't wait to introduce you to my parents."

"Sure," she replied with awe.

Paisley cleaned up the rest of the seafood platter on autopilot. She was speechless with happiness. The afternoon felt like magic, it was so perfect. She was almost glad when Bernie stood up to declare he couldn't stomach one more mocha latte and announced they had to head back home. Spending any longer with Lance meant chancing something could go wrong. She wanted to remember this day in her dreams forever.

Lance declared he would pay the bill. Bernie gave half-hearted dissent before making a show of agreeing reluctantly. The best part – which left tingles of delight circling around her heart and tummy during the whole drive back to Lower Teasel – was Lance's kiss. Right before she got in the car. As if it was the most natural thing in the world to do. On the lips. Gentle, indicating his soft, romantic feelings, but with enough pressure to hint at a possessive passion still to come. Perfect.

Chapter Thirty-One

Convict Crust's dining area began to fill up with regular customers – mostly male – at the same time every afternoon. Right before MM was due to come back after her siesta. Anita stood at the cappuccino machine watching it spit out slurry into two well positioned coffee cups. She leisurely filled each cup with warm milk, swirled the bakery's bespoke rose pattern on top and dusted each with pink sugar crystals. There was a backlog of orders, but she was relaxed. From the sounds of avid conversations and the accompanied raucous laughter, no one was in a rush or tracking their orders.

To alleviate boredom, she counted the hours until the weekend when she'd see Bernie. The waistband on her jeans rubbed the tramp stamp that was healing, making it itch. Wriggling to reposition the band, she smiled remembering his reaction when seeing the completed motif – a Steampunk version of the Jules Verne kraken inspired by Light Up's octopus door knob.

Breaking her reverie, a man in a charcoal suit with a brocade tie threaded with gold sauntered up to the counter. He appeared to be a businessman, or maybe a salesman; not from around Lower Teasel. Sophistication and self assurance oozed out of his pores.

His eyes scanned the room with a casual air before focusing in on Anita. She didn't recognise the man; a new customer then. The social media site was working. She beamed her widest, friendliest smile.

"What can I get you?" she asked in her most professional waitress voice.

"Actually, I'm looking for *Monique* Swan." A tiny smirk creased the edges of his mouth. "Would she happen to be available?"

She detected a faint New Zealand accent. "No, not at the moment; we are expecting her soon." She carried the two coffees to diners at a nearby table and then returned. He waited. "Can I help you?" she asked.

He leaned forward as if to take her into his confidence. He wasn't a tall man, a couple inches above her height at best. Nor was he conventionally handsome. But similar to Monique, his presence seemed to fill the room. His breath smelled of cinnamon lozenges.

"This is somewhat of a surprise visit. We have business to discuss – of a confidential nature. Related to property. She'll know what it's about."

Anita knew it. Her step mum was putting the bakery on the market to sell. "Are you a real estate agent?" she asked to be polite. Inside she was fuming at the unnecessary secrecy.

"More of a silent partner than an agent. Monique's been investing on my behalf. You could say we share property in common including the bakery. It's opportune to sort out how she's been running her affairs."

Running. Interesting choice of word. Knowing Monique, there was no way she'd admit the bakery was on the brink of financial ruin to this supposed partner of hers. She'd sooner pack up and do a runner. Tobin beat her to it first off, but Anita knew Monique would follow suit. Eddy was most likely the mug who'd rescue her and take her in. She always found a man to pay the bills.

The fact Convict Crust was partly owned by another party was an interesting twist. She always thought Tobin had thrown in all his payout from the Army to buy his share of Convict Crust. It was a mystery how MM found the money for her half. Her parents hadn't died in a car accident; they'd retired to New Zealand years ago. There was no insurance money from an inheritance. All fat lies told to Paisley when they first met. Whether to win sympathy or just because she was a compulsive liar, it was hard to tell what motivated her step mum to tell such tall tales.

She wondered if Tobin knew about this other silent investor. Even after disappearing from the scene, his pension was deposited regularly into the bakery bank account which was the only way the business remained afloat. She knew this because she helped MM with the business accounts.

"My name's Thayne Swanston by the way." He reached out to shake her hand.

"I'm Anita, Monique's step daughter."

"Ah, interesting. Would you mind if I walked around and took some photos for my portfolio? I can see you're busy, otherwise I'd ask you to accompany me."

Anita felt it was in everyone's best interests to portray the bakery in its best light. Maybe Mr Swanston could be persuaded to make a cash injection if she impressed him with their ideas about growing the business. This visit must have been in part precipitated by the social media site going live.

"It's okay. I can ask Paisley to watch the counter. Give me a minute."

Paisley was out the back in the patio area cleaning tables and chatting away with Noelle. Mr Swanston followed at Anita's heels. Once through the kitchen and out the back door, he pulled up short and stared at Noelle.

"This is Mr Thayne Swanston."

"Hello. And you are?" he asked Noelle, giving her a shark tooth grin and reaching out to shake her hand. He ignored Paisley as if she were of no consequence. Noelle fidgeted under Swanston's hungry glare and didn't respond to his overtures. Abruptly, he got the message and withdrew.

"He has an interest in this real estate," Anita explained. "I'm about to give him the grand tour. Paisley, could you take over from me at the front counter please?" She put on an officious manner acting the supervisor. "Noelle, could you find MM and ask her to attend this meeting?"

Noelle ran off without a word. Paisley gave Mr Swanston a suspicious look before gathering up the last of the rubbish left on the tables and taking the tray to the kitchen.

Monique sat up against the carved wooden headboard of her antique bed with Kathy Reichs' latest novel in hand. The page zoomed in and out of focus after the second paragraph. She was having trouble concentrating. There was a niggle of apprehension in the pit of her stomach. It had been there since Anita's bombshell – going live with the social media pages without asking permission. Who would have credited the girl with any independent initiative? Tossing the book onto the pillow-soft feather quilt, she reached for the phone and pressed the speed dial. Eddy promised to get back to her about arrangements for a weekend at the cabin but she'd heard nothing so far. The clock was ticking; she needed to assess whether it was suitable without raising suspicions. The phone went unanswered. She left a breathy message, trying to sound sexy rather than anxious.

Looking up, Noelle stood in the doorway to the bedroom. "Well, what is it? Can't it wait a few more minutes," Monique growled, taking out her frustration on the kid.

Nonplussed, Noelle teared up. "Anita said to get you. There's a real estate man."

"Right. That's sooner than I expected." She'd left messages with a couple of agents wanting some quotes on what the bakery would be worth in the current market but no one had returned her calls.

Noelle looked sullen. "Does this mean we're moving again? I like it here. My friends are nice."

"Look, it's nothing for you to worry about. Keep a lid on it. We don't want our customers to start gossiping," she instructed. "How about you stay here and play Minecraft. I'll come and get you after I've dealt with this man." Monique waited for Noelle's reluctant nod of acquiescence before kissing the kid on the head and racing past.

No sooner had she exited the residence and entered the kitchen than she caught a whiff of a distinctly expensive European aftershave, worn by only one man. Moving forward in slow motion, she saw the back of the *real estate* man casually chatting to Anita. Time stopped dead. *Thayne.* She knew him from all angles, front, sides and back, dressed and undressed. And he scared the devil out of her. Her knee jerk reaction was to run back through the security door, grab Noelle and disappear before he saw them. A nice fantasy.

The reality of her predicament asserted itself in the blink of an eye. The fact he was here, much sooner than anticipated, meant the window of opportunity had firmly shut. It was too late to escape. His net was cast, even if they were not entangled just yet.

Thinking frantically, she knew the best tactic was to remain calm and try to negotiate a way out. If she paid him back, maybe he'd leave them alone. Tobin would help; except contacting him could be a problem. Damn Eddy for being so slow about the mountain hide-away. Even so, maybe that option could be kept open as a last resort.

Hearing the security latch click open, Thayne turned around. "Monique! As beautiful as ever!" he enthused before Anita could utter introductions. He strolled over, arms out as if meeting an old friend after a long parting.

Defeated before the battle began, a resigned Monique smoothed her skirt and took steps to meet him halfway, braced for the hug of possession. "Thayne, you're early," she blurted as he squeezed the breath from her and held the hug longer than necessary. She struggled to get free. He laughed.

"Ah, yes. I stopped by on the off chance I'd catch you. Just letting you know I'm in town. I wanted to make sure you weren't planning to run off before we have a chance to discuss arrangements. My young friend here has been giving the grand tour. Impressive." He winked.

Anita took this as her cue. "Why don't you both sit down and I'll make hot drinks."

Thayne cocked his head. "Good idea. We have unfinished business to discuss, but that can wait. First, let's be civil over cups of tea in the manner of our British ancestry." Thayne gripped Monique's elbow and pushed her along to the café dining area.

Monique looked as if this was furthest from her mind but acquiesced without a sound. Anita headed for the coffee bar and began to line up saucers, cups and dangling tea bags in pots of hot water on a tray. She watched the dynamic between Swanston and MM with curiosity.

"Tell me how you and Noelle are? I was beginning to think I'd never see you again," he said with aplomb. Then as if testing for a weak spot, he asked smoothly, "Would Noelle care to join us?"

"Not today," Monique barked; displaying an attack of nerves. This was a first, Anita observed. When it came to handling men, her step mother was usually the one with cool, self-possession.

Thayne picked up on her loss of composure and laughed. His laughter was softly executed but hard edged, hinting of someone in complete control of their relationship. Involuntarily, Anita shivered. A wordless instinct registered the sinister undertones but had not yet worked its way to her conscious brain.

How did these two know each other? What was his real interest in Convict Crust Bakery?

Setting the tea tray on the table, she began unpacking it. Ever the conscientious waitress, she asked, "Mr Swanston, would you care for a sweet pastry or a piece of cake to go with your cuppa? MM makes the best chocolate eclairs."

Swanston folded his hands across his chest in a parody of delight. "My heart weeps at such talent. This woman captivates and is *captured* – by my undying admiration and ever faithful regard. Please, one éclair accompanied by a short black, double shot." He pushed the tea cup to one side.

Sure. Whatever. What was this guy's game? she thought.

Anita passed a silent look towards Monique asking what she wanted. Her step mum paled as if about to be sick and simply shook her head.

✿ ✿ ✿

Swanston sipped coffee slowly and began to entertain them with stories of recent travels to Western Australia visiting cousins, uncles, nephews, stressing how the family was scattered far and wide – even New Zealand, he reminded her. *They asked about you and Noelle*, he mentioned in passing. He stressed how close and loyal the family was, which registered like a veiled threat to Anita's sixth sense. Monique kept her gaze on the table top and contributed nothing to the conversation.

It seemed he dragged out finishing his coffee and éclair, as if deliberately prolonging an atmosphere of discomfiture. It wasn't what he said so much as the manner in which he said it. Anita watched her step mum folding in on herself more and more during the conversation.

She was dumbfounded at MM's docile demeanour. Where were the tittering giggles at his lame anecdotes; the batting eyelashes and meaningful long held gazes into his eyes; the seemingly unintentional brushes against his arm; all the flirting that was second nature to a professional femme fatale? MM acted as if she wanted to diminish her presence, become invisible, be a non-entity. This was not the woman Anita knew. She wanted to poke her to wake up, take charge. MM was scaring her. What was going on?

Swanston finished his drink to an awkward silence. Anita was too confused about the dynamics at the table to attempt polite banter. Not in the least perturbed, the man actually sighed with satisfaction, as if he'd completed what he'd set out to do – put them off balance. Job done; he could strategically exit.

Pushing back his chair, he stood to brush imaginary crumbs off his immaculate suit. Addressing Monique's cringing figure, he said, "I'll come later to discuss what you owe me. We can go through the terms of your payment options. Don't do anything stupid in the meantime." With a flourish, he walked out of the bakery. It was at this point Anita knew with certainty that this Swanston character was dangerous.

Monique fled the room, not bothering to give Anita an explanation. She was left wondering how much trouble her step mother had gotten herself into, and how she was going to get out of it. And what this meant for her own future living at the bakery and attending university.

Putting bits and pieces together, it was beginning to make sense to Anita. MM must owe him money for the bakery. He'd come to collect. And she couldn't pay. What would happen now?

❁ ❁ ❁

Monique ran to her bedroom and bolted the door. With Thayne gone for now and the security locks on her residence, she felt safe temporarily. Pressing speed dial on her phone, she cursed Eddy for being slow to make arrangements. *Hurry up and answer*, she swore to the empty room.

Finally, his slow and stupid voice came on the line apologising for not returning her earlier call. She cut him off. She didn't have patience to listen to a drawn out explanation about work pressures. "Can we get away this Friday? I need to know now!" she demanded.

Silence for frustrating seconds.

"Um, I guess it will be alright. It's not fly fishing season …"

"I don't care about the fishing!" she shouted. "Just pick us up after work tomorrow. It's vital."

Another long pause.

"Sure. No worries. I can arrange it. Maybe." *There it was again; he kept saying he could arrange it. How hard could it be to take her to his cabin.*

"What's there to arrange?" She took a deep breath, noting her tone was sounding more desperate than intended.

"Well, do you want the whole weekend or just an overnighter?" Eddy sounded huffy.

Monique couldn't afford to get him offside. If he got into a sulk, it could be days of working her wiles before he cooperated. She changed tact. "I mean, I can't wait, darling. I've been fantasising about my mountain man in his wilderness habitat, stripped naked under a full moon, pleasuring him until he howls like a wolf. I'm panting right now, hungry for you. I need you with such an urgency you cannot imagine."

Eddy bought it. The nerd affected a growl like a Tassie Devil, attempting to sound sexy. "Tell me what you'd like me to do to your smouldering body. I'm picturing you erupting in a blazing inferno under the stars," he crooned, getting into the mood. It was so lame she would have burst into laughter under normal circumstances. Thayne's presence had caused her to lose any sense of humour.

What counted was that he was on board. Relief washed through her. "No spoilers," she grunted. "Pick us up at six tomorrow." She ended the call abruptly, in no mood to spend the next half hour talking dirty. If the call had continued, more than likely she would have ruined everything by saying what she really thought of men and their claims on her body.

Chapter Thirty-Two

They'd gotten away on schedule. Eddy picked them up exactly at six. Her mountain man had come through for her. She should never have doubted. The sun was bright in the sky; it wouldn't get dark until around nine, giving them plenty of time to travel to the cabin and get settled before the pitch black of night. Her Land Cruiser sat parked outside the bakery and a light left on in her bedroom gave the impression they remained at home.

Not wanting to alert any nosy neighbours or passing customers about going away for the weekend, Monique packed light. She dressed as if on a date wearing a summer dress and sandals, and carried an oversize handbag with a few toiletries and a change of undies and socks for Noelle. A summer weight cardigan slung over her shoulders. Eddy noted her attire and warned that the air chilled in the mountains even in Summer, but she brushed off his caution. "I'm expecting you to keep me warm," she quipped, thinking surely the cabin would have blankets in the cupboards and a fireplace to burn logs for heat.

This was a reconnaissance trip to check out the fishing cabin. If it turned out to be safe and secure, she'd prepare more thoroughly when she and Noelle made a run for it. Thayne was sure to find out about their disappearance eventually, but a false run might allay his suspicions and delay the inevitable. She wanted tonight to look like a family outing, not part of an escape plan.

Once off the main highway, Eddy's ute bumped along rough corrugated dirt roads, dodging native animals, skidding, kicking up dust, and taking curves wide around the mountain side leaving Monique's stomach in her throat. Every minute that passed, every teeth jarring bump along the way, reassured her that his mountain cabin would be the perfect hide away. She'd lived in big cities all her life and the rural community of Lower Teasel had been the closest to what she thought of as remote. Viewing the dense rain forest wilderness growing down the ravines on either side of the ute gave new meaning to the notion of isolated and inaccessible. As far as the eye could see, there were no signs of human life; no other cars; no houses; not even telecommunication towers or power poles. Thayne would never find them up here. This was perfect. Her judgment about her mountain man had been infallible.

Noelle sat in the backseat complaining she was hungry; she was going to be sick; she needed to pee; could she have a drink. It was getting tiresome. There was nowhere to stop and pull over on the narrow road. The kid would have to wait. Monique replied over and over again on automatic, "Soon, sweetheart. When we get there."

Heath dug into his backpack and broke a chocolate nut bar in two to share with Noelle, along with sips of water from his drink bottle. This kept her quiet for a while.

They'd left quickly without eating dinner or grabbing a snack. She'd spun a romantic notion of eating under the stars by a campfire, not wanting to alert Noelle to the urgency of their predicament. Not packing much in the way of supplies, she assumed Eddy would bring the basics required for the weekend. Although she expected to buy top up groceries as her contribution on the way. When Eddy stopped in one of the small towns to fill the tank with petrol, she'd drop into the village supermarket for sophisticated fare such as smoked salmon, brie, and a good bottle of red.

Not realising until it was too late this was a fanciful thought. Since turning off the main highway there hadn't been townships or shops or petrol stations. It began to dawn on her that they had left civilisation behind.

Eddy's ute powered along, familiar with the roads. Silence filled the cabin for long periods, until he decided to prattle off the top of his head. "When we first met, you seemed like such a city girl – I was thinking it would have to be expensive hotels with spas and fine dining. I wondered what we had in common and if I could afford to date you. But then you were so keen to come up here – I couldn't believe my luck. Even though it wasn't fly fishing season, you wanted to experience the great outdoors and camping with me. You are a star."

Monique roused from a hypnotic stupor caused by the endless line of monotonous trees and the shuddering vibrations from corrugated roads. A flirtatious response was required but her brain was sluggish. "Anything to please my mountain man," she said sweetly.

Eddy frowned, as if thinking about something. "I hope you're not expecting it to be a glamping experience." He gave a nervous laugh.

"Glamping?" Monique asked.

"You know, glamorous camping for tourists where it's a five star experience in a tent. Fold out beds with mattresses and fluffy pillows. Gourmet food. Music. That's not what you'll be getting this weekend. When I come up here with my mates to fish, we live rough. We sit around a fire, play cards, drink beer and fry up what we catch. Eat off the pan using our fingers. No washing up." He gave a short laugh. "That's what I call real camping."

A first whisper of intuition, Monique began to wonder if Eddy's earlier bragging about his fly fishing experiences had overstated the truth. When he spoke about a fishing cabin in the mountains, she pictured a log cabin straight out of an American movie. A large stone fireplace with deer antlers hanging above the mantle, polished oak floorboards and scattered braided rag rugs, with an overstuffed grandfather-plaid couch in an open plan lounge room; an upstairs with bedrooms and bunk beds. Wasn't fly fishing a gentleman's sport?

Lulled by the ute's sleep-inducing shaking, this daydream became even dreamier. There would be a rocking chair on the front porch draped with a hand crocheted blanket. A walk in pantry stocked with canned goods and long life milk. A kitchen with cast iron fry pans and a copper kettle. Nothing glamorous, but a place with rustic charm, cosy and warm. A perfect hide away. She kept these thoughts to herself. To be on the safe side, she sent a quick prayer to all the gods in heaven for Eddy's cabin to come close to match the storybook vision.

Eddie kept prattling, digging a deeper hole. "I haven't told my mates we're coming up this weekend. A man's fishing spot is sacrosanct – a man's territory – secret – like a claim on a gold mine. For males only. No women allowed." He glanced to check her reaction and received a blank look. Monique made an effort to keep her breathing even and calm. "It should be right, being off season. But if we're caught, play it cool. Let me sort them out."

This was news. No wonder he kept telling her that *arrangements had to be sorted*. "Caught?" she asked.

"If they happen to be there when we arrive."

An inferno of outrage burned in her throat as she stifled a scream of frustration at the glib omission of the full story. Why hadn't he clarified this from the start? In a pinched voice, she attempted to assert girlfriend rights. "I'm not happy about sharing. Eddy. I thought this weekend was all about us being together." If his mates could show up at any moment, then the cabin might not be as ideal a hide away as she thought. This was a wasted trip. It was too late to turn around and go back home. The sun was about to set and grey shadows crossed the road. It would turn dark soon.

"It is. It will be. Don't worry. I'm sure the cabin will be empty." He looked flustered, not wanting to disappoint her. "Look, here's the driveway. We're almost there." The ute turned into a partially hidden dirt track, overgrown with wattle branches. It bumped and ground gears along an ungraded narrow strip of ground rutted with deep trenches carved from run off, a trail only a four wheel drive could manoeuvre.

Crossing a wooden bridge over a shallow river cascading over moss covered stones the road rounded into a bend. Through the window, sounds of a forest's night life began to come alive. The last of the day's fading heat scented the air with eucalyptus. Headlights lit up a cabin partially hidden amongst the shadows of tall gum trees.

Monique held her breath, not from excitement but more from abject disappointment. Calling it a cabin was an over statement. From the outside, classing it as a shack was too generous. In reality, it looked like a shabby, run down hut – rotten grey wood planks, dirt encrusted opaque windows, a rusted tin roof that didn't look waterproof. Sleeping overnight in it would be little different from camping out in the open.

As Eddy pulled up alongside the front door, Noelle jumped out. "Where's the toilet? I have to go!"

Heath ran after her, waving a roll of toilet paper and yelling, "It's outdoors."

Eddy looked apologetic. "What he means is, the outdoor toilet is actually ... well, we go outdoors – in the bush. Not flash but environmentally friendly."

Monique gave him a look that said without words *you've got to be kidding me*. If it wasn't so late and the drive down the mountain so winding and treacherous in the dark, she'd insist he take them home immediately. As it was, she extracted the oversize handbag resting under her legs, exited the ute and stalked towards the 'accommodation'.

In a blink the last of an orange streaked sunset dimmed to grey dusk and the summer night air chilled. An ice-cold shiver coursed through her body. Not just from the change in temperature.

"I'm going to need a fire lit as soon as possible," she told Eddy who was busy unpacking items from the back of the ute. He carried a case of Bramley Range bitter brew and two large packets of cheese and onion potato chips into the hut. Was that his contribution to their dinner tonight? "Is that it for food?" she asked. If so, they were going to be hungry.

"What do you mean? This is all we ever take with us when the guys come fishing." He patted a pocket checking for his smokes. "I thought you must have eaten when I saw you hadn't packed a picnic." He tossed her a bag of chips. "Here you go, if you're hungry."

The bag went wide and fell onto the ground. Ignoring it, she followed him through the door.

The inside of the building was as primitive as it looked from the outside. A rusty cast iron wood stove featured in the square room that made up the entirety of "the cabin". Two single cots rested against cobwebbed walls. Eddy dropped a case of beer on the floor. Pulling a box of matches from the back pocket of his jeans, he lit an oil lamp and turned the flame up, placing it on the stove. The room took on a shadowed glow. Hardly enough light to read by but it kept them from tripping over each other.

"There's a fire ban on this time of year. I'm thinking it may not be a good idea to light the stove. It's a tinder box out there. Sparks could shoot out the chimney and start a bushfire. There's no way we'd get a firetruck up the driveway," he stated with authority.

Monique nodded. Of course. No fire. What next? She scanned the room for blankets and pillows, but there were none to be seen. Where did Eddy expect them to sleep? Clutching her arms against her chest for warmth, she walked across dirt covered floorboards to the kitchen sink, turned the tap, to find it spurted water the colour of tea and stopped abruptly. "No water either?" she glared at Eddy accusingly.

"It's been a dry summer; I expect the water tank's empty," Eddy explained. "Sapphire River is not far. I'll get a bucket from out the back. If we boil the water, it should be fine. We won't need any tonight; I've brought beer." He strolled out the door and returned after a few minutes carrying sleeping bags and a deflated blow up mattress. "Heath and Noelle can take the cots. We've got the mattress." Sitting on his haunches, he proceeded to blow into a nozzle on the side of the mattress.

It was slow going. From the looks of it, Eddy would be at it all night. All the puff would be out of him before he dropped into bed. Which was good because the man had never seemed less attractive than he did at this moment. She considered sleeping on the back seat of the ute, curled up in a sleeping bag – on her own.

Heath returned, eating from the packet of chips found at the doorstep. Noelle followed. "Want some?" he offered to everyone and no one in particular. He held on to the packet possessively. Noelle pushed in to grab handfuls to scoff down.

"That's your dinner," Monique stated, giving Eddy another glare. Noelle and Heath looked aggrieved, as if they were being punished but didn't know what wrong had been committed.

Opening kitchen cupboards, she searched for anything edible. A dried out jar of vegemite as old as the hut itself held some scrapings. There was a tin of condensed milk, which would have been useful if someone had thought to bring tea or coffee, but no one had. Then a Eureka moment! At the back shelf, an unopened packet of Sao biscuits was pulled out. Its use-by stamp was a date from last year but, to paraphrase an old saying, *hungry buggers can't be choosers*.

She sat on the dusty floor and rested against a cobwebbed wall with a sleeping bag wrapped around her shoulders, holding onto a parody of civilised dining by eating from a chipped china plate. It was loaded with crackers and chips. Of everything she'd imagined about this outing to Eddy's mountain hide away, she never expected to be so relieved to be eating dry, chalky stale biscuits smeared with black yeast paste washed down with a bitter brew. To her disgust, she even tried to eat some of the Sao's smeared with condensed milk. It was another humiliation to add to an increasing list of blackmarks against Eddy.

Finishing the lot didn't ease the hunger pangs either.

Or, perhaps the empty ache in her stomach came from a different source. One she couldn't face at the moment. Despair. Knowing she'd lost. Blaming Eddy's deception but cursing her own stupidity for imagining she and Noelle could ever escape.

She popped the tab on another can of beer. If there was any chance of sleeping through this evening's disaster, it was to get well and truly trashed on alcohol before the night was through. In the morning, Eddy would drive them home at first light and they would never speak of his mountain cabin again. If she ever spoke to him again at all.

The worst thing about this shemozzle, and what frightened her the most, was knowing this hut could never be used as a hide away from Thayne, not even on a temporary basis. This had been the escape plan, Plan B, if all else failed.

This left Plan A only. And that was not reassuring. Negotiating a way out of her debts to Thayne was never going to work. The man escalated his demands as soon as he won a small concession. He'd come for Noelle. The money was secondary. Monique vowed she'd rather die than lose her daughter.

She began to hate Eddy from this point on. For all his big talk and Paisley's reassurances that he was one of the *good guys*, the guy lied like all the rest of the men. A big fat liar, all promises and no substance. Leaving her alone and unprotected. How useless was that? What could she do now?

Chapter Thirty-Three

Just past seven in the morning, Eddy dropped off Monique and Noelle at the front of Convict Crust and drove off gunning the motor and spitting gravel. She'd refused to talk to him the whole way home which probably explained why he ended up in such a bad temper. Good. He deserved it, especially when he was clueless as to why she was in a temper, too. She looked a wreck, smelled of Eddy's sweat and cigarette smoke – not having changed clothes nor showered in twenty four hours – and she hardly got any sleep the night before with Eddy pestering her to *get in the mood*. She was starving, hung over, and angry as a possum with a sore head. A can of beer and half chocolate nut bar for breakfast shared with Noelle barely touched the sides.

Noelle ran ahead to open the back door to the kitchen and then continued through to the residence yelling '*I'd die for a bowl of cereal*'. Monique flung a hand bag on her shoulder and dragged her feet to the patio, not the least anxious to start the day. The kitchen was cold and clean, ready for the day's baking. Anita promised to take on the role of baker for the day. If the ditzy girl remembered, she was making a late start. The wood fired oven should have been alight with hot coals long before now.

Monique fumed, realising she had to do everything around here. All she asked for was a one day break and she couldn't rely on others to do even half the job. She imagined posting a For Sale sign and closing the doors for good. Why work so hard; it only delayed the inevitable?

In the process of keying in the security code, she found her body forcefully pushed into the door before she completed the sequence. Hot breath on the back of her neck smelled of cinnamon lozenges. "I've been waiting; thought you'd fucked off without a kiss goodbye," Thayne hissed.

"Don't start. I'm not in the mood." She expelled a huge sigh. "I've got work to do, but first I need to take a hot shower." Wriggling to free herself, she found Thayne kept her trapped. He laughed at her struggles as if it were a game. "You're hurting," she whined.

He rubbed his hard-on against her rear, pressing his torso into her back so that her breasts flattened against the cold door. Her traitorous nipples protruded like rock candy.

"I like you best unwashed, smelling of another man, damp and slutty," he whispered. A hand crept under her dress and up her bare thigh, finding its way to the sweet spot where he began an expert finger massage.

After all these years, he still possessed a confident familiarity of knowing her body so much better than any other man. Her sex swelled and throbbed with memories of him, their volatile, insatiable lovemaking; the treacherous ways he found to make her come over and over until pleasure turned to pain and she fainted when it became too much. This time, as before, she fought against it; helplessly hating the control he wielded over her; his knowing touch unwanted, rejected, irresistible, too vivid to spurn. Thayne had the ability to send her spiralling into an abyss of ecstasy where morals, decency, self respect – everything good she thought herself to be – vanished into the heat of his demonic passion. He was like a magician with magic fingers; a magic tongue; a magic wand. Unable to stop, a deep moan of pleasure escaped, giving him permission to continue.

"Ahh, I see lover boy didn't meet your expectations last night," he breathed, taking tiny nips at her ear lobe and then sucking it as it began to throb. "I'll wager a bet, fucking has never been as wildly satisfying with anyone else, my Moaning Mona." A waft of his unique scent – musk, vetiver, amber mixed with male pheromones – set her womanly hormones on fire. "Or should I call you *Monique*, mon Cherie?" He feigned a French accent.

Fuck, he was right. She wanted to experience him again. Not just a couple fingers; his full length inside pounding her like a meat mallet. She blamed the build-up of frustration from the night before, her anger towards Eddy, the disappointment of her plan crumbling. And the fact Thayne knew her body and all her triggers too damn well. "Not here," she gasped. "Anita will be down any minute to start the sandwiches."

"Is that a challenge?" he panted, not as controlled as he wanted to be. "The risk of getting caught in the act always intensified your climax and mine. I can make this quick." Unzipping trousers, his erection surged free. He lifted the back of her dress and pulled down her panties enough to jab the moist tip of his prick in her back passage.

A sense of her own power as a woman rushed free like a religious revelation. Sexual gaming was part of her skill set. She knew how to perform to enthral men; the precise instance to vocalise cries of praise and exaltation to touch their egos at their weakest moments; tactics to soften their cold, hard hearts like putty in her hands leaving them obsessing about her and no other woman. Thayne was just another simple man, not a monster to be frightened of, but a bloke easily manipulated if she played this right.

Leaning against the door, she stuck out her butt to make it more accessible and squirmed to help with insertion. He grunted approval, pulling her hips towards the length of his shaft. Moaning *this was how he remembered it*.

From the other side of the door, the lock buzzed and disengaged, the door partially opened. Monique fell forward, attached to Thayne's shaft. His hands caught her around the waist and pulled her up against his chest. A belt buckle dug into a butt cheek causing an unexpected ripple of sexual electricity. Like a branding, it would leave a purple bruise as a reminder.

Anita yanked the door fully open and was confronted by the two locked in an unusual embrace. "Oops," Thayne joked. "We were on our way to …" he motioned with an airy wave towards the residence. With a tight hold across Monique's breasts, he turned her with him to allow Anita to enter the kitchen. They rushed through the closing door before the girl saw too much.

Their titters left little question in Anita's mind about what was going on. Since meeting Bernie, no one could accuse her of being a naïve virginal teenager.

But why was MM doing it with Thayne suddenly? Yuck. Sure, he claimed they had some history, but the guy was a sleaze. Anyone could see that. She had serious doubts about MM's judgment nowadays, especially after what happened with Mr Two Score.

So much for MM's grand passion for Eddy. The mountain cabin and the great outdoors experience was obviously a fizzer. Maybe he refused to open his wallet to pay off her debts. How quickly her fickle step mom latched on to another man to rescue her from a failing business. This had to be the only way she'd hook up with Thayne.

She wondered if Eddy knew he'd been dumped. Or like poor Simon, would he discover the news in a similarly humiliating fashion.

Anita didn't want to be around when it all went bust. There was an image in her head of Thayne being the detonator and MM the bomb. Convict Crust destroyed in the fall out.

Chapter Thirty-Four

By the time Monique re-appeared in the kitchen freshly showered and glowing from a thorough work out with the sleaze bag, Anita and Paisley had crimped the Cornish pasties ready for the wood oven and started on the no-bake slices. Anita decided not to bring up the Thayne hook-up, in case it was a one-off, spur of the moment thing. She had no idea if Paisley held any sense of loyalty towards Eddy after all that had gone on but she didn't want to chance it. A melt down was the last thing they needed this morning with everything else going on behind the scenes. The unspoken issues created tension in the room.

"You're back early but I'm not surprised," Paisley said, unfortunately choosing to ignore Anita's earlier advice not to mention MM's date with Eddy. Mean spirited, the foolish girl pretended to offer sympathy. "I wondered how you'd go when I overheard him *over promoting* the virtues of his shack. In fairness, he loves going up there with his mates. Being a bloke, he doesn't comprehend that women experience the primitive camping stuff differently."

Anita's stomach fell. Today was not the day to provoke her step mum by rubbing it in. She braced for a confrontation.

"Well, I wish he'd been more upfront about it before …" Monique stopped what was going to be a tirade, deciding not to admit to her humiliation. "Look, it doesn't matter. Things have moved on." With more force than required, she slid a paddle of pasties into the hot oven.

Noting MM's mood, Anita set a timer just to be sure. The bakery couldn't afford to burn another batch.

Unfortunately, Paisley wasn't quite finished poking the sore. Oblivious to the implications caused by Eddy's big, fat lie – that being MM's crushed illusions about her mountain man and the disappointment about the cabin's lack of suitability for a hide away – all this leading to a knee jerk response to ditch the guy and take up with Thayne. The worst plan ever. It was a disaster waiting to happen.

"I suppose I should have told you it wasn't *his* cabin. One of his mates from work owns it. Which is why it's so run-down. The bloke's a slob, but he's Eddy's hero for letting them use it when they go fishing."

This was belated news to MM, from the expression of suppressed rage on her face. It was a deliberate act of omission on Paisley's part. Revealing it now was petty and mean and wouldn't go unpunished. It would never occur to MM that she got what she deserved with Eddy, her *mountain man.* Instead it would backfire on Paisley. She'd bear the blame for the weekend disaster instead of Eddy, the braggart who deserved MM's ire.

MM could be spiteful if a person got on her wrong side.

As if on cue, the woman's face contorted into a ruddy mask of suppressed rage. Paisley smirked; mission accomplished. Not realising it was a declaration of war.

MM was not one to forgive easily. Anita looked to her step mum expecting an explosive reaction. Instead, she witnessed MM pull in the rage and store it in a memory compartment with Paisley's name written in large letters. A narrowing of eyes indicated MM had made a decision and it was already in train. To Anita, that look was more disconcerting than an emotional outburst. It meant MM was planning payback.

Anita spent the rest of the day on tenterhooks, sensing trouble was on its way. It wasn't until the café closed and she was cashing up, and Paisley had grabbed her handbag ready to head off that MM initiated the first move in a larger strategy.

Thayne made a lazy appearance crawling out from the residence where he'd been lurking all day. Unshaven, hair askew, he wore track pants and a tee shirt, no longer intending to impress and instead making himself at home wearing Tobin's cast offs. MM motioned him to join them.

"Before you go, I have an announcement to make," she said, putting her arm around his waist in an act of possessiveness. "Thayne and I are married." This was boldly pronounced, daring anyone to challenge her statement.

"Um, congratulations?" Anita said with some doubt but polite as always.

Paisley spluttered in shock. "Hellfire! You must be joking! When did that happen? He's only been here for a few days and through all that you've been dating Eddy!" Thayne had the gall to smirk at her high-minded condemnation. Anita waited for the meltdown.

Monique remained cool, calm and collected, the same composure she displayed on the day Simon caused a scene at the bakery. "Yeah, well that's a mistake I won't repeat!" She smiled at Thayne as if it had been worked out previously and all was forgiven. "In point of fact, Thayne and I have been married for many years. Due to unfortunate misunderstandings a history ago, we separated. He's been searching for us ever since and finally found us. Thank you, Anita, for your clever social media site."

Again, was that sarcasm or sincere appreciation? Anita was never sure. One thing was certain: Anita did not feel the least proud of her contribution towards putting these two together. Unlike Eddy, this guy was not one of the good ones. As far back as they went, MM had been smart to put as much distance from him as she could. Her lapse in memory must be due to desperation if she was hooking up with him again.

"Although parted, we never divorced because deep down, we remained in love."

Thayne kissed her cheek as an endorsement. Very chaste. It conveyed a gesture of mockery nonetheless.

"So, by the Eternal. Do we crack open a bottle of champagne – or are you planning a party later?" Paisley asked in a sarcastic tone. Thayne's eyes lit up approving both ideas.

Anita didn't believe their story. Monique's account sounded rehearsed as if attempting to weave a romantic tale. It made no sense. Paisley nailed it – this had happened too quickly to be legit. Thayne had some hold over her.

She vaguely recalled MM mentioning years ago that Noelle's father was abusive and she ran away in an attempt to disappear off his radar. Knowing MM to be a compulsive liar, she put this down to another tall tale and promptly dismissed it from her mind. True, MM had moved constantly around different States in Australia, hooked up with various men, Anita's father being one of many. A step mum for a few years until she ditched her dad for Tobin. Being *on the run* seemed an overly dramatic excuse for erratic behaviour.

But maybe it was true. Suddenly Anita understood the significance of the social media site she'd created. Recalling MM's first comments about it being a game changer of the first order. Shit. It had led Thayne straight to them. OMG. This was her fault.

Unnecessarily, Thayne added his own version of their story. "After reuniting this morning ..." he winked suggestively "... we discovered our passion had never died. Once again, I've become obsessed with this arousing, invigorating woman. There's no one else who compares. One hour alone with her and I looked fate in the eyes. This was my chance to make her mine ... again ... forever."

There was stunned silence. From Paisley's purple face, the girl was about to have a paroxysm.

Anita wanted to vomit, it felt so grubby. "Does this mean you'll be moving in with us?" she asked, unable to disguise a sullen tone of voice. *Oh god, please say no.*

"Ah, good question." He stole a glance Monique's way whose smile froze in rigor mortis. "We haven't discussed future arrangements as yet. I live in Perth. Depends on what *we* decide about the bakery. What I own; what stays here. I can only hang around Lower Teasel with all of you for a short, few days. Business commitments, you understand." He yawned.

Paisley had heard enough. She stalked out of the bakery without saying goodbye.

"Bernie and I will see you at the pub tonight," Anita called after her. She had a bad feeling about all of it. Turning to MM, she asked one last question – the elephant in the room question. "Have you told Noelle about you and Thayne being married?"

Thayne exposed shark-like teeth in an evil grin. "Yes, *Moaning Mona*. How much does *our* daughter know about her father? It's been ages between access visits. Don't you think we should balance the books and return my equal rights? I want a chance to know her a whole lot better."

Monique went pale and visibly shrunk. This was when Anita became very scared.

Chapter Thirty-Five

A typical Saturday night at the Draught Horse Pub – crowded, noisy, with lots of families in the dining area and all the bar stools occupied with blokes good naturedly yelling at the footy on a television screen that spanned half the wall space behind the bar. Paisley was run off her feet which should have kept her mind from obsessing about the Monique, Eddy and Thayne threesome – but didn't. Bernie and Anita ate schnitzels and chips at a round table in the middle of the chaos. As an excuse to talk to them, Paisley carried over complimentary beers (which she put on her personal tab).

"She's been married the whole time!" she whinged to Bernie. "All through the *he's left me* Tobin drama; then Simon's scene in front of customers – all that *please come back to me* shit; then the pressure and threats to get her *Mountain Man* to go out with her. And she was married!" After plonking down two schooners, she raced back to the bar.

Tolerant of the brief interruption, Anita resumed her conversation – filling in Bernie on recent events at Convict Crust starting with MM's disastrous camping date with Eddy after which they weren't speaking to one another. "Paisley never told her that his cabin was actually an uninhabitable hut without water or a toilet. MM will never forgive her."

"I get that she was unhappy about Eddy dating Monique but it was a bad call on Paisley's part to not say anything beforehand."

"I've worked out that MM owed Thayne money for the bakery. She was going to do a runner if he caught up with her, using the mountain cabin as a temporary hide away," Anita explained.

"When Paisley went on and on about Monique using Eddy to gain a hide away, I called her an idiot and told her to butt out and get a life. It never occurred to me with all her obsessiveness, Paisley could have been onto something." Bernie looked contrite.

They stopped abruptly when Paisley returned with a jug of water and two glasses, which were once again plonked down with force. "Eddy and Heath were my only family! She ruined it. Making out she'd be Heath's new step mother, pushing me out."

While Paisley took in a deep breath, Anita mumbled in the interlude *tell me about it; she's my step mum too apparently*. This caused a pause in the rant for a split second before she went on.

"Making out we were *like sisters*. I'm such an idiot. Can you believe it? I cleaned Eddy's house trying to be a good sister and friend." She paused to consider the enormity of her stupidity. "How can I ever be friends with someone who's a big, fat liar. I'll never forgive her. Or Eddy." Paisley huffed off again.

Turning to Bernie, Anita gave a guilty shrug. "It's my fault about Thayne finding them. The social media site tipped him off. He's Noelle's biological father – did you know that? It sounds like he's returned to claim access rights and MM's not wanting that to happen."

"How were you supposed to know?" Bernie patted her hand in a show of support.

"Paisley's not going to come back to the bakery after this, is she?" She looked to Bernie wanting him to disagree. His eyes said it all. "They'll never cope without help. I'll bet MM and Thayne will sell the bakery and move to the Mainland. Where will I live if that happens? Uni starts back in a few weeks. I've got two more years to go."

Bernie glanced to the bar where Paisley was busy with customers. "Let's not get ahead of ourselves speculating about what might be. We don't know much of anything for sure yet." Anita was unhappy at this response. He resumed eating his meal in thoughtful silence.

Anita was stacking their finished plates when Paisley loomed over them brandishing a mobile phone. "One thing's solved. I don't have to worry about resigning. Have a read." She thrust the screen under Anita's nose.

A text message read:

> Don't come in on Monday. You are excess to reqts.

> PS My customers will learn who you are. A liar and a sneak.

It was Monique's revenge. Anita knew it was coming. Fired by text was the ultimate insult. What rumours was she going to spread? She handed the phone across to let Bernie read.

"I'm so sorry it came to this Paisley. After all you've done for her," Anita said.

Paisley wilted. All the steam had been vented and left her numb. "I've never been fired from a job before." She looked like a vulnerable ten year old, unable to comprehend how horrible the world can get. "Don't tell Mel. I don't want her to get the wrong impression about me."

"She won't," Anita said.

Bernie didn't like seeing his old friend regress to being a sad foster kid. He wanted to shake her up. "Auntie Sheryl warned you that working at Convict Crust was a mistake. You never listen."

She showed a bit more spunk. "I'll bet Monique will expect her new lover boy to replace me. She'll be in for a shock. There's the Steam Fest catering coming up in a few weeks. They won't cope."

"Well, I'm not doing your share and mine too. Stuff them. I don't trust the guy. Something's going on behind the scenes," Anita exclaimed.

"What about Noelle? Does she even know Thayne is her dad supposedly?" Bernie asked.

"Yeah, is that another one of Monique's lies! She made out that Tobin was the father – one happy family and that was another porkie." Paisley checked out Mel and saw her frowning. "I've got to get back to work." She grabbed the phone and pocketed it.

"Coffees and two sticky date puddings with ice cream," Bernie announced loudly to give Mel the impression they were discussing a dessert order and not personal stuff. Paisley gave him a grateful look and dashed back to the bar. "Paisley might look tough but underneath she's a terrified street kid longing for a stable home to belong. This will hit her hard."

Anita agreed. "Anything could happen once MM gets offside with someone. Paisley needs to watch her back."

"And we'll be watching for her, too," Bernie said.

Chapter Thirty-Six

Late morning, Anita leaned over an open laptop resting on Light Up's front counter, scrolling through posts on Convict Crust's Facebook page. The tobacco shop was quiet and Bernie allowed the intrusion into his space in a gesture of support. She was upset and was taking out her grievance by analysing in focused detail what changes had been made to the site.

With Monique's agreement, Thayne had taken over as the Administrator of the site a couple days ago which left Anita out in the cold. She could add her own remarks and respond to others' posts as a subscriber but wasn't able to delete any negative or derogatory remarks from the site in a controlled manner. When Anita argued for control, Monique dismissed her indignation with a shrug – a total lack of caring. It was a payback of sorts, for creating the site and going live before being given permission, and gratefully, Anita got off lightly so far. However, it made her wonder about Thayne's agenda because he definitely had one from the get go.

For days, she'd waited for the signs of Paisley and MM's falling out to go public, for her step mum to wreak havoc and destruction to demonstrate no one crossed her and got away with it. Bernie kept an ear to the ground amongst his business colleagues ready to come to Paisley's defence, if required.

When nothing became apparent, Anita wondered if she'd misread her step mum's character. Maybe MM had too much else on her mind to carry out the threats. Within the Lower Teasel community, Paisley was a nobody. Ruining her reputation would be of little consequence to anyone but Paisley.

The lie of omission was actually a fairly petty matter and not worthy of expending energy on revenge. Eddy's mountain hide away was a disappointing non-starter but not hugely significant in the scheme of things. As Bernie explained, Thayne would have found Monique and Noelle eventually because he'd been very determined. There was no place to really hide forever. For years, MM ran but ultimately couldn't disappear off the map – not even in as remote a place as Eden Isle. It was better to face the man once and for all. Reimburse what she owed him to get him off her back. There were more important matters to deal with, for example, keeping the bakery afloat.

Scrolling down the Facebook page, the first hint of trouble was an announcement that Thayne Swanston from Western Australia's culinary capital had joined Convict Crust as part owner and new baker. A photo of him dressed in a white apron and chef's hat showing a wide row of shark-like teeth in a cheesy grin signalled the bakery's new direction. He was quoted as saying *My plan is to tempt our customers' appetites with sweet things too irresistible to refuse. I draw upon family recipes of old classics: pork pies; toad in the hole; spotted dick pudding; tarts and crumpets – taking these to a whole new extreme of sensory delights.'*

Anita doubted the man had ever cooked in his life, let alone qualified as a baker and chef. He planned to take credit for MM's hard work. His tone made a mockery of what had been an artisan bakery with a boutique image and turned it into a low class double entendre. Is this how he saw MM? Ugh. Was he trying to run the place into the ground before selling it off cheap? She and Bernie discussed this at length but finished up undecided.

It was mid afternoon when Anita spotted the first damning post started obviously by Thayne, the new site administrator, on Monique's behalf.

Convict Crust is sad to advise our barista was let go after an inventory uncovered unexplained missing items.

An outright lie but it didn't take much to encourage a barrage of sympathetic supportive comments from loyal customers. She turned the screen towards Bernie. "It's started. Take a look," she said. They began to read and scroll through the posts.

Dressed like a freak. Never trusted her.

It's so hard to find good honest help these days. My sympathies to you.

From Thayne:

We tried – staff discounts; bags of leftovers – never enough!

Responses:

> You try to do the charitable thing. These kids let you down every time.

> Once a stray always a stray.

> You give a street kid a leg up and she takes an arm and a leg.

> You share a few leftovers and then they think it's theirs for the taking.

Bernie cursed. As soon as they reached the end, more comments of a similar nature were posted. "Paisley will be devastated. Can't we do something?" he asked Anita.

"We can write something to support her. What should we say?"

He typed:

> One is innocent until proven guilty.

Thayne must have been waiting because he responded straight away.

> Not laying blame. Our Steampunk stray's fey innocence is appealing. But is it a defence?

Anita decided to go all in, heavy duty. She typed:

> Heard the owner was fucking her ex.

This started an avalanche of posts, missing the point.

> Boo hoo, no one gives a shit.

> Stealing's a crime, fucking isn't – if between consenting adults

> I got even with my ex pouring sugar in his petrol tank.

> Cool. Does it have to be any particular kind of sugar? I'm vegan.

Anita jotted down stats in a notebook. "Amazing. I didn't think we had that many bakery customers. Wow! It's exceeded the population of Lower Teasel. Followers have increased exponentially since these posts started. Look at the numbers! People are forwarding the page to their friends and we're getting new subscribers every minute."

Bernie gave a quick look at the numbers but wasn't that fascinated. "How sick is it? So many people getting off on the bullying and harassment," Bernie said.

"It's good for Convict Crust's business. And it's entertainment. They all assume she's guilty on one person's word – Monique's. Or more likely, Thayne's behind it, being the administrator."

"Yeah, well Paisley is a real human being, not someone's entertainment for the day – or week." He'd seen enough. He slammed shut the laptop lid.

Anita left it until the end of the day when she couldn't help but have a peek at the stats. There were hundreds of comments and thousands of followers. It was an insane result for her social media creation. If only her university professor could see her work now for grading! When she set up the loyalty program for Convict Crust, never did she imagine in the space of half a day its uptake could surge to such heights. It passed the test. Despite being based on a lie and at the expense of Paisley's reputation.

Chapter Thirty-Seven

This was the first time Paisley had ventured out in public since Convict Crust's Facebook posts began several days ago. Like poking a sore tooth, she'd been glued to the page for hours, addicted to reading and re-reading each comment, focusing more on the nasty ones, trying to make sense of how quickly her smiling-faced customers turned into hypocrites – leaving no benefit of doubt that she could be innocent. Burning with indignation, she wanted to face them head on, in person, confront them with the real truth and ask for compassion, empathy, some human connection, not be treated like a label – stray, street kid, foster kid – but they hid behind stupid pen names, anonymous and unaccountable. Like it was some game, not her whole life turned upside down.

Despite crippling trepidation, she decided to attend the Steampunk Club meeting. Steam Fest and the challenge were only a couple weeks away. It was a critical stage in the project plan if it was going to be a success. Her job was more than Committee Secretary. She was their trouble shooter which meant liaising with sponsors, caterers and volunteers to ensure all the tiny details were in place ready to go and, if not, fix up problems or loose ends. The

Guinness Book of Records challenge was at a critical stage and she needed to drum up more enthusiasm to increase the numbers. She had a few ideas to put to members to garner community support. The more entry fees, the larger the donation to the Street Kids Appeal. This was the whole point of the festival this year.

Taking a deep breath before entering the Draught Horse, Paisley relaxed somewhat convinced the pub's bouncers would ensure it remained a congenial place for customers and staff alike. Mel – *the best boss ever* – would not tolerate the town's vitriol to turn to physical abuse within its walls.

Except – what she didn't expect was Mel to pull her to one side of the bar before she escaped to the meeting room for a spur of the moment performance review.

"How are you doing?" Mel asked with a frown. Paisley read that as sympathy.

"Awful. The black-hearted skulduggery isn't stopping and I can't defend myself or tell my side of the story. No one cares about me. I'm afraid to leave the house."

"Are you saying you didn't do it?" Mel asked rather harshly in Paisley's opinion.

"Hellfire. Do you even have to ask?" This was the first time Mel had disappointed her as a boss.

"Yes, I do." Mel shifted uncomfortably. "Sorry, but I have noticed you pinching peanuts during Happy Hour. Not recently, but ..."

"By the Eternal. If you thought that was a big deal why didn't you say something straight away?" Paisley was incredulous. She turned her back ready to walk away. Mel put a hand on her shoulder to stop her.

"If customers complain, sorry Paisley, but I'll have to cut back on your shifts until the hullabaloo dies down. It's not personal."

In fairness, her old boss did look sorry. Not that it helped one bit. "Yeah, well fantastic. Thanks for your vote of support." Teary eyed, she refused to show vulnerability in front of this woman who'd been a friend. Mustering dignity with a straight back she walked away.

The club room was in chaos. Bernie stood at the committee table with his hands held up for quiet. Anita was flushed and distressed. Members were yelling at her to tell them the truth. Convict Crust was her family's business; what did she know? Conan started beating his shield to call the meeting to order. When they noticed Paisley enter, someone started booing and others joined in.

Ready to turn and run, Lance grabbed her arm. "Why haven't you called me? I saw the posts. If you ever need anything – food, money – you never have to resort to ... I mean, you just have to let me know."

"Bedamned. I didn't do it," she responded with an angry yank to get her arm back.

"That's not what I'm saying!" Before he could apologise, Bernie came up and shadowed her other side. Between the two men she was chaperoned to the front of the room. They forcefully made her sit in the Secretary's chair to make a point to others in the room. Lance stood by, not being on the committee but not wanting to leave Paisley's side.

"The power granted through the Sanctum of the Grand Mechanism, Order! This meeting is called to order!" Bernie yelled above the rabble. "We have a full agenda to get through. The Steam Fest Challenge is not far off and there are a lot of outstanding issues."

"No! First, what about *her*?" the Mad Hatter shouted. He received cheers of support. Paisley sunk in her chair wishing for a steam-driven time machine to whisk her away to another era.

Bernie stood and eyeballed the crowd, not saying a word. He waited until the mutinous mob quietened into an uncomfortable shuffling. "By the heart of the Alchemist's truthstone, our *Club Secretary* has come under attack from a smear campaign. She is the victim here. If you can't see that she needs our support, and not our condemnation, then I don't know what to say."

Mad Hatter was not convinced. "Strewth! I've heard sponsors are pulling out and businesses have started to take down our posters – all because of her!" He pointed accusingly. "She threatens to destroy all our hard work to make Steam Fest a success. I say, she has to go!"

Paisley sat up in her seat. *All their hard work! She was the one doing most of it.* Lance put a comforting hand on her shoulder. Bernie sat down in frustration.

Adam, bless his cotton socks, stood up as a voice of reason. "Please, everyone. Calm down! The whole point of this year's festival is to support street kids in Lower Teasel. And we're allowing our own to be too easily painted as a stereotype – the one that says street kids steal and cheat and lie – and they don't deserve our compassion or help. This is the exact perception we're trying to deconstruct and re-write through the challenge for the Street Kids Appeal. Don't succumb to the saboteurs."

This caused pause for thought, until Marianne took a deep breath and added her own two cents worth. "It is fair to say we are dealing with a distillation of perceptions from the crucible of Lower Teasel's residents – and not the Alchemist's truth stone per se. But can our club afford to separate the alloys from the base metal right now – when it's clear the compass bearings are steering our Steam Fest galleon into the reef of destruction?" Where had these words come from out of Marianne's mouth? Paisley shook her head. This did not sound like the Marianne she knew. It was obvious the girl was trying very hard to win support from the crowd. But why?

Her speech brought a round of applause and louder shouts of *She's got to go!* which mutated into a monotonous chant. *She's got to go! She's got to go!*

There was no point in trying to debate the issue further. At this rate, nothing would get done at the meeting and decisions needed to be made. The project's hour glass was running out of sand.

Bernie cast a quick 'sorry' towards Paisley and then yelled over the crowd, "Hail, members of the Alchemist's Sanctum. I beseech – let us follow proper protocols under the instrument of the Guild Masters Watch Works. Will one of the Club's querents propose a motion?"

Mad Hatter put up his hand. "I propose Paisley is replaced as Club Secretary and in her place, we vote in Marianne." To her credit, Marianne looked surprised at this but also rather pleased. The motion was seconded by a pipe smoking Sherlock Holmes.

"All in favour, show your hands."

Anita counted and whispered to Bernie. He stood and in a tone of regret announced, "The motion is passed by powers of the Guild Masters Watch Works. Marianne, please take your seat at the table. Paisley is excused from duties. Godspeed," he stated in an official tone. Cheers and clapping deafened the room.

Paisley was forced to walk down a gauntlet. She didn't wait to be asked twice. She leapt out of her chair and stalked out of the room without a second glance. Lance ran after her.

Marianne worked her way through the applause to sit in Paisley's vacated spot. Satisfied, the mob broke off into smaller groups to murmur rather than shout their opinions.

Anita looked stricken. "This was Monique's plan all along," she whispered to Bernie. "She wants to bring the festival down; if she can't succeed in business, she doesn't want anyone else to."

"I'll bet she closes the bakery before having to fulfil the catering contract."

"Thayne's up to something. Steam Fest and helping out local businesses is the last thing on his mind. He's moved into the residence and spends his days sucking up to Noelle. There's a big yuck factor to it. I hate being at home these days."

Marianne tapped Bernie's shoulder. "Right. Where were we with the agenda? Should we get started?" Opening her handbag, she pulled out a pocket notebook and a pen with a pink pom pom attached to one end. Holding it to her lips, she grinned, ready to begin.

Anita rolled her eyes.

"Hellfire. This is going to be a disaster," Bernie mumbled before calling the room to order.

✿ ✿ ✿

Lance ran after Paisley. The pub's front door slammed shut behind him with a crack. "Wait up. Where are you going?"

"As far away as possible," she replied, continuing a brisk walk down the sidewalk.

"Slow down. Talk to me," he called out.

When he caught up, she stopped abruptly and turned to him. "I've been booted off *my own club*! It's *mine* and Bernie's – we started it. The Steam Fest challenge was *my idea*. Those people have known me for years. And they still sided with Monique. What is it with me and people?"

"It's not about you. They're caught up in the drama of the moment and have lost sight of common sense and reason. Monique has deliberately orchestrated this to get to you. Don't let her." Lance could see the pain of rejection in her eyes, and worse, the acceptance of it as her *life as usual*.

"I'm over it. Let go and move on – that's my motto." She stalked off to Rolla parked a half block down the street.

Lance decided to let her go and blow off steam. There wasn't much comfort he could give without adding further to her humiliation. At the back of his mind, he began to formulate a plan to redeem Paisley in the eyes of the community and in the process rescue what appeared to be a Steam Fest train wreck on the horizon. If he could pull it off, maybe he and Paisley had a chance too. *Trust me – I won't let you down*, he whispered watching her drive off down the road, praying this was true.

Chapter Thirty-Eight

Paisley couldn't face staying in the small, sad flat staring at the walls, obsessing for days on end about how the world had done her wrong. Hellfire and be damned. She'd lost two jobs in the space of a week. She'd been booted from the club she founded, supplanted by Marianne of all people. Her BFF facilitated her demise; she'd never forgive him. Humiliating her in front of a new boyfriend as well. God only knows what Lance must think of her. And where was Anita in all this – supposedly a friend meant to stick up for her? Silent as if one of Monique's shadow recruits!

Residents of Lower Teasel branded her a petty thief and an outcast. This would never change; they'd never see beyond that corroded patina to the gold beneath. Even after all she was trying to do for their community through the Steam Fest challenge – attracting tourists to the village and pouring dollars into their businesses. It was the moment of truth to face reality – she did not belong in this place. Maybe once, she'd had a chance to make this a home but Monique had put an end to that fantasy. It was crucial to clear her head and consider future options.

The problem with living by the motto *Let go – and move on* was where to go and how to get there?

Not to her parents at Crows Marsh. That would be an admission of total defeat, and the end of life as she knew it. Not to Stubblefield where Bernie and his family lived. She was too mad at Bernie to ever want to see him again, even if his family were lovely. Whaler's Cove? Yeah right. Lance would think she was stalking him. Associating with a girlfriend who was labelled a criminal would be a bad look for his business. She couldn't do that to the guy.

Then there was the issue of moving and how she was going to afford to pack up and leave. How much could she pack into Rolla? She'd need to get a job at the other end. Where were the more likely places to have job opportunities? Could she pursue her Steampunk dream, or would her future forever more be pulling pints at another pub, always putting her creativity on hold. What life path was she to follow? *Letting go* was the easy part. *Moving on* was starting to get complicated.

Like the wise words from the Cheshire Cat in Alice in Wonderland, if she didn't know where she wanted to go in life, then it didn't really matter which path to take to get there – wherever *there* was. She wanted friends. Family. A place to belong where she was seen true and fair. Where people liked the individual that she was. She had to earn a living, but money wasn't a priority. Living poor was a constant. She'd survive.

Except survival was a lonely business without people to love. Eddy and Heath no longer made up her small family, eternal curses to Monique. And her friends? Could she leave them behind?

As if she'd already packed up and left, she began to miss Bernie, Anita, Adam and Lance.

Knocking her head with frustration, she decided to tackle first things first. She needed a place to disappear in order to think about her life in its current state of play and what direction she wished to *move on*. Follow her bliss, as the counsellors would say.

When the answer came, she had a chuckle at the irony. It was only a temporary solution but for now, it was perfect. Eddy didn't have to know. It was off fly fishing season so there was a strong chance no one would find her there. It was as far from human contact as she could get – and cost nothing, which considering she was broke was the best part.

She started packing Rolla with pillows, blankets, clothes, tinned food, boxed food, cooking utensils and anything else that seemed reasonably handy for camping out at Sapphire Creek. There was a niggle of doubt about whether Rolla would make the climb up the dirt track to the hut once she turned off the main road. It didn't matter. If the worst happened, she could always park the car and backpack the rest of the way. She had all the grains of sand in the hour glass.

Unlike Monique, she was used to sleeping rough. It reminded her of the old days when she was that wayfaring street kid – a defiant teenager treasuring freedom, independence and seclusion over the judgements of the virtuous and the upright. Except this time around, the stray had a perfect hide away.

Chapter Thirty-Nine

It was embarrassing. Anita did not take any pleasure in the evident success of her social media site if the number of customers packed into Convict Crust Bakery was any measure of accomplishment. From the hum of gossip and the phone scrolling to check out new posts steadily venting hurtful comments about Paisley, the hate campaign continued its wildfire conflagration. It was obvious Thayne fuelled the ire posting witty responses and new angles of character assassination about their former barista's reputation timed to coincide with each gradual tapering off of comments, setting off a fresh set of trolling.

Monique sat at a round table in the middle of the café surrounded by groupies offering support and nagging for every gory detail. She was happy to comply, playing the hard done by employer. In the meanwhile, Anita was run off her feet making hot drinks and plating up sweet orders. Noelle helped serve customers and clear tables but orders backlogged. Thayne was a no show – probably sitting at a laptop in their living room orchestrating the hate campaign – and therefore no help.

Towards the end of the busy afternoon, Anita turned to scold Noelle about pinching jam tarts from the display counter when she noticed Heath standing nearby. Which meant Eddy must be somewhere around. OMG. Was this going to be another Mr Two Score scene? She cast around the room looking for Eddy. He was sitting at a table quietly waiting for Monique to acknowledge his presence. He shared Simon's lovesick puppy look.

"Where's Paisley?" Heath asked innocently. Anita wasn't sure where to begin. Luckily, Noelle answered.

"MM said she was sick and tired so Paisley needed to go and leave."

"You mean go *on* leave." Anita corrected, aiming for a positive spin. Noelle shrugged.

"Can you make me a hot chocolate with marshmallows the same as Paisley does? She makes the best," Heath pleaded.

"Me, too," Noelle said. "We're going to play in my room. Come on."

"Hold on. I want to ask your dad first." Anita wasn't sure if it was a good idea to play behind locked doors where Thayne was in residence. The way his eyes glazed when staring at Noelle creeped her out. Moving between tables, she worked her way to Eddy.

He smiled. "Hi, Anita. Where's Paisley?"

Could it be that Eddy had not followed the social media campaign? "Um. She doesn't work here anymore, since last week."

"She's on leave," Heath contributed helpfully. "Can I play in Noelle's room please?" He dragged out the please.

"Before you say yes, you should know that Thayne is staying with us." Anita screwed up her face trying to convey a telepathic message that the man was trouble. Eddy looked blank.

"Thayne?"

"My dad," Noelle chirped. "MM and he married long ago and now they found each other and love each other and are back together. We're going to move to Western Australia."

"Oh," Eddy said, clearly confused. He looked to Anita. "I came to apologise for the misunderstanding about the mountain cabin. Guess I left it too late."

"Let me get you a cup of coffee and I'll explain a few things," Anita offered.

Thayne entered the café area wearing jeans and a sleeveless tee, barefoot and unshaven. Making a beeline to Monique, he came up from behind and squeezed her neck with both hands in a covetous hold. Maintaining it, he pulled her head up and sucked her lips, drawing out the kiss until she was breathless and turning blue. She squirmed and, when he finished, gasped for breath. Not protesting exactly but clearly not enjoying his possessive public display. Her groupies around the table giggled uneasily.

Eddy flinched; his natural instincts were to protect her. Anita braced for an altercation. "Is that Thayne?" he asked through clenched teeth. "Kids go play. I'd like a few words with this guy." Heath high fived Noelle and they ran off. Pushing back his chair with a screech across the wood floor, Eddy stood to full height and strutted over.

Thayne took notice of his rival with the grin of a white pointer, not perturbed in the least. In fact, when Eddy was close, he held out his hand as if enjoying the drama. "Mate, gid-day."

Eddy declined the handshake and addressed Monique instead. "Is this the abusive ex you've been running from? Do you need my help to get rid of him?" he asked bluntly.

Monique turned away and ignored him.

Thayne was more verbose. "Hey, fuck off man! This is my woman, my property – got it?"

Monique stirred. "Don't start, Eddy. You're making a fool of yourself like some whipped stray. To tell the truth, you were a non-starter. You were totally forgettable – like Simon. It's pitiful to see a man begging for it. Don't be a dick. Walk away with some dignity." It was cruel and left no ambiguity.

"Yeah, think of yourself as a piece of trash in her trashy past. She's traded up. You couldn't get her off so move aside and leave it to the real stud." Thayne egged him on like a cock fighter. Anita waited for Eddy to slug him.

For a tense moment, Eddy stood there eyeballing the guy. Then, he gave Monique a pitiable stare as if to say she and Thayne deserved each other. With a rueful smile he said, "We've all been there, done that with Monique. You're the one being played for a fool. My advice? Best to move on. This is how to do it." He walked out of the bakery without a backward glance.

Anita trotted after him. Once outside, she tugged on his sleeve to make him pull up. She began to fill him in on the background story as far as she knew the details: how MM owed Thayne money; he found them through the social media site she'd created; they were married and Noelle was his daughter; he wanted access rights; he'd moved in and she thought MM was planning to sell the bakery and move to WA with him. Catching her breath, she added a few details about what was going on with Paisley – getting fired and Monique on a campaign to destroy her reputation. Eddy listened without saying a word. She could sense the heat of anger radiating off him.

"Get Heath," he ordered in a gruff voice. That was it. No more was said. It was weird.

After releasing the kid from the residence, Anita's intuition said this would be the last she saw of them.

Chapter Forty

At one in the morning, a shivering Anita dressed in lightweight cotton pajamas and running shoes without socks pounded on the back door of Light Up. When Bernie failed to open, despite hyperventilating from stress, she had the presence of mind to send a text.

It's me @ door

She had no idea if he was a heavy sleeper, or if he turned the phone off before bed. Slumping down onto the back step, all she could do was wait. Outside at Bernie's backdoor, a few steps from an unlit Council laneway and a dumpster, felt safer than her bedroom at Convict Crust. Hugging the phone, her breathing and pounding heart calmed. It was going to be okay.

A light came on and a groggy Bernie opened the door and peered out, not sure what he was looking at. "Bedamned. Anita? What the ..." he asked. He wore boxer shorts and a short sleeve white tee crumpled from sleep. His hair stuck out in all directions.

Anita leapt up to hug him as if he was a lifejacket she wanted to crawl into. Peeling her arms away, he managed to say, "You're like an icicle. Come inside. I'll make us a cup of tea." She refused to let go of his hand and they stumbled together into the kitchen of the shop's small accommodation area. Making her sit before answering questions, he put the kettle on and rattled through the cupboard for mugs and dangled a tea bag into each.

"I got scared and had to get away," she said, trembling. Bernie unhooked a jacket from a coat stand near the door and placed it around her shoulders. He looked alarmed.

"What do you mean?"

"They were shouting, Monique was screaming, and then fighting broke out." Anita's breathing became ragged and she doubled over, rocking on her knees.

The kettle whistled and Bernie filled mugs with boiling water, added a heap of sugar and milk. Carefully, he placed a mug in her hands and made her sit up. "Hang on, start at the beginning. Who was shouting?"

Anita blew on the tea and steadied her nerves. "It started at around ten thirty. I was in the bakery kitchen sneaking brandy for my hot milk before bed and this pounding started at the back door. That freaked me out and then shouting started. This guy was yelling at the top of his lungs, "I want my money back, Monique. I know you're selling. Open up!" It sounded like Simon. I peeked out the kitchen window but he was in the shadows. But I knew it was him. From the psycho scene he caused a couple weeks ago, there was no way I was going to open the door."

"Good to know." When she didn't crack a smile, Bernie asked, "Did you call the police?" He pulled out a chair and sat facing her braced for a long story.

"No, I sort of stood there frozen waiting for him to go away. I guess I expected Monique or Thayne to come out and deal with him." She took a tentative sip from the hot drink. "But they didn't hear – being otherwise engaged. After a while, his voice went hoarse and the yelling toned down to a normal voice. When it all went quiet, I thought he'd given up because no one opened the door. I thought he'd slunk away, rejected and embarrassed at causing another scene." She pulled the jacket around tighter for comfort.

"But he didn't?" Bernie probed.

Anita gulped the tea as if bracing for a confession. "I poured extra brandy in my milk and waited just to be sure. Then knocking started up again but more normal. And a voice was saying, '*Monique, open up – it's me, Tobin*'. I turned on the patio light and looked out the window. It was Tobin. I was so relieved seeing him, I opened the door straight away."

"Fair enough. I mean you hadn't seen him for a while and never got to say goodbye," Bernie said.

"He made me feel safe. Tobin was there because Monique got in touch with him and begged for help to save her from Thayne, calling him a thug. I think she was expecting bail out money. Instead, Tobin rocked up for a *big-production-all-out rescue*. But it went horribly wrong." Tears fell into her tea. She rubbed her wet cheeks with the sleeve of Bernie's jacket. He patted her knee but didn't push for an explanation.

Sniffling, she raised her head. "The problem was Simon hadn't gone. He'd waited in the shadows on the patio and when I let Tobin in, Simon barged in after. Weirdly, Simon was more composed and he started explaining stuff to Tobin who was quite interested in what he had to say. From what I gathered, when I saw that windfall land in the bakery's bank account ages ago, it wasn't from Tobin selling off his Harley. It was from Simon falling for Monique's sob story about needing a loan to keep the bakery afloat."

Bernie interjected. "Hold your horses. From what you're saying, Monique owes money to Simon, Tobin *and* Thayne!"

Anita nodded vigorously. "All from a bakery that is well above its over draft and surviving on the good graces of the bank. If I thought she could fit another man into her busy schedule, I'd wager she'd shag the bank manager to delay foreclosure."

"Hellfire and skulduggery!" Bernie laughed in horror. "She's like a scammer."

"I don't know about that."

"Sorry. She's your step mum."

Anita gulped down the rest of her tea. Staring into space, she continued. "What happened next is sort of my fault. They were talking so normally with each other in the kitchen. You know, about their work and what money they were owed, comparing notes quite civilised. I decided if their issues were going to be sorted, Monique needed to sit down with them and talk like business people do. So, I opened the security door to the residence and invited them into our lounge room. I went to get Monique, and of course, Thayne came, too." Her voice took on a distressed whine, as if beseeching Bernie to absolve her of what happened next.

"It started out reasonably tame. Monique was happy to see Tobin and gave him a big hug as if they were still together which was weird. This did not impress Thayne; his eyes turned into black slivers like he wanted to kill the guy. I thought, this can't be good." She took in a deep breath.

"And, it wasn't. It didn't takc long before everyone was shouting about what they were owed and that they were more entitled than someone else. *Show me that in writing*, Thayne was shouting. *If you don't have a signed agreement, then too fucking bad*. He kept shouting *too fucking bad* over the top of everyone."

"Hellfire. He didn't want to share any of the money from the sale of the bakery even though Tobin and Simon had vested interests." Bernie summarised.

"It got out of control when Monique decided to step in between the lot of them, siding with Thayne and denying she owed Tobin and Simon anything. She kept repeating like a broken record *'gifts don't need to be repaid'*." Anita looked into Bernie's eyes. "That can't be right?"

"No. It's not good," Bernie agreed.

"I stood in the doorway; they'd forgotten I was there. But it was like I was stoned. I couldn't look away or even move. Then a three-way punch up started between the guys. I couldn't say who was punching who; it was indiscriminate and crazy – but seriously bad. Monique tried to break them up and was getting hit in the process. That scared me. The spell I was under broke and I ran to my room. Then I heard a loud bang – maybe like a gun being fired,

I don't know – and Monique started to scream like she was in grief or something." The shivering started again, more uncontrollable.

Bernie pulled her close and murmured soothing sounds as if she were a little kid. "I threw on runners, jumped in my car, and got away as fast as I could. And came here because it was the only place I could think of as safe." She snuggled into his arms.

"Do we need to call the police? If you heard a gunshot, anything could have happened." Bernie reached for his phone. Anita cried into his shoulder. "And what about Noelle? Do you think she'll be alright?" Bernie asked.

"OMG! I forgot all about her. She was fast asleep when I left." Anita paled. "I don't think it's wise for us to go back there tonight unless the police come with us."

He was dialling as she spoke. "I've got a recorded message. They are attending a motor vehicle accident." He shook his head. "They say to call the police at Plover Point if it's an emergency." He re-dialled and listened. "Hellfire. I've got the same recorded message from Plover Point police. It must have been a pile up on the highway. What do we do now?"

Anita looked stricken. "I can't go back there tonight in the dark. I'm sure everything is fine. The bang I heard could have been anything … a lamp falling over, or a door slamming." She hugged Bernie so tightly he had trouble taking in a deep breath.

"Maybe things will look better in the light of day. If you feel up to it, we can check in on Noelle tomorrow." He was worried about her little sister but agreed in order to soothe Anita's nerves. Intervening in a domestic dispute could be dangerous. There wasn't much they could do without the police present at any rate.

"I'll never forgive myself if something happened to her," Anita whispered, distraught.

"I'm sure she'll be safe enough tucked into bed." Bernie said the words but frowned as if his heart said something else. "Talking about getting tucked into bed, it's very late and you're shivering. We could both use some sleep." Leading her to his bedroom, he was true to his word. Tucked in and cuddled, she fell fast asleep, secure under his protection.

Chapter Forty-One

The next morning, Bernie was preparing the cash register for opening Light Up while Anita washed the breakfast dishes. The aroma of bacon and maple syrup waffles wafted through the shop from the residence out the back. Daydreaming about the night before, he was caught by surprise when pounding started at the front door. "Bernie? Open up!" a man shouted.

Recognising the voice, he rushed to unlock it. "Come in. What's going on, mate?" He ushered Lance inside.

Hearing the commotion, Anita stepped into the room holding a dishcloth. Lance was too overcome with concern to notice Anita wearing an off the shoulder pirate shirt, a brocade corset, and herringbone breeches taken off the shop's Steampunk clothing racks and completely out of character to her usual dress style, nor Bernie's goofy smile as if bewildered at his good fortune finding his girlfriend wandering around in the morning after what was clearly a night of canoodling. Nothing about this scenario struck Lance as out of place.

"Have you seen Paisley?" he asked, forgoing niceties and focusing on only one thing after pushing through the door breathless in a state of panic.

"She's been incommunicado since the meeting," Anita answered looking puzzled at his frame of mind.

To sound reassuring, Bernie added, "After all that slagging, she needed time out."

"We've been giving her space," Anita added.

"I know all that but she's not been at home and she hasn't been returning my text messages for days. I haven't been worried until … It's just …" Lance stopped and instead of explaining opened his phone and scrolled through a few screens. "Have you seen this? It pinged on my phone early this morning." All three huddled around the phone.

Bernie reacted first. "Hellfire, man. She'll be devastated."

As if she couldn't believe her eyes, Anita read out another social media comment, a new one posted from Thayne:

> Not bad enough stealing our food. Now our
> dog is missing, too.

"She wouldn't steal Missy, would she?" Anita asked. "Like some sort of revenge on Monique? You know, like, she's already been accused of stealing, so one more thing won't matter?"

"Don't be a buffoon. Paisley loved that dog but she wouldn't do anything that stupid even if she believed Monique didn't deserve Missy."

Lance cut in. "It's not about whether Paisley's taken the dog! It's about how she'll react knowing Missy is gone. This could be her breaking point. I'm afraid she'll confront Monique —"

"— and that would not end well," Bernie completed the thought. "By the Eternal, we have to sort things out with Thayne and Monique once and for all. They have to stop harassing Paisley already. Enough is enough."

"At least find out how they explain the dog going missing," Lance remarked.

"OMG. I want to check on Noelle," Anita said. "We'd better go asap. While you grab your car keys, Bernie, I'll lock the cash register for you."

Lance shuffled his feet with excess energy wanting to do something and not just stand around. The front door opened with a gush of cool air. Paisley walked in looking pale and lost. She glanced at Anita working behind the counter dressed like a Steampunk girl and her face froze. Bernie dashed from out the back, keys in hand, and stopped dead seeing Paisley standing stiff as a statue.

Lance was first to respond. "Thank the gods, Paisley, you're here. We've been so worried." He hugged her rigid body trying to imbue warmth and life into it. "Have you seen the comment about Missy? Stupid question. That's why you are here." He was rambling, not sure how to read her mood.

"I came to say farewell. I'm moving away." Paisley glared at Bernie. "But I guess no one cares." She stared up and down at Anita dressed in Steampunk standing at Light Up's cash register and winced as if in pain. "I see Anita's replaced me. Funny how quickly she's moved in and started working for you. That was fast pushing me out of the way, even for a Swan." In the background,

Anita flinched from the hurtful jab, not understanding what Paisley was on about.

Bernie got the message even if Anita didn't have a clue. Arriving and taking things out of context, all Paisley saw was his new girlfriend at the cash register 'working' in a position that should have been hers. From the beginning when he took over as owner of Light Up, he'd made a standing promise to Paisley that as soon as he could afford it, there'd be a job here for her. His BFF, having lost two jobs in twenty four hours, was understandably ultra-sensitive about the motives of any member of the Swan family under the circumstances and had jumped to the wrong conclusion. Unfortunately, there wasn't time for a long drawn out explanation, so he kept things simple.

"She's here because of all the crap going down at Convict Crust."

"Tell me about it," Paisley sneered. "No one answered when I drove there half an hour ago. In fact, the place looked deserted. There's a For Sale sign in the window. But I guess that's not news to you." She stared at Anita with disgust. "Missy's gone. The gate was left open."

Anita blanched as if she was about to faint. "Shit. Do you think they've done a runner so soon?" She looked to Bernie who affected a carefully constructed neutral expression. A prescient shiver of doom, something much worse than Monique doing a runner, caused her to stand at this spot and not want to move from Light Up. All her instincts screamed to stay put if she wanted to continue a normal life blissfully uninformed, and safe.

Disregarding the undercurrents in the room, Lance became a voice of reason. "What are we waiting for? If we want to find out what's happened, we need to get going." He grabbed Paisley's hand and pulled her with them as they all piled into Bernie's SUV. "We'll talk later about your moving away, Steampunk Girl."

Paisley didn't want to be in the car with Anita and Bernie. As far as she was concerned, they were both traitors, not friends. It was bad enough what Bernie had done to her at the meeting; how easily he was now replacing her for his girlfriend, forgetting all the promises he'd made. She couldn't really blame Anita for moving in on the dude. She was acting out of her best interests – with a step mother and role model like Monique what else could one expect? On the other hand, in fairness, Paisley could see the girl truly cared about her BFF and the feelings were mutual.

She knew this day would come when *three's a crowd*. Today happened to be the day to bow out, move on.

There wasn't any point returning to Convict Crust. Missy wasn't there. She'd searched the Town Common, hoping for a déjà vu moment but life did not repeat itself. The dog was well and truly gone. She didn't care if Monique and Thayne had done a runner, absconded from paying their local suppliers, and reneged on the Steam Fest catering contract. None of those issues were her problem now that she was leaving Lower Teasel, the Steampunk Club, and her friends behind forever.

In the back seat, Lance leaned in to whisper in Paisley's ear. "Where have you been? I tried texting but they bounced back. When I found out about Missy, I was so worried. You love that dog."

"I've been camping out at Sapphire Creek, thinking about stuff. I came back today to say goodbye and tell Bernie of my decision to move to Plover Point to start again. Everyone hates me here in Lower Teasel ... so ..."

"No. No. No. Things will change. Trust me. I've worked out a way to put things right. You are going to love it. You'll see there's no need to continue to feel cut about what others think – or to worry about moving anywhere!"

"Sure, right. Well for now, the main thing is to find Missy." Paisley easily dismissed Lance's offer of help. She couldn't see how any one person could change a whole village's opinion of her. It was kind of heroic of him to try. And very sweet. Any romantic notions had to be put on the back burner. They had to focus on finding Missy.

Bernie drove the SUV into Convict Crust's driveway and parked in front of the shed. They'd all seen the 'For Sale' sign in the window listed with the distinctive teal and gold branding of Eden Isle Real Estate Co., a company specialising in expensive, boutique sales to mainlanders. Monique had been busy to organise this so quickly.

Anita leaped out of the car and ran across the patio to the back door. Bernie called after her to wait 'just in case'. It was decided to go in together. The place had a deserted quality and yet something felt off.

Entering the kitchen, Paisley first registered the cold and then the smell of bleach. From the first day she worked here, the kitchen was always toasty warm and smelled of baked bread and sourdough starter. It was always in organised chaos, with the long table covered in flour dust and rolled pastry, sandwich ingredients, plastic cartons, and baking tins. Now it was empty and sterile. Anita flitted around opening cupboards and checking the walk-in pantry, finding bare shelves. 'Where's it all gone?' she kept asking. The wood fired oven had been cleaned of wood ash. The baking paddle leaned against a wall. Likewise, chairs in the dining area were stacked on tables which were pushed into the corner; the fridge and display counters emptied and wiped clean. The cappuccino machine sparkled from a recent clean and polish.

Bernie and Lance gave each other meaningful looks. Anita acted as if reality hadn't caught up with what her eyes were seeing. Keying in the security code, she entered the residence. At first it appeared nothing had changed. Furniture was in place; curtains closed; the scent of polish and cleaning product hung in the air. "MM? Noelle?" Anita called, more hope than common sense.

"Is there a note or anything left for you?" Lance asked. Each of them scanned the living room but found nothing left of a personal nature.

"Let's check out Noelle's room. I'll go with you," Bernie said to Anita. Same story there: empty drawers and bare clothes hangers in the wardrobe, floors vacuumed, shelves dusted. The bed looked to be made up with a quilt and comforter set on top of the mattress, but on closer inspection, the sheets and blankets underneath had been removed. Left to give the appearance of a lived-in home for potential buyers but in reality, it was more like a bakery in a ghost town.

Suddenly Anita gasped. "My room," she said, running off to see what was left of her stuff. Making an escape the night before, she'd left most of her precious belongings behind. Paisley heard her crying.

She and Lance hurried to see what had happened. Much like Noelle's room, it was clean and dust-free; the bed was covered in a bedspread but all blankets and quilts had been removed. Likewise, they watched Anita opening drawers and wardrobe doors to find them emptied. Two cardboard boxes marked with her name sat in the middle of the floor.

"They knew I'd be back, but didn't leave a note," Anita whispered in shock. "They just left me." Overcoming inner resentment about the vagaries of her own life, Paisley reached out to gather Anita in a comforting hug. Bernie and Lance hefted the boxes onto broad shoulders and left to pack them in the boot of Bernie's car. There was not much else to see within the residence.

With sudden resolve, Anita whipped out her phone and punched the speed dial. It rang out. She tried again with another number. It rang out. "MM isn't answering the phone. Neither is Noelle," she said slumping in anguish. "I'm all alone."

"Not even remotely true. You have us," Paisley said. She slowly walked a weeping Anita through the residence and out the kitchen door. Lance met them at the patio. "Come and see the back yard," he said.

Bernie was poking around what used to be the compost trench. "It's been completely filled in and tamped down," he stated.

Grabbing a shovel from the shed, he dug out a couple shovelfuls of dirt. A spray of white powder flung into the air. "Flour," he announced. Digging in another shovel load, the sound of metal hitting tins resonated across the garden. "Just as I thought. All the kitchen supplies have been buried in the pit." He tossed the dirt back into the holes and packed it down with the back of the shovel. Conscientiously, he returned the shovel to the shed.

"What a waste," Paisley noted.

"You could say they were thorough in the clean up despite it being a remarkably quick job," Lance commented. "Such a long and deep trench helped their efforts."

"Weird. All four of them must have pitched in," Bernie noted.

"Couldn't get away quick enough," Paisley said.

Anita looked about to collapse. Bernie came up and placed an arm around her shoulders. "This is the fastest get away I've ever seen MM carry out," she whispered in awe. "I know she could be secretive, but this takes the prize." There was a collective pause as each considered the circumstances and consequences of Monique's runner. Anita started to murmur over and over *'what am I going to do now?'*

Paisley took control. "You are not to worry. Bernie and his family will take care of you. You can stay at Bernie's for as long as you need. Isn't that right, Bernie?"

"By the Eternal. Of course." Bernie hugged her tight. "It's going to be alright. I'll take care of you. My whole family will take care of you."

Chapter Forty-Two

Back at Light Up, Bernie and Lance deposited Anita's two boxes of what constituted all of her belongings onto the floor of the shop's single bedroom. She sat on the bed lost in a daze. Bernie suggested making everyone a cup of tea and disappeared into the kitchen clanking dishes.

Lance offered to order pizzas for lunch. Anita was unresponsive. Bernie gave him both their preferences and then Lance walked out to the shop floor where Paisley shuffled about looking like the odd one out. He got it. She was feeling ultra-sensitive about rejection given what Monique had done. She wasn't sure about her place within this friends' group.

But he was here for her. She had to know that and start trusting him. There was no way he was going to let her disappear out of his life without a serious conversation first. But rather than lecture, he asked if she could drive him to Stubblefield Pizzas. Carrying pizzas on the back of his motorcycle was not much fun, he quipped, and received a wan smile in return.

"Actually, I was hoping to get you alone because I need to discuss my plan to make Steam Fest the best ever. It's an awesome idea and my mum agrees. But it all depends on you. I need your approval," he said. Before she could open her mouth to argue, he barrelled on. "Don't say you're not part of the festival any more – or that you don't care, because I know you. You care about Lower Teasel and the Steampunk Club is still yours and Bernie's, even if things have gone to shit temporarily."

Paisley shrugged, not arguing but not building up any enthusiasm either.

"You know what? Instead of trying to explain anything right now, let's just get the food and eat. Then, this afternoon I'm going to take you to Whaler's Cove to meet my mum."

"Rolla would never make it there," Paisley said this matter-of-factly as if that decided the matter.

"I know. You're going for the ride of your life on the back of my Harley."

Paisley arrived at Lance's home in Whaler's Cove with a throat hoarse from screaming in terror and exhilaration throughout the whole bike ride. She'd never experienced anything like it. Clinging to the back of Lance's leather jacket for the best part of two hours was only half the thrill. The roar of the engine, holding on for dear life as they flew around curves in the road, the wind on her face – the full force of the sense of freedom – it was the ultimate. At the end, she considered trading in Rolla for a motorcycle as traitorous as that sounded. That's how fantastic the ride was for her.

Unfortunately, standing at Lance's front door with the thought she was about to meet his mother, the famous Skye Mandala – her hero – brought her back to earth with the speed of a Tesla coil.

"Mum said to take you around to her studio before we sit down for afternoon tea. She wants to give you the tour."

"By the Eternal," an awestruck Paisley managed to say. Like walking through a dream, she was shaking hands with a smiling Skye Mandala and being shown process design books and unfinished pieces of sculptures in a welder's workshop with running commentary on her choices of materials and the technical difficulties with cutting and welding and joining various metals and shapes.

On this day, Skye Mandala's appearance was very different from the television version when opening one of her exhibitions or unveiling a sculpture in a public square. On those occasions she dressed in flowing frocks in vivid colours, high heeled boots and dramatic jewellery, with her hair wrapped in velvet hairbands. Today long, strong legs fitted snugly into a pair of old jeans, a plain tee shirt exposed muscled arms, and steel cap work boots replaced high heels. Her ghost white hair was short and styled in a pixie cut, like Alice from the Twilight movie. No airs or graces of a celebrity; simply the artist in residence.

Skye had a way of making her feel welcome. Paisley relaxed into the dream.

At one point, Lance nudged her out of reverie when his mother had asked a question about Paisley's own jewellery design. "Steampunk fascinates me – how it repurposes old timepieces, chains, cogs and mechanical, industrial ugliness into an organic artform. Very much a miniature version of what I do on a larger than life scale," she prompted.

Although humbled by the thought that *Skye Mandala* was in the least interested in her amateurish jewellery designs, she couldn't help but share her passionate goal to one day make a living off her work. They discussed composition and selection of objects. Skye asked insightful questions, respecting Paisley's artistic choices.

"I'm not a coggler who takes a piece of jewellery and applies cogs and clockwork mechanisms onto it. I create original works of art. This makes me an artificer within the Guild of Prima Cogglers." Working up the courage, Paisley opened photos of some of her favourite pieces saved on her phone to show Skye who made gestures and noises appropriate enough to sound impressed. *My life is complete*, Paisley sighed with happiness.

She beamed a hundred watt smile towards Lance to show appreciation for arranging this meeting. He in turn gave his mother a sign to indicate she was to move on to the real purpose of their visit. Skye winked conspiratorially.

"I think we should sit down to enjoy a nice cup of tea and some bikkies," she suggested. "Lance, why don't you take Paisley over to the back porch while I get our afternoon tea ready. You can start to discuss your awesome plan for the Steam Fest. I won't be long."

Lance was brimming with excitement. Dusting off leaves from the wood and wrought iron table, he sat opposite Paisley and grabbed both her hands in his. "I've been thinking about how to win back the support of Lower Teasel businesses for the Steam Fest Challenge after all the damage caused by Monique and Thayne. I spoke to mum and she's completely on board with my idea. But now it's up to you, whether or not you agree. I so want you to say 'yes'."

"What's all this?" she asked, suspicious but smiling at the idea of a surprise coming.

Lance took in a deep breath and plunged in. "Mum wants to create a Steampunk sculpture for Steam Fest to be auctioned off after the challenge with proceeds going to the Street Kids Appeal. But that's not the best part! She wants the sculpture to be a collaboration with you!"

"With me?" Paisley couldn't have heard him correctly.

"You know how she loves to support artists on the island, particularly young ones new to the art world. Steam Fest is perfect because it's a community event that brings tourist dollars to local businesses and raises money for charity. Just the kind of thing mum loves to get involved in."

Paisley's gaze wandered past the porch and across to the Mandala's backyard. It wasn't what one would describe as a garden, more a gravelled courtyard. Near to Skye's studio was a pile of random rusted metal items ranging from small things such as buckets filled with bolts, nuts, screws; old hammers and wrenches, wire coils, bike chains; up to large sheets of iron and even an ancient tractor with missing tires and cracked windows out in the open exposed to the elements. If she didn't know better, the area could easily be mistaken for a junkyard. In the centre of the courtyard, a wood stump took pride of place, surrounded by scattered wood chips. Although there wasn't a chainsaw to be seen, she knew this was Lance's father, Monroe Mandala's workspace where he sculpted out of wood. Lance had explained his dad had his own shed to store his tools of trade.

A tinkling of china forewarned that Skye had returned with a heavy tray of pots and cups and biscuits. Lance jumped up to take the load and place it on the table. Immediately, she asked, "Is Paisley happy with the plan? I'm thinking of a small sculpture, for an individual garden or patio – not one of my huge installations that go in public parks and town squares. That's why I need your help with the design. You work with small, detailed pieces, something that I'm not used to doing. Together we can make something special."

Paisley was dumbstruck. Any association with Skye Mandala would be like a gold card. "I don't know what to …"

"If you're happy with Lance's idea, I'd like to start straight away at fleshing out the initial sculpture form. There're not many days before the festival. Once we agree on a design, then we can work on all the parts needed and how to put them together. What do you say? It would be my pleasure," Skye said encouragingly.

A sketch pad and pencils magically appeared on the table. They began to discuss some ideas in line with this year's Steam Fest theme. Lance contributed suggestions. Soon Paisley was caught up in the artistic enthusiasm around the table and began to fully participate. Two hours and two pots of tea disappeared in a flash, lost in a creative zone that artists know defies the laws of physics.

"That's it! We have our design," Skye announced. All three gazed at the drawing with satisfied smiles.

"It's perfect," Paisley agreed. "Now the work begins."

"One suggestion is to bolt and screw joints rather than soldering. Paisley, with your skills in intricate details using clockwork mechanisms, cogs and wheels, I'd like you to focus on the head. I can start on the larger parts of the body."

Lance looked at his mother. "It's getting late. I was wondering if it would be okay for Paisley to stay with us while you both work on the sculpture? Like you said, there's a lot to do before the festival."

"Not a problem for me. Paisley can have the guest room. I can lend you some pyjamas for tonight. Tomorrow you and Lance can go back to Lower Teasel and bring back some clothes and your tool box."

"What do you say, Paisley?" Lance looked at her with hope and adoration.

"I say power to the Eternal Clock Maker."

Chapter Forty-Three

Lance and Paisley held their breaths and waited as Skye Mandala walked around the rusted sculpture of welded, riveted, and screwed scrap metal for a final inspection. It had been a rushed job, not helped timewise by Paisley's amateur assistance. She'd soldered before, but welding was next level. As a mentor, Skye possessed Zen-like patience coupled with an insistence on technical precision. Working with an expert, Paisley began to appreciate how much skill and dedication it took to become an artistic luminary. The woman was awesome.

Unashamedly, Paisley worshipped at her feet with all the reverence of an initiate towards a master. Resolved to dedicate the hours of practice required to achieve even a fraction of Skye Mandala's talent, Paisley vowed to spend the rest of her life trying to emulate this woman through her own Steampunk jewellery designs.

Turning to face Lance, she smiled shakily and held up crossed fingers. In return, his eyes shone bright with pride. She hoped some of that was meant for her and not reserved all for his mother.

Bedamned. Skye Mandala was Lance's mother. Too much to think about with all the hype around Steam Fest: collaborating in creating the sculpture, redeeming her reputation in Lower Teasel through association with an Isle icon, and getting back in the good books with the Steampunk Club members by auctioning off the sculpture for a huge amount of money, attracting masses of tourists and thereby saving the day. Lance was another of her heroes after making all this possible. She owed him big time. In fact, if thinking too deeply about all of this, she probably loved him. In terms of *the future* it was best not to go there.

Despite all the awe and worship going around, Paisley glanced at her watch surreptitiously. The morning was getting on. It was a two hour drive to Lower Teasel Showgrounds. Not that the Steampunk organising committee would dare criticise them for arriving late, Skye being the star attraction. But Paisley was anxious, wanting to get it over and done with. The suspense was getting to her.

Being a perfectionist, Skye would not allow delivery until absolutely satisfied. Peering closely at the statue as if holding up an imaginary magnifying glass, she prodded an index finger at its screws and rivets to ensure stability and blew puffs of air at any remains of filing dust caught between mechanical parts. Finally, producing a small hammer from her pocket, she gently whacked one corner on the rectangular name plate that was raised a fraction to flatten and secure its attachment to a heavy iron base.

Paisley's heart throbbed in her throat seeing her name next to Skye's embossed in black on the name plate's oxidising copper. Unlike other moments in her life where she felt life was about to change for the better, this time she knew without a doubt her credibility as an artist – after the Skye Mandala association –

would be firmly established. This was a game changer. She would no longer consider her craft a 'hobby'. From now on, it meant business. It was up to her to rise to the occasion and 'join' the Artificers of the Guild as a maker.

Skye straightened and a frown lifted from her forehead. "Righto, I'm happy with it. Are you happy with it, Paisley?" she asked, as if it was perfectly natural to ask her opinion as the co-creator. She even waited for her response, *so* respectfully.

"By the Eternal, absolutely," Paisley gushed.

"Then, I guess, we're good to go. We'd better pack it up and get going. Fashionably late is one thing but we don't want to appear arrogant and rude by keeping them waiting too long."

Lance's dad, Monroe, arrived with a roll of bubble wrap and tape. Between the two, the sculpture was wrapped and ready in a few minutes. Clearly, they'd worked together before on this type of job. The piece was heavy but Lance easily carried it to the back of Skye's van, positioned it on a mound of old blankets and secured it with straps to keep it from moving around. Monroe stowed his chainsaw in the back as well. He was a regular at rural shows and fairs, a popular drawcard demonstrating his death-defying wood sculpting technique. The Steam Fest organisers had booked him months ago. His dad's involvement in the festival was the inspiration behind Lance asking his mother to help out Paisley.

Skye insisted Paisley accompany their sculpture all the way to the Lower Teasel Showgrounds as a rite of passage. Bruiser, her youngest son, pleaded to ride on the back of the Harley with Lance. After some discussion about being careful, Skye agreed as long as he wore a helmet and didn't muck around. Monroe and Paisley piled into the front seat of the van with Skye as the driver.

The trip to Lower Teasel was an experience in itself. Paisley started off feeling slightly queasy from nerves and Skye's driving didn't help. She and her son shared a common love of taking mountain curves fast and fearless, albeit skilfully, even if the van was less agile than a motorbike and therefore way less exhilarating. Sitting in the middle between Monroe and Skye meant she couldn't roll down the window to feel the force of the wind on her face unlike on Lance's bike. And she felt a need to be polite next to Skye and therefore sensibly suppressed the screams threatening to bubble up every time the van rounded a curve on two wheels. When they parked at the Showgrounds, she was drained of energy from shot nerves.

Bernie and Anita were there to meet them. Their excitement was palpable. The couple were dressed in matching top hats with feather plumes and coat tails accessorised with an over the top array of dangling pocket watches, braces holding up herringbone trousers, plus monocles. Anita's stage makeup glittered with a butterfly design around her eyes and complimented the green fringe poking out from under the brim of her top hat. Bernie wore a silk cravat in shiny greens and golds.

"Salutations from the Alchemist's Sanctum!" Bernie greeted, paying homage to both sculptors.

Paisley replied with their ritual response. "Greetings from the Artificers Guild of Prima Cogglers." She'd come dressed in her go-to Amelia Earhart leather jodhpurs, bomber jacket, aviation cap and goggles, with killer boots crisscrossed with buckles.

Her attention diverted to the sounds of steam engines hissing and tractors hooting their whistles, kids running around squealing with joy, the aromas of corn dogs frying in hot oil, popcorn and fairy floss wafting from a line of food stalls, and best of all, large crowds of characters strolling around in Steampunk costumes.

"Great scott! This is awesome!" Bruiser exclaimed behind her.

Bernie snorted, equally surprised but for different reasons. Addressing Paisley, he said, "By the Eternal, your nemesis Marianne came good after all. When she realised Convict Crust was a no show, she got some market food vans to fill in at the last minute. Village Spice and the CWA are in the main pavilion where there are tables and chairs, so the food vans are happy with the more upmarket placement within the showgrounds."

"Best of all, she surprised us by using her connections at the shire council to secure the club a grant for marketing at the last minute. Got us a couple advertisements on the TV where we could promote the art auction," Anita explained.

Paisley was too relieved to be jealous of her rival's stunning success at organising and troubleshooting at the final hour. This only went to prove no one was indispensable, not even one of the Club's founders, she noted ruefully. In the distance, she thought she saw Eddy and Heath sauntering through the showgrounds holding onto colourful balloons.

A bit disappointing that they weren't wearing Steampunk gear, but at least they showed up. She also recognised the young, exhausted mother who came to the bakery each Thursday with a screaming baby, pushing a pram fancied up to look Victorian, wearing a black frock with a pleated bodice, a black cap with lace and ties, and face makeup resembling a zombie version of a nanny out of a Sherlock Holmes film. Her support was an awesome surprise. She wondered if a Steampunk baby would be included in the final count.

Anita was eager to share more success stories. "I've started counting Steampunk costumes and I'm pretty sure we've almost reached a record. By this afternoon when we do the official count, I reckon we'll make the numbers."

"It's largely due to the art auction. That stirred up masses of interest on social media. Funny how your reputation did a one eighty suddenly, once people saw you were being supported by the island's celebrity artist." Bernie smirked.

Skye waited with Monroe next to the van, not wanting to interfere with the reunion, sensing it was an important milestone in the lead up to this event. Taking fashion advice from Paisley on what was suitable for the occasion, she shunned the usual soft flowing colourful dresses the public expected of Skye Mandala 'the artist' and instead wore her work gear: a heavy leather welder's apron over a linen shirt with rolled up sleeves, worn jeans and steel cap boots, assured her look was sufficiently old industrial-blacksmith for the day. To be on the safe side, she smeared black soot across her cheeks and pulled on a brown leather cap with goggles over her pixie white hair to give the impression of arriving straight from the forge.

Paisley waved at Skye, Monroe and Bruiser to come and meet her friends. Bernie and Anita looked awestruck when they shook hands. This gave her a momentary twinge of self importance – and vindication. She had connections. She wasn't that foster kid from Stubblefield any more. She was somebody recognised by somebody. She belonged to this festival regardless of what her club members thought.

Lance stood holding the bubble wrapped parcel. "Where do you want this?" he grunted. It was heavy.

"The Main Pavilion where the auction will be held," Bernie said. He led the way and they traipsed along with Lance hugging the sculpture. Skye locked the back of the van, kissed her husband, and ran to catch up with Lance. Bruiser followed his dad.

Paisley watched a rakish Monroe hitch up the chainsaw and wander in the direction of the demonstration ring mumbling about checking out the set up. He'd dressed in the spirit of the day in Western Steampunk, wearing a red neckcloth under a cowboy shirt, leather holsters with revolvers, moleskin breeches, and knee high boots with spurs. Bruiser dressed to match. Monroe's chainsaw was decorated with cogs and clockwork mechanisms.

Upon entering the Main Pavilion, Marianne in her cutesy Alice in Wonderland attire ran across the hall to greet them. "Over here, please, on this stand." She motioned towards a stage with a lectern, a large canvas screen and a cement 'Grecian' column. "This is so exciting."

Paisley suppressed a laugh, imagining the contemporary scrap metal sculpture being displayed on such an inappropriate stand. Although she took back her ingratitude when Lance and Skye unwrapped the art work and Marianne gasped in delight. "Why it's a Steampunk dog! How original using bent tines from a pitch fork for a ribcage! I love it," she gushed.

"That's why we named the piece 'Steampunk Stray'," Skye remarked. "The design was Paisley's and we worked on it together."

"Of course. Now I see. How appropriate for the Street Kids Appeal." Marianne was nothing but professional. All credit to her aplomb.

Skye fussed about arranging the sculpture to its best advantage. Paisley stood by 'helping'. While that was happening, Marianne went through the schedule of events. A loudspeaker would draw in the crowd to the pavilion and the Guinness Book of Records count would happen first. As costumed people came through the door, they'd be given a number. The event was time limited so the doors would close when the clock struck twelve. The last person to arrive would hold up their card to indicate the final total. She looked quite pleased at her plan. Reluctantly, Paisley admitted it was more brilliant than what she'd intended to do, which was to hold the event outdoors on the oval for everyone to watch a simple headcount.

Marianne explained that after the event was adjudicated by the officials from the Guinness Book organisation and the result verified, the doors would re-open ready for those wanting to bid at the Art Auction. The interest in Skye Mandala's small sculpture was unprecedented. Already, they'd accepted closed bids in writing from businesses that were unable to attend and registrations for interstate telephone bidding.

"Sight unseen? In collaboration with an unknown artist?" Anita asked.

"That's how cool my mum's reputation is," Lance bragged.

"It's a first working with another artist and to such a small scale which means the price will fall more in the realm of individual collectors and not only municipalities and corporations with deep pockets," Skye reasoned. "I suspect this is why all the interest. And of course, it's for a charitable cause which makes people more generous."

Marianne scrolled down on what looked like a 'To Do List' on her phone. "It looks like you're settled. I'd better go around and check on the rest of our sponsors, make sure they're happy and sort out any last-minute issues, before the count. See you later." She swished off in a whirl of white petticoats and striped stockings.

The rest of the day passed in a hectic blur of monumental success. The Steampunk crowd not only passed the Guinness Book of Records' challenge of becoming the largest gathering of costumes at a single event in Australia; they surpassed the record for New Zealand as well which was an achievement. Marianne stood up to the podium to accept the accolades which, on balance, Paisley thought was fair enough, given the young woman only had three weeks to rescue the event from disaster. She deserved the praise. Graciously, in Marianne's speech she credited Paisley for the original idea and for making it a charitable event with donations going to the Street Kids Appeal.

Apparently, it was okay to mention Paisley by name again in public. Bernie was right in saying that Lower Teasel's residents had memory loss around the abusive posts and bullying gossip, and with all forgiven, embraced their Steampunk Stray back into the community.

Then it was time for the art auction. A local antiques dealer from Plover Point, Mr Bradley, conducted the show starting with a rundown of Skye Mandala's academic qualifications, art awards and commendations, features in national and international magazines and exhibitions, and summing up with a slide show displaying a selection of her sculptures in various Eden Isle art galleries, mentioning in passing the estimated value of each in the current market and broadly hinting at these being an intelligent investment. He continued to stir up the crowd's excitement by describing in fine aesthetic detail the merits of the Mandala-Wildmoor 'Steampunk Stray' sculpture. After his introduction, people were begging to throw money at it.

In the end, the final bid was won by a private collector on the Mainland through a telephone bid. Spontaneous clapping broke out when Mr Bradley confirmed the huge amount of money for which the sculpture sold. Skye pulled Paisley up to the podium, grabbed her hand and lifted their arms to the roof in a signal of success, accompanied by ear shattering applause and more cheering.

The whole auction was filmed by Meridian News for the evening program. Their journalist, Mariel McGuirk, cornered Skye and Paisley as they stepped from the podium and thrust a microphone at their faces. "Ms Mandala, congratulations on setting a new standard for your art."

Skye smiled into the camera, used to giving impromptu interviews. "Today has been such a lot of fun and I am delighted that our sculpture sold for a respectable amount. This was a first for me, working on a small piece and I relied heavily on the expertise and skills of Paisley Wildmoor in order to design and complete the sculpture. Paisley deserves equal credit for today's success. She is truly a talented artist."

Mariel turned to Paisley for a comment. "Working with Skye has been the biggest thrill of my life. Equal only to the large donation the Steampunk Club will now be donating to the Street Kids Appeal. I hope we will collaborate again sometime in the future for a similar cause."

Skye leaned into the microphone. "I look forward to it, Paisley. Apart from creating art, my joy is supporting community arts and mentoring up and coming local artists." At that, Mariel signalled the cameraman to cut. She thanked them and wandered off to see what else was of interest at Steam Fest.

As soon as the journalist and cameraman left, Paisley and Skye were surrounded by Bernie, Anita and Lance hugging and congratulating them. Then Adam appeared out of thin air and was hugging her, too. Marianne patted her on the shoulder, not yet admitting they could be friends. Nonetheless, it was a heady experience.

Waiting in the wings was the club's Mad Hatter. *Oh, god, what does he want?* Paisley thought with trepidation.

When released from all the hugging, the man approached. Bernie stiffened and Lance stood guard expecting a scene.

"I wanted to congratulate you on the success of the art auction. It raised a phenomenal amount of money for our charity. I don't know how you managed to convince Skye Mandala to participate but she clearly is one of your biggest supporters. Thanks to you, this year's festival is the best yet." His delivery was stiff and formal.

Paisley gave him a double whammy look and didn't acknowledge the compliment.

Clearing his throat, he looked chastened. "I'm sorry to have doubted your credibility at the last meeting. In real life, I own the newsagent in Lower Teasel. My accountant, Simon Shepley, set me straight about Mrs Swan."

For some reason, Paisley felt compelled to abide by Monique's code of 'what's said in the bakery, stays in the bakery'. When she didn't indicate knowing Simon, he explained. "He dated the woman and got caught up in her duplicity. Found out too late she bought the bakery with money stolen from her husband's business account. Simon lost not only his pride and his sanity temporarily but also his relationship with his partner, Joan. And a lot of money. When he tried to get it back, Mrs Swan threatened to ruin his reputation with his clients and in the community. That husband of hers was intense, too. Simon decided it was too dangerous pushing the issue. He let it go."

Paisley wished to hold on to the feeling of being top of the world and the last thing she needed was to be reminded of the skulduggery of Monique's smear campaign, not to mention being booted off as Club Secretary. Magnanimously, she accepted Mad Hatter's apology, wanting him to get on with it and leave.

"Yeah, okay; no hard feelings. It all worked out in the end. Marianne made a leviathan of a Club Secretary – better than me, in fact. She pulled off what looked like a steam train wreck in the making and turned things around to attract this massive crowd. So, you know what? I'm happy she's our Secretary and festival trouble shooter. It's only right to hand over the job to an enthusiastic member." She gave a wan smile to Marianne to prove the point.

Lance squeezed her hand. Bernie looked proud of her. Adam looked doubtful. She wanted to get away and get fresh air.

Mad Hatter wasn't easy to get rid of, however. He had more to say. "I feel bad about what happened. Our club members have a lot to make up to you. At our next meeting I wanted to suggest a motion to vote you into a new position – as the club's 'Artificer Liaison'. If you don't mind?"

"Sure, no worries," she replied. He looked so chastened and hopeful, Paisley agreed to his proposal, even if she didn't have a clue what 'liaison' in the title meant. That could all be worked out on another day.

Bernie decided to go for it. "By the Eternal, that's a brazen idea, dude."

"I'll include it in the agenda under New Business," Marianne said, getting in on the act and sealing the deal.

Lance and Anita grinned like idiots. Paisley was back in the fold. Steampunk Club was one happy family again.

Skye glanced at her watch and signalled to Lance. Suddenly anxious, he began to pull Paisley away. "We've got to go. Dad's demo is about to happen." As they raced across to the other side of the showgrounds with Skye keeping pace, a loudspeaker announced Monroe Mandala's chainsaw spectacular was scheduled in Area Four in five minutes.

Nearing the roped off arena, Skye pushed through the rows of on-lookers. Cowboy music piped through the loudspeaker. One handedly Monroe held a chainsaw above his head to the cheers of the crowd. Paisley breathed a sigh of relief; they'd arrived at the start. Bruiser saw them and waved them over to reserved seats.

In his element and a showman at heart, Bruiser's dad played to the audience. He began a slow walk around a rough chunk of log stuck in the middle of the stage. After a thorough inspection, he rubbed his chin deep in thought, perplexed about what to do with it. Then, tapping his head as if experiencing a lightbulb moment, he pulled down his safety goggles and pulled the start up chain. With an almighty roar, the chainsaw came to life.

The crowd grew silent. The volume of the music pumped up. Wood chips went flying through the air.

… *Roll-um, roll-um … raw-hide!* blasted across the stage.

Making her way to a seat next to Lance and Bruiser, Paisley stopped short, caught by surprise. "Hellfire, the Rawhide song," she laughed.

"I know, right. It's dad's favourite song when he's creating," Bruiser said proudly.

Chapter Forty-Four

Two months later ...

With a secret smile, Bernie observed Paisley flourish a feather duster over shelves of Light Up's new range of Steampunk accessories exhibited in the window. This was the second time in the last hour she had fussed with the displays which demonstrated an obsession with getting everything just right. Since the success of Steam Fest and her collaboration with Skye Mandala, it seemed everyone wanted a piece of Paisley's collection. *'Wildmoor Embellishments'*, her start-up business in the corner of Bernie's shop, proved to be her dream come true.

Underneath the signage sparkled Paisley's latest Steampunk range of jewelled phone cases, elaborate, old worldly hair ornaments, lengths of necklace chains hung with repurposed copper buttons, mother of pearl bling, and tiny clockwork mechanisms, and wide corset belts with straps, buckles and lace. She'd also created a series of sculpture desk ornaments in the shape of Alice in Wonderland-style mechanical snails. With Bernie's business support, it seemed her ideas were limited only by the amount of hours in the day available.

The feather plumed duster danced through the air like a silent orchestral conductor spinning music out of thin air. Paisley was happier than he'd ever seen her. Her Wildmoor look mimicked a conservative shopkeeper from the late 1800's: a brown frock coat in tweed, trousers to match, a worsted waistcoat dangling numerous pocket watches, and a man's shirt as white as her goth face make-up. She'd taken to wearing gold wired spectacles accentuating heavy black kohl lined eyes. A halo of cherry red braids on top of her head contrasted with the minimalist Steampunk brown. In Bernie's eyes, his BFF had constructed the image of a true artist: contemporary, mature and yet exuding her own aura of outrageousness. A new styling of the old Paisley. He was proud of his BFF and new business partner.

A couple months back, the duffer had taken a break to decide her future options. She'd lost two jobs in so many days. In a knee jerk, emotional response to rejection, she announced a decision to burn bridges and leave all her friends behind to move to Plover Point. Forgetting about all the people who cared about her. Bedamned. *As if.* They were never going to let that happen.

On one compass reading, he understood Paisley's need to *let go and move on* from the horrid memories of Convict Crust and Madam Monique's betrayal. He carried guilt over his own collusion in that skulduggery allowing Paisley to get booted off the Steampunk Club as their festival organiser. He owed her big time for that misguidance and since then had apologised ad nauseam. Bless the Eternal, she did not hold grudges. All was forgiven and forgotten. But he knew something had to be done to stop her restless spirit running if and when times grew tough down the track.

Lance wasn't the only one who loved the Steampunk girl, prima coggler within the Guild of Artificers (even if Bernie's affections were more accurately described as brotherly, not at all the same as he felt for Anita, but still …). There were lots of people who cared about her – Bernie's and Lance's families, as well as Anita, and even Marianne and Adam these days.

She had deserved a chance to make her dreams come true. Lance may have been the cosmic spark that set the cogs and gears in motion. But her BFF, Bernie, took the opportunity to crank up the Grand Mechanism and establish a platform for her industriousness.

When they'd sat down in the shop kitchen and discussed Paisley's options about making a living around Lower Teasel, he soon realised it would be undignified to offer his BFF a job working behind the counter of Light Up. She needed work – but deserved so much more than a shop assistant job.

He had to admit to a stroke of genius convincing Paisley to establish a range of original Steampunk accessories – jewellery, timepieces, hats, braces, masks and clothing creations, all and sundry – to sell from her own retail corner of Light Up – cutting himself out as the middleman and setting her up in her own modest business enterprise.

The best was that they'd work alongside each other like two peas in a pod. He wouldn't be a boss. He'd act as a mentor and provide guidance and advice on the boring bits such as pricing strategies, keeping accounts and taxation law. Paisley would have a place where she could be totally her own person; a place where she belonged.

Chapter Forty-Five

Three months later…

"Here's something funny," Adam said as he spun the lazy-susan and used chopsticks to spear another salt and pepper squid from the centre dish to add to his own plate. The gang, which included Marianne, Bernie, Anita, and Lance, were sharing the banquet at Stubblefield's Chinese Restaurant. They'd become friends and this dining experience was a regular event since the success of Steam Fest much to Paisley's amazement.

Before he could continue, Marianne cut in knowing what he was going to say. "Are you allowed to tell?" Being a stickler for 'the law' she didn't want him to get in trouble. Adam was working as a police officer again. He re-joined the service after his children went to live with their mother and her marriage partner. Unhappy as he was about it, his mood swings seemed to lift. Paisley couldn't recall when in the last few months he'd man caved. She wondered if the reason was being back on the job. No. Her bet was on Marianne and him hooking up as a couple, at last.

Adam ignored Marianne's advice. "The Mainlanders that bought Convict Crust Bakery are planning to turn it into a Bed and Breakfast. They were digging in the backyard —"

"— looking for Old Chugg's tins of gold, I'll bet," Anita interrupted and created chuckles all around the table.

Bernie laughed the loudest. "That old con never fails!"

Adam tried to continue. "— they found bones in the compost trench and reported it in a state of panic. Me and my partner, Kyle, rushed over with a roll of crime scene tape ready to call in the forensic team ..."

"OMG. What happened?" Anita yelped, looking sick to her stomach.

Adam burst out laughing, as only a hardened cop would. "Turns out, the city slickers couldn't tell the difference between human remains and dog bones!" He whacked the table several times and continued a belly laugh. The others, all born and bred on Eden Isle, joined in mocking Mainlanders. Except Paisley who turned white and left the table to go 'to the ladies'.

"What's wrong with her?" Adam asked.

"It'll be Missy's bones. The dog disappeared the day Monique and Thayne did a runner," Bernie explained soberly. "She'll be devastated, she loved that dog."

Anita was pale from shock as well. "I knew they planned to go to Western Australia and I guess taking a dog with them would have been too much trouble. But I never thought Thayne would kill Missy rather than let her go."

The table went quiet as each friend processed that observation.

Changing the subject to a more positive one, Anita said, "Did I mention I got a text message last week from Noelle? It's the first I've heard from her. Nothing from MM so far. I keep leaving texts but get no response. Noelle's message implied she and her dad were visiting family in New Zealand. I texted back to ask about MM and got an oblique response saying *MM was on her way*. Whatever that means. Noelle hasn't returned any of my texts since then."

"At least you know where they are and that they're alive and well," Bernie said.

"I don't suppose Paisley needs to know?" Anita asked, unsure of what to do but not wanting to keep secrets either.

After a moment of reflection, Lance said, "Best to leave it alone, with what's happened to Missy and everything." All heads nodded.

Adam cleared his throat. "I guess it's the wrong moment to tell Paisley that I know who bought her Steampunk Stray sculpture?"

"No way – the new owners bought it?" Marianne asked, uncannily reading his mind.

Adam nodded. "Pride of place on a huge stone in the middle of the bakery patio."

Chapter Forty-Six

Ten months later…

The door to Light Up jingled and Lance burst in, brimming with excitement. "Bernie, is Paisley here by any chance? I tried her at home and her phone's not charged as usual. I've got the best news ever!"

"In the kitchen having a cup of tea with Anita," he said, locking the cash register and following Lance around the back.

Anita and Paisley were giggling like two school friends when Lance rushed into the kitchen. "You're not going to believe it!" he said. They stopped and gaped at him.

Catching his breath, he willed to slow down. "I rode past the Village Green today on my way to Paisley's and guess who I saw? Eddy and Heath walking a dog." He waited for this to sink in. "I stopped to be absolutely sure. It was Missy!"

Paisley put both hands to her heart. "Bedamned. Are you absolutely positively sure?" she asked.

"You'll never credit it. I decided to speak to Eddy to check out what was going on. He wasn't the least embarrassed. On the day Monique dumped him, Noelle decided to open the gate and let Missy escape because Thayne said they were moving to Western

Australia and wouldn't be taking the dog. When Heath told Eddy what they'd done, he searched for Missy, found her wandering the street and took her home with them."

"Bedamned. They stole Missy! That doesn't seem like the Eddy I used to know." Paisley sounded surprised.

"Eddy said he was so pissed off at Monique, it was sort of an act of revenge."

"Good. Heath loves Missy and Monique didn't deserve her," Paisley said. And then she leapt up and hugged Lance, crying tears of joy into his shoulder. "I can't believe it. Missy's alive. I thought she'd been composted."

"By the Eternal, everything worked out fine in the end," Bernie stated for the record.

The front door to Light Up jingled again. Bernie walked out to the shop to see to the customer. He returned a minute later with Adam, standing tall and all official in his police uniform. Everyone expressed happiness at seeing him so unexpectedly.

On the other hand, Adam looked sombre and not friendly. "Sorry, but this is police business. I'm glad I've got you all in one place. Makes this easier. I need to know where each of you were on the night Monique and Thayne disappeared from the bakery."

"What's this all about?" Lance asked.

Adam winced. "You know how I joked a few months ago about the owners of the old bakery digging up their backyard looking for Old Man Chugg's gold. They found those old dog bones. This time they dug up bones that turned out to be human. In the compost trench under a lot of rotting bags."

"Hellfire. They killed Tobin and buried him under the compost," Paisley cried out. "I knew from the start that was going to be Tobin's fate."

"I probably shouldn't be telling you this but it's true we haven't been able to locate Tobin. He seems to have disappeared off the map. Finding out his real name has been a problem. The Queensland police are checking their records."

"The bones can't be Thayne's because I got a text message from Noelle saying she was with her dad in New Zealand." Anita pulled out her phone and began scrolling through old messages.

"We know. He's making no attempt to hide and has been cooperating with the police. We've received a full statement from him about the night in question. Apparently, there was nothing special about it. All was quiet. No visitors. They went to bed as usual."

Anita screwed up her face. "That's not true. I was there when an almighty fight broke out between Thayne, Tobin and Simon. Monique got between them. Then she screamed and I heard a loud bang like a shot being fired. At least, that's what it sounded like. I got out of there as fast as a startled whippet. Drove to Bernie's. I was so scared." He nodded confirmation.

"What about Simon? Surely, he's a suspect?" Paisley asked.

Adam acknowledged this but shook his head. "Unfortunately, he can't be questioned at the moment. When the body was discovered, he had a breakdown and is in hospital heavily sedated. We tried but can't get any sense out of him. He keeps mumbling stuff about loving Jezebel and being a minion of Satan."

"Poor guy was very religious until he was thrown in the crucible by a black hearted doxy," Paisley said with sympathy.

Suddenly, Bernie stiffened. "I just remembered. My prints may be on the shovel. That night, I used it to dig into the compost trench to see if that was where they'd thrown all the stuff from the kitchen. I couldn't understand how they were able to clean up the place so quickly. The digging churned up clouds of flour dust, which confirmed my theory. I put the shovel back against the shed after that."

Adam shuffled uncomfortably. "Um, it probably was lime, not flour dust. Someone dumped bags of the stuff into the trench before covering it. It accelerates decomposition and lessens the smell." Bernie turned green realising his shovel missed hitting a dead body by centimetres.

"We'll have to take your statements back at the station, especially now that it contradicts Thayne's." Adam hesitated as if about to confide unpleasant information. "Forensics on the body came back. Death by gunshot. Only, the body wasn't that of a man." He shuffled his feet uncomfortable with the shocked faces in the room. Anita started weeping. Bernie put his arms around her.

"By the way, her real name was Mona Swanston. She changed it a few years ago to Monique Swan. I guess she thought it sounded posh," Adam said helpfully. "But it was true, she and Thayne never divorced. He is Noelle's father. She didn't fabricate that."

Anita looked up from Bernie's wet shoulder. "MM was a compulsive liar and after all the tall tales, half-truths and outright lies she told, at least we can now be sure of a few facts."

"That's something." Bernie's face crinkled. "I wonder which of the three guys did her in? If it was Thayne, we can only hope Noelle won't be in danger living in New Zealand with her father."

"Thayne wouldn't hurt her. He's been searching for his daughter for years and came all this way to re-establish a relationship. And," Anita speculated, "Tobin wouldn't hurt a fly. He truly loved MM and wanted to rescue her from Thayne's clutches. I reckon it was Simon; he's a bit of a loose cannon."

"It's going to be hard proving it one way or the other," Adam. "Personally, I think all three are guilty."

Anita wiped her nose with a tissue. "I wonder when Thayne will tell Noelle what happened to her mother? He can't keep up the pretence forever that *MM is on her way*."

Paisley shook her head. "If Thayne is anything like his wife, he'll keep lying until he can't get away with it anymore. That could be years. Monique's ending was horrible and she didn't deserve to die, but the woman's fabricated stories and outright lies affected so many people ..." She thought about how Eddy and Heath were lost to her, never to be part of her family circle again. This was very sad, and so unnecessary. If only she hadn't stopped for a stray on a dark and stormy night ...

If there was one shining light amongst the clouds, it was Missy finding a good home with them. Heath loved that dog as much as she did. Someday, maybe she would have a dog and a home of her own. If not for Missy, she and Lance would never have met. Fate had a strange way of working.

Bernie put the kettle on and started setting up mugs and tea bags, the Eden Isle solution to any unpleasant news. He noticed

Paisley had a quizzical look on her face studying Lance. The dude seemed unusually anxious. Paisley had mentioned they were having dinner with his family later on, but that couldn't be the reason for his nervousness. She got on amazingly with his parents.

He shrugged it off, not concerned about his BFF's relationships any more. Lance was a steadying influence. He'd convinced her to let go of the crazy notion to move to Plover Point to start over. She seemed settled within herself and her circle of friends. Her Steampunk accessory business was doing a fair trade and gaining momentum as her reputation grew. The stray, foster kid personae was fading away. Paisley was maturing into a confident business woman.

The friends sipped tea in silent camaraderie processing past events and aiming for a philosophical perspective. Paisley was the first to share.

"After a harrowing Alchemist's crucible of distillation, by the magic of the Master's truth stone, my leaden heart now shines as bright as a diamond. I'm so grateful for you guys. You're more than friends – consider yourselves my kith and kin," she gushed giving Lance a secret smile. Bernie and Anita cheered.

"In fact, I will go so far as to admit, *I'm happy to be stuck with you*."

"Like an old tattoo," Anita chimed.

"You can never brush us off; we won't allow it," Bernie stated unequivocally.

A sense of relief washed through Lance. Nervously, he fingered a small velvet covered box in his pocket. Inside was a Steampunk ring designed by him; a ring his mother helped make. Tiny clockwork wheels riveted onto a band made of gold scrollwork in the shape of a Jules Verne styled octopus, with multi-coloured jewels randomly embedded in its tentacle suckers. After hearing Monique's fate, the timing was shit and it was a risk taking this next step, but he was betting Paisley wasn't the type to want a guy that played safe.

They sat around the table drinking tea, more relaxed now that the initial shock of Monique's death had been processed and the aftermath put into perspective, when suddenly Adam started laughing. It broke their contemplative mood, being inappropriate for the sombre moment, and especially with Adam's role at the table being that of a police officer on serious police business.

"I suppose it's the wrong time to tell you, with all that digging going on, the new owners of the bakery actually uncovered one of Old Man Chugg's tins."

"OMG!" Anita gushed. "They'll be rich. Won't that piss off Thayne." She began to chuckle.

"Bedamned," Paisley muttered. "The urban myth proved true!"

Bernie joined Anita's laughter. "Auntie Sheryl will be stoked."

Adam put up one hand like a cop stopping traffic. Timing it perfectly for comedic effect, he said, "Except, it was filled with coppers – not gold coins."

That brought the house down.

Chapter Forty-Seven

Later that afternoon, Paisley clung to Lance as they rode off to Whaler's Cove. The thrill of the ride never faded. She loved it so much, it crossed her mind again to trade in Rolla and buy a bike of her own. It only took half a second to dismiss that thought. Clutching tight to Lance's leathers riding on the back of his Harley, she decided, why let go of a good thing? By opening her heart, she could continue to do this on a permanent basis.

In fact, she felt confident enough to modify the motto she lived by. 'Letting go and moving on' didn't have the same ring to it these days.

Hmm.

Riding into the setting sun with Lance, she had an inspired moment. Her new motto had to be *'hold tight and move on'*.

Yes. By the gears and cogs of the Grand Mechanism, that had the perfect feel to it.

Book Cover Art

Painting 'A Rain Soaked Westbury Day' by Kataraina Koroheke

Kataraina Koroheke is a Tasmanian landscape artist known for her emotionally expressive abstract works. Despite living with Advanced Keratoconus, which distorts her vision, she continues to create vibrant, conceptual art that explores the connection between art and humanity. Born in Hamilton, New Zealand, she now lives in Tasmania.

This book cover features a scene from the village of Westbury in Northern Tasmania.

About the Author

Kaybee Pearson

Kaybee Pearson relies on a life rich in human dramas to write stories challenging mainstream narratives. She shares a property in the wilds of rural Tasmania (Latikikithika country) with feral and native creatures including her small family and a scruffy poodle named Bailey.

Kaybee holds a Bachelor Degree in Communication Studies (Journalism).

Published work to date includes:

- The Diminishment of Joy – The Rural Publishing Company 2023

- A feminist cartoon book 'Good Vibrations' co-authored with Wendy Newton, illustrated by Mark Godfrey (National Library ISBN 09587168 0 3)

- Short stories published in anthologies – the Devonport Writers' Workshop 2018 and Speculative Fiction 2021 Anthology on Survival. Her poems have been shortlisted in Tasmanian competitions

The Rural Publishing Company – books out soon:

- **Steampunk Stray – 2025**

- Quamby Bluff Gold

- Dystopian Women in Power Trilogy: Book 1 – The Score (co-authored with Zaire Hammond)

- Family of the Silent Lie

- The Bells Writing Circle – How to Write a Memoir